Random Precision

Random Precision

Tales from Within and Beyond

By

Rick Chambers

ISBN-13: 978-0-578-68020-0
ISBN-10: 0-578-68020-3

Cover design by: GreenStreet Marketing & Design
Printed in the United States of America

To Kailynn and Rowan,
each of you a story I treasure

TABLE OF CONTENTS

INTRODUCTION

I don't think writers are sacred, but words are. They deserve respect. If you get the right ones in the right order, you might nudge the world a little. —Tom Stoppard, The Real Thing

Stoppard is right: Writers aren't sacred. We're flawed. We're angst-ridden. We talk too much, or too little. We drink too much, or not enough. We wallow more in our alternate worlds than in this one, indulging our made-up characters in the places where they live and breathe and demand our attention. Then we cower as they laugh at our futile attempts to direct their imaginary lives.

Yet we carry on. We open our veins and bleed (as Hemingway probably didn't say) because we must.

Therein lies the dirty little secret, perhaps the real reason why writers aren't sacred. Writing is less about creating than relating. We tell the stories that form within our minds and hearts.

Stories that connect. Stories that, left untold, would tear us apart from the inside, like John Hurt's Kane at the dinner table. Stories are made of words. Sacred words. Words that inform, that rouse emotions, that spark imaginations, that inspire hope or summon horror. Words that can nudge our world.

I credit my late mother with showing me the sacredness of words. She was a voracious reader, a gene I inherited. I learned to ride the city bus on my own, and by age 9 I was making solo trips to the public library and various bookstores. Around that time I began experimenting with placing sacred words in some sort of order.

Science fiction was (and still is) my main inspiration. Books and TV shows—*Star Trek* chief among them—played the muse. At age 11, I discovered C.S. Lewis and his Space Trilogy: *Out of the Silent Planet, Perelandra* and *That Hideous Strength*. These, along with his Narnia books, challenged me to look at my heart, at my motivations, at my faith while on this journey of life. As a writer, I've sought a similar path.

While I've penned three novelettes plus a novel, *Radiance*, of which I'm quite proud, my first love is writing short stories. A novel is like swimming laps; a short story is a leap from the diving board for a quick, refreshing dip. In a short story, every word carries meaning. Every word is … sacred.

The stories in this book emerged from within, sometimes unbidden, sometimes prompted by an event or contest. In fact, several of these tales earned honor in writing contests. Some are straight science fiction; others are odd twists on everyday life. I'm a big fan of Rod Serling's *The Twilight Zone*, the way he and his writers used fantastic tales to make telling points. You'll see that influence here.

Mostly, I hope you find these words speaking to you at some level. I hope they cause you to question your assumptions and biases. I hope they connect you with every emotion—love, anger, sorrow, empathy, compassion, whatever they may summon from within.

The title for this book (and one of the tales herein) comes from a line in a Pink Floyd song. "Random precision" is counterintuitive, like many of my stories. They may take you places you didn't expect to go. Sacred places, perhaps. I hope you enjoy the journey. And then go out and nudge the world a little.

Rick Chambers
March 2020

COVETING FIELDS

Lila Cooper grew a watermelon, and Ella Dasch threw a fit.

Nebraska hadn't seen a genuine watermelon in nearly a decade, yet there it was: *Citrullus lanatus*, its green-striated glory taunting Ella through her spotting scope.

The gush of saliva it prompted seemed especially cruel, like waterboarding.

Ella spun away from the scope, seeking comfort from her own spectacular farm. Neat squares of plump soybeans, succulent tomatoes and other delights rolled out before her. The sweet corn thrilled her the most, with towering stalks bearing ears as big around as her bicep. A splash of yellow wheat, a gnarled vine heavy with grapes, even a small apple tree graced Ella's two-acre world.

Autumn gave the cloudless sky a chill-blue cast, but Ella was comfortably warm. She buried her feet in the buffalo grass and felt her skin tingling under filtered sunlight. Bordering the long grass were daisy-like asters and purple gentians, common blossoms of the fall. A few bees hovered; she kept a hive, sustained by the nectar of seasonal wildflowers. The bees pollinated her crops and left her some honey to boot.

Ella had far more than most Nebraskans. Yet she couldn't get over Lila's watermelon.

Not that she was jealous, not at all. Ella was just … well, stunned. From her frequent snooping she knew Seth and Lila Cooper possessed weak farming skills. Besides, to her knowledge no one had preserved a viable watermelon before the Contagion. All hope for that sweet treat was lost in the coffee-colored sludge stretching beyond the horizon.

The Contagion left nothing else.

No one saw it coming. Indeed, the news was upbeat when biochemists at a small lab in nearby Hastings celebrated an incredible achievement: a synthetic virus that destroyed every farm-threatening insect, from aphids to wireworms. Carefully engineered, the virus prompted the insects' cells to generate chaotropic acids that shattered molecular bonds. *Voilá*, dead pests!

But the gleeful scientists forgot one thing: Viruses evolve.

Within four years, their creation began liquefying the crops it was designed to protect. A year after that, it invaded all other plant life. Government researchers scrambled to develop an antidote. Luckily they did, saving the rest of the planet, but not before Nebraska's Great Plains collapsed into a flatland of rotted, gelatinous plant proteins, a gooey morass where the virus still lurked.

Folks called it the Kool-Aid Contagion, to the great annoyance of Kool-Aid's maker. Because both were born in Hastings, the association seemed inevitable, albeit unfair. At worst, Kool-Aid caused a few childhood cavities. Its namesake spawned an environmental disaster.

Some farmers, Ella among them, saved what they could, using precious cash reserves to build huge, transparent agridomes. Strict access protocols kept the climate-controlled shelters free of infection, preserving a slice of the Cornhusker State's legacy.

Enough to keep their families alive, anyway.

Ella's agridome was among the largest, a source of pride she reveled in at rare social gatherings. In contrast, the Coopers' dome was one-third the size and significantly weathered despite its relative youth. If any of its seals failed, the Contagion would swoop in and consume the farm in less than a season.

Of course, Ella would never wish such a fate on her neighbors, even if they didn't deserve that luscious watermelon.

"It's not fair!" Ella whined. She returned to her spotting scope, zooming in on Lila's emerald fruit. "Mine is the best farm for a hundred miles. I could grow dozens of watermelons! She only managed one!"

She'd never thought of the Coopers as selfish, but this new development said otherwise. They had grown and hoarded a watermelon, then shamelessly taunted people by leaving it easily seen—at least by anyone who happened to spy on them.

Ella believed something must be done. The community should share in this bounty. True, one watermelon didn't come close to satisfying even the much-diminished population of Adams County. But what if Ella planted some of its seeds, tending them with greater care than Lila Cooper ever could? Why, the harvest would be the talk of the region! She envisioned an Ella Dasch Watermelon Festival in Hastings, with children devouring the red, watery flesh, some for the first time, their faces alight with smiles and wonder.

What right did the Coopers have to keep such a prize from their neighbors? Where was their compassion, their sense of charity?

Ella wouldn't stand for it.

Her plan was simple. She'd sneak across the jellied landscape that evening, slip inside the Coopers' agridome and rescue the watermelon for the good of all. She would gather the seeds and plant them in two of her available plots, with an eye toward a harvest celebration three months later.

Best of all, Ella would eat the evidence.

* * * *

Standing in her agridome airlock, Ella donned safety goggles and waited patiently as the system cycled through its two-minute exit procedure. Like many of the dome's functions, access was controlled by computer. Whenever Ella went outside—an infrequent event—the system increased the air pressure to push contaminants out, then flashed the airlock and everything inside with purple laser light, just 100-quadrillionths-of-a-second long. This rendered any virus impotent, including the Contagion.

A chime sounded softly. The cycle was over. Ella removed her goggles, turned the handle on the airlock door and stepped into the night.

The air was crisp and damp, but it lacked the aroma of autumn. There were no trees to cast off dying leaves or fuel cozy fireplaces, no late-season blooms to perfume the breeze. Only the endless slime remained, now colored a disturbing black under the blue-gray light of the harvest moon.

Ella kept a pair of modern snowshoes near the airlock door. Their aluminum-and-neoprene makeup was perfect for crossing the knee-deep goo without sinking. She secured her feet in the bindings, eyed the quarter-mile trek ahead and set out.

A farm girl from birth, Ella missed the sounds of a stroll across open fields. The squishing noise of her snowshoes on the semi-solid gunk swept away that pleasant memory. Indeed, the flat landscape, still air and otherwise silent surroundings were all a bit creepy. Never had 400 yards seemed so far.

And then she was there, standing at the airlock door of the Coopers' agridome.

Peeking through the glass, Ella eyed the small living quarters on the far side of the dome. No activity meant the Coopers were asleep. She touched the door handle and twisted it slightly. It moved. This was no surprise. Few Nebraskans locked their domes. Theft wasn't a problem; either you had your own farm with your own food, or you lived somewhere else.

Ella slipped off her snowshoes, stepped into the airlock and immediately faced a dilemma she hadn't considered. If she engaged the lengthy entry process, the noise might awaken the Coopers. If she didn't, she might set off an alarm—or worse, allow the Contagion to invade the farm.

Despite her resentment, Ella wouldn't risk infecting her neighbors' crops. So she compromised, instructing the computer to engage the laser without recycling the atmosphere in the airlock. As she put on her goggles, the system complained but obeyed.

Seconds later, Ella slipped quietly into the dome.

While smaller and not as diverse as Ella's, the farm was surprisingly pleasant. Plots were arranged in ordered rows, weed-free and competently tended. Only the dome's triangular segments of nano-ceramic glass showed lack of attention, with a thin film proving they hadn't been cleaned in months. Seth Cooper had been an office worker before the Contagion, a pudgy man who tended toward laziness. Ella snorted. His sloth was probably costing their farm 20 percent of life-giving sunlight.

A scattering of small overhead lamps shed just enough glow for Ella to find the watermelon patch. She gasped as she saw the single, bulbous fruit. It looked to be about 20 pounds, roughly average size, but being the first watermelon she'd seen in years, it seemed enormous. Ella splayed her fingers across the green rind; its cool, firm skin sent shivers up her arms.

She lifted the melon and saw a yellow patch on its underside where it rested on the soil—a sign that it was ripe. The tendril nearest the watermelon had turned brown, which was another good indicator. Ella smacked the rind with an open palm, smiling at the deep, hollow response. No doubt about it, this melon was ready for picking.

Ella snapped the stem and lifted her prize.

Success!

And then she heard a single, sharp "yip."

Were she not in the middle of a brazen theft, Ella might have cooed over the golden-brown Australian terrier. The cute canine stood six feet away, wagging its docked tail in celebration of her company.

"Hey there, puppy," she whispered with exaggerated cheer. "I didn't know Lila had a dog. Really, really wish I'd known that."

The pup yipped again. It skittered away a few feet and then came back, panting hopefully. It was an invitation to play.

"Oh, I can't do that right now, little guy. I … sort of have my hands full."

Two barks this time, in a slightly scolding tone. Ella mourned the dog's lack of humor.

"Skeezy! Here boy!"

Lila! Ella dropped to the ground, somehow managing to keep her hold on the hefty melon. The terrier hesitated, as if torn between this potential new playmate cowering in a melon patch and the comfortable assurance of food and affection from his owners.

"Skeezy!"

At last the dog settled on the sure thing, streaking along the pathway toward his master's voice.

Ella waited a good five minutes before peeking out of the greenery. The dome was silent once more. That was her cue to head for home.

She passed through the airlock, instructing the computer to again skip all but the laser. Donning her snowshoes, she clomped quickly across the gushy landscape, lungs burning, her arms aching from the weight of the watermelon.

At the door to her agridome, Ella risked a glance back at the Coopers' place. All remained still; they hadn't been alerted. The moonlight showed her footprints slowly fading into the sludge. Seth and Lila would never know she was the thief.

This time Ella went through the complete entry protocol. Minutes later, she placed the watermelon on the counter outside her living quarters. Wax paper covered its surface, and a huge knife awaited her.

Grasping the knife, Ella made the first cut.

It was like opening a treasure chest, but instead of gold doubloons there was the vibrant red of a ripe, juicy watermelon. Ella eagerly shoved a wedge into her mouth, moaning in delight as the sweet taste exploded in her mouth. She nibbled every bit of the red flesh from the rind, pausing now and then to spit seeds onto the wax paper. Then she sliced free another hunk and continued her ravenous assault.

By the time her stomach called for a halt, she'd eaten half of the watermelon. The rest would keep in her refrigerator, awaiting the next feast.

And then there were the seeds, promising many feasts to come.

Ella guessed they weren't hybrids, which wouldn't germinate. Not even the Coopers would waste precious soil on a one-time crop. She took the pile of seeds she'd gathered so far and placed them in a dish of water with a small drop of dish soap. A short soak removed any remaining sugar. Then she removed them from the liquid, patted away the excess moisture and spread them out on a paper towel. After drying for a week, they would be ready for planting.

She stared at the seeds, smiling at their potential.

The work ahead was daunting—watermelons needed lots of water and tending—but Ella knew the harvest, and the accolades, would be worth it. She heaved a tremendous yawn. The future began tomorrow. Now was the time for sleep.

* * * *

Ella drifted up through layers of slumber to serene consciousness, dreams of watermelons still ripe in her head. She smiled. What a wonderful way to begin the day!

Her head was awake, but her hands were asleep, lightly zinging her with that prickly sensation. Ella endured it, her eyes still closed so she could linger on visions of luscious fruit and admiring friends.

As glorious as her dreams were, a small sting of guilt dimmed her smile a little. By now the Coopers would have discovered their loss. How would they react?

She doubted they would accuse her. If they did, she'd deny it. No one would believe such a tale. Why would Ella, owner of the best agridome and richest crops in the region, steal from a neighbor, even something as rare as a watermelon?

Fear of being caught didn't concern Ella. The realization that she'd taken something precious from those who already had less—that, admittedly, was a little unsettling. The Coopers struggled far more than Ella did. No doubt they saw that single watermelon as a rich reward for their labors. But in Ella's view, she had done them a favor. In three months, they and the other farmers in Hastings would have all the watermelons they wished.

Lila and Seth would thank her in the end. She was sure of it.

The pins and needles poking her arms grew more insistent. Ella sighed. Time to leave the dreams behind, shake her limbs awake and get on with the day.

Ella opened her eyes, sat up and looked at her numbed hands.

She gasped in stunned horror.

Her hands weren't asleep. They were missing.

So were most of her forearms.

What remained was covered in a thick, pinkish syrup that oozed from the stumps. A puddle of this goo covered her thighs where her hands had rested. Staring down, she saw her feet leaching the same substance. Viscous droplets formed a slow trickle, pooling around her ankles. As the pink drool grew, Ella saw her toes begin to contract, shriveling from sight.

Her body was melting before her eyes.

Just like the crops when the Contagion came.

The virus hadn't lain dormant. In the gloppy gruel of Nebraska's long-lost farmlands, it had continued to evolve, invading the Coopers' dome—perhaps through a gap in the poorly maintained glass—to find its way into a single crop. That crop flourished somehow, unaffected by a virus that had learned to dissolve something other than plants.

Ella realized all this just before she screamed.

And screamed. And screamed.

Until she couldn't.

Until there was nothing left to scream.

THE CHASM

A Carolina pulled pork sandwich makes lunch at Virgil's Real Barbecue worth every bump, dodge and weave required to cross Times Square for one. Add a dash of job stress, though, and that sandwich ignites like a pound of napalm.

But heartburn was the least of Derek Vayne's problems. His lunchtime pitch to a key client had ended in failure. Now, with an unsatisfying tap on his smartphone to cut off his furious boss, so had Derek's career.

Derek stormed up West 44th Street, away from Virgil's, clutching his smartphone and debating whether to fling it into traffic. In the end, he decided to hold onto it, along with the tattered remains of his self-respect.

As Derek began to pocket his phone, someone bumped his elbow. The phone flew out of his hand and skittered across the sidewalk. A moment later, the clod who had knocked it away was reaching down for it.

"Leave it alone!" Derek shouted.

But the man already had the phone in his hand. He was shorter than Derek and much thinner, clad in stained, ragged jeans and an Army jacket with the name "Lazare" stenciled over his left chest. From the look and smell of him, Mr. Lazare hadn't been near a shower recently.

The stereotypical homeless man. There were thousands of them on the streets of New York City. And this one was about to make off with Derek's smartphone.

Or so Derek thought until, amazingly, the man handed it back to him.

"Nice phone," Lazare said in a soft voice.

Derek snatched it from his grasp. "It was a lot nicer before you knocked it onto a concrete sidewalk!"

"S-sorry about that." Lazare hesitated. "Hey, uh, you wouldn't have a couple of bucks you could spare, would you? I haven't eaten in two days."

As a New Yorker, Derek had been hit up by his share of panhandlers. On the rare day when he felt generous, he gave whatever loose change was jingling in his pocket. Today wasn't one of those days.

"You nearly break my phone, and now you want me to give you money? What I ought to do is kick your ass!"

Lazare was streetwise enough to leave such a volatile man alone. But he couldn't hide the look of disdain that crossed his face as he turned away.

It was the worst thing Lazare could do. Enraged, Derek grabbed him by the arm, spun him around and punched him square in the—

—nose exploded in agony, filling his vision with darkness and stars. Derek's legs melted, and he fell to his knees on the cold sidewalk. The stars slowly faded from view, replaced by splatters of blood on concrete.

I can't believe he hit me! Derek lifted his head to glare at his assailant.

And gasped in astonishment.

Gone was the bedraggled beggar. In his place was a young man, handsome and sharply dressed, like countless other businessmen on the streets of New York City. But this particular man seemed to be in shock. He stared at his bloodstained fist, then down at his cashmere overcoat, then into Derek's eyes.

The man looked exactly like Derek Vayne.

"Th-that's impossible!" Derek stammered. Frightened, he clamored to his feet and reached for the man who looked like him. But the stranger was even more terrified than Derek. With a cry of fear, the man turned and ran, slipping through the river of mildly curious people that streamed along the sidewalk.

Derek gave chase, calling for help and demanding that his twin be stopped. Few paid attention, and none acted. In moments, the imposter vanished in the crowd.

Despite being a fitness freak, Derek found that he couldn't keep up. Strangely, he had no energy. In fact, despite the big meal he'd consumed at Virgil's, his stomach felt empty. Painfully empty.

As if ... as if he hadn't eaten in two days.

A moment later, a whiff of broiled kielbasa pushed through his blood-clogged sinuses and gave his unfilled stomach a stir. Derek's brief pursuit had ended near one of the ubiquitous hot dog carts found throughout the city. The vendor, a pudgy man with too much body hair, attended to an attractive, well-dressed woman, pouring on equal amounts of compliments and condiments.

Derek paid no attention. He'd found something much more mesmerizing: his reflection in the acrylic shroud of the vendor's cart.

The face he saw wasn't the one that stared back at him in the mirror every morning. Instead, he saw the face of the scrawny beggar whose Army jacket named him Lazare.

"What the hell is happening?" he whispered, frightened as he watched the strange lips move with the words he spoke.

"Hey! You gonna buy something?"

Derek's eyes shifted and caught the suspicious gaze of the vendor. Suddenly, despite his shocking reflection, food was the only thing on Derek's mind.

"Two dogs," he said. "Mustard and relish."

"You got any money?"

Derek's eyes widened. He'd never been asked such a thing.

"What kind of question is that? Do I look like a bum?"

The vendor looked him up and down. "Not saying nothin'. We're a prepay business here."

"Since when?"

"Since now."

Muttering, Derek scrounged through the pockets of his—Lazare's—tattered jeans. He came up with 27 cents. Anger quickly turned to desperation.

"Please," Derek pleaded, "I'm really hungry. I can pay you back tomorrow."

But the vendor wasn't interested in Derek's IOU. Yelling loudly, he grabbed the nearest nonlethal weapon—a used, wadded-up napkin—and threw it at him. Derek caught the napkin and, strangely, couldn't part with it. He stuffed it in his pocket and trotted away, still weak and hungry.

He didn't go far; he didn't have the energy. Derek's head whirled from lack of food and lack of understanding. He finally sat down on the sidewalk on 42nd Street, tantalizingly near the happy sounds of Bryant Park, and tried to reason through his impossible dilemma. "Impossible" was the right word. Exchanging bodies—it was right out of a cheesy Disney movie. It defied all logic. Was this a dream? A hallucination? Had someone slipped something in his drink at the restaurant? Implausible theories, perhaps, but far easier to swallow than a literal out-of-body-and-into-someone-else's experience.

The mystery stubbornly defied explanation, but Derek had more immediate worries. He had nowhere to go. His apartment was in Brooklyn, and he had no money for a subway ticket or taxi fare. Even if he walked there, he had no key to get in, and he doubted the landlord would believe his crazy story. Without his ATM or credit cards, without ID or even change for an all-but-extinct pay phone, Derek Vayne was just another homeless person among thousands in New York City.

Hour after hour he wandered the streets, stopping in front of windows to marvel at the image that wasn't his. Then a store manager would wave him away, or a cop would grunt in his direction, and Derek was obliged to resume his aimless trek.

He needed help, at the very least a meal, but no one offered him one. Not that he didn't ask time and time again. But pedestrians passed him by, pointedly looking away, drawing coats and purses tight against their bodies. It wasn't that New Yorkers lacked compassion; the horror of September 11 had proven their heart. Nor were they different from people in any other city where the poor roamed. Some didn't grasp the depth of need. Some doubted the need was legitimate. Many simply felt powerless to make a lasting difference, and so they did nothing. In truth, a sandwich would have been enough for Derek.

Of course, there were some who just didn't care. At one outdoor café, an annoyed couple hurled a pat of butter at Derek and told him to get a job. Derek picked up the butter and fled.

The day wore on. Soon the sinking sun cast a fading orange glow against the glass and steel of the city's skyscrapers, and the concrete canyons gradually sank into shadow. By the time darkness fell, Derek gave up his wanderings, plopping down on some grass not far from the Sherman Statue in Central Park. The cops would chase him away eventually, but for the moment it was a place of rest for a vagrant like him.

A vagrant like … me.

There had been a time—just a few hours before, in fact—when Derek would have cast all such vagrants into oblivion, were it within his power. He would have cheered the roundup of human trash from the otherwise unspoiled streets and parks. Put them to work or put them away, that was his motto. He had no sympathy for the poor. He believed poverty came from laziness and bad choices, none of which was Derek Vayne's responsibility.

Right now, a different belief overwhelmed his mind and heart: hopelessness. He'd never suspected such utter despair and aching loneliness were so real here in the heart of the crowded city. Nor had he thought about how awful it felt to be hungry, painfully hungry. Anything at all was better than that horrible emptiness in his stomach.

Anything.

With little forethought and much desperation, Derek pulled the wadded napkin from his pocket, carefully frosted it with the melting pat of butter, and devoured it. Just to have something in his stomach.

Then he hung his head and wept.

That was a mistake; sorrow made his damaged nose hurt all over again. But at this moment it didn't matter.

How Derek wished he could tell everyone the truth! How he longed to warn friends, relatives, even strangers, that Hell was real, achingly real, and not as far off as they thought. But it was as if he stood on the far side of a chasm, light-years apart from the people he loved and the world he once knew. He couldn't cross that chasm, and it wouldn't matter if he could.

No one in his world was interested in what Derek Vayne had learned. In his heart, he knew they wouldn't listen.

"They used to tell me God cared about people. They used to say he was merciful." Derek looked up at the few bright stars that cut through the city's glare. "If ever I needed mercy, it's right now. Please …"

He waited, pleading silently. But the heavens didn't open. No dazzling light shone from above. The song of angels didn't resound across the sky. There was only his own sobbing, his own pain.

He hung his head again and kept praying. There was nothing else left to do.

Then, after what seemed like an eternity, there came a gentle touch on his shoulder.

Derek looked up, expecting to see a scowling cop. He was ready to protest, to offer his excuses, to beg for help, to weep and hope that someone would make things right.

What he saw was a face. His face. The face of Derek Vayne.

"I couldn't forget," Derek heard his own voice say. "I don't think God would let me. Not after all I've been through—the hunger, the loneliness and pain. I wouldn't wish that on anyone, no matter what. I had to find you."

Derek watched, speechless, as the man in the cashmere overcoat reached down, grasped his arms and helped him stand—

—lifted Lazare to his feet. The homeless man wobbled, weak from hunger and from whatever had happened to the two of them.

"It's okay," Derek said, steadying the man. "I know what you need. And I'm going to help you."

Lazare smiled. A tear glimmered in his eye—no longer the glint of sorrow, but of happiness and hope. Then the two men began to walk, holding onto each other, toward the lights of the living city.

A Speck of Sawdust

Greta peered through gritty eyes as the steel-and-glass door moved left into the slotted wall with a solid "thunk." Freed from the jail's detention cells, she stepped toward her carefully coiffed, pinstripe-suited lawyer. He, on the other hand, moved backward, glancing at her vomit-stained blouse, wrinkled pants and matted brown hair, and shielded himself behind his briefcase.

"Where have you been?" Greta snapped. "You were supposed to spring me last night!"

Lance Guilford offered a small, apologetic shrug. "Couldn't be helped. Your trial was fast-tracked. It happened an hour ago."

This caught Greta by surprise. "Fast-tracked? For a simple DWI?"

"Nothing about last night was simple."

Greta couldn't argue—mostly because she remembered little of what happened.

"Why didn't I get to testify?"

"You did, sort of. The DA posted video from your interrogation."

"You mean when I took responsibility for my actions?"

"Or, put another way, when you admitted everything, insisted it all be on the record, and then asked for a lawyer. So much for my one good argument." Lance sighed. "The verdict didn't take long. Rarely does these days."

Greta posed her next question with a lift of her eyebrows.

"Guilty, of course," Lance replied. He ticked off the list with his fingers, starting with his pinkie. "Driving while intoxicated. Destruction of public property. Reckless driving causing serious injury. And you came this close"—Lance ended with his index finger and thumb in a near-pinch—"to vehicular manslaughter."

Greta's head, already pounding, felt as if it would explode.

"What's the sentence?"

Lance took a deep breath. "Your blood alcohol level was over 0.3, Greta. It's a wonder you were even conscious. You were clocked driving 110 miles an hour through residential streets where the highest speed limit is 35—and with half a dozen police cars wailing behind you, by the way. Then you crashed through a Veteran's Day display and nearly ran over a 78-year-old former Marine. He'll be in the hospital for at least a week."

He paused.

"Every member of the virtual jury did search-engine research. Not one found a sentencing precedent. So, they gave you life."

Greta wheezed as the air left her lungs. She leaned against the wall, bent over and retched. Lance patted her shoulder awkwardly.

Greta couldn't fathom the verdict. Why such a high price for a single mistake? She was willing to take responsibility for her poor judgment. Yes, she had far too much to drink. Yes, she drove when she knew she shouldn't. Yes, she drove recklessly, doing so on a drunken (and stupid) rationale that the faster she drove, the less time she posed a risk on the streets.

But ... *life*? What a cruel irony, describing the death of her freedom with that word!

Greta slowly lifted her head, jaw set, anger flashing in her green eyes. She refused to accept this. A few dozen people voting in an online poll, without giving Greta the chance to defend herself, was no means of justice. It was cruel. It was crass. It was wrong. She would fight it.

"Alright," said Greta. "What's our play?"

Lance looked surprised. "Our play?"

"Yes. How do we get this overturned? How do we get in a real courtroom, in front of a real jury?"

"What are you talking about? Did you forget how this works now? There are no courtroom trials anymore. We did away with them. The system couldn't keep up. Not enough judges, not enough juries. Now that it's all online, we have the swiftest, most efficient justice system in the world. Trial, verdict, sentence—boom!"

He shook his head. "There is no play, Greta. Life in prison. Minimum 15 years, then maybe you get a shot at parole."

"But … can't we appeal?"

"Appeal what? You admitted your guilt on video. The cops have dashcam footage. You put a veteran in the hospital."

Greta curled her hands into fists and stomped a foot.

"This is bullshit! I want my day in court!"

Lance snorted. "As far as the law is concerned, today was your day. And you lost. Look, you delivered this jury a unique lineup of violations without precedent. They had no past sentence to follow. Remember, this is an online world now, where the trolls consider every violation of the law egregious. They fashioned a punishment to fit your crime. That means you have nothing to appeal to."

Frustrated, Greta started to pace the confines of the small visiting room. "You can't possibly agree this is just! Who says my sentence must be an apples-to-apples comparison? Lots of people drive drunk and crash their cars. Maybe the details differ, but the basics are the same. Can't we appeal based on that?"

"Horseshoes and hand grenades," said Lance. "Close isn't close enough. It's not just the laws you broke, it's how spectacularly you broke them. That got you trending online, and not in a good way."

Greta rubbed her face vigorously. Like most people, she hadn't objected to the change in the justice system—hey, no more jury duty!—until it had come around to bite her in the ass. Now the new system was poised to throw her in prison for the rest of her life.

"Okay, we need grounds for an appeal," said Greta, thinking hard. "You claim we don't have one now. What would it take to create one?"

"Create a case?" Lance was genuinely puzzled. "I don't get your meaning. Online sentencing is about two things: precedent and outrage. To change it, we'd have to find a case where someone did exactly what you did, or nearly so. If that person's sentence was less than life, that's an argument for leniency."

"Good. And what if we went after outrage?"

Her lawyer took a deep breath. "That's a tougher nut to crack. Someone else's crime can generate outrage simply enough, but getting it to go viral … well, you need the right level of exposure. Put it out there with a solid SEO, and that could work. Leniency, maybe. An outside chance of a pardon."

"Perfect!" said Greta. "I vote for outrage."

"Greta—"

She put up a hand. "Don't start, Lance. I'm not going to settle for a lesser sentence. I want out of here. Full pardon! If you can't find a precedent to do that, I'll go find a worse case than mine."

"But there isn't one, Greta! I looked. My team looked. The jury looked."

For the first time that day, Greta smiled. Lance thought it an ugly, conniving smile. "No problem," she said, chuckling at her own cleverness.

"If we can't find a worse case, we'll make one."

* * * *

The club was a maelstrom of darkness and light, of human shouts, clinking glasses and the obnoxious *boom-bff-boom-bff* of dance music. Bodies moved, some to the beat, some to the contortions of navigating a viscous sea of flesh.

Greta gently sipped a mango margarita—her first and only, she promised herself—and eyed the crowd. Her anxiety grew with each passing minute. After much legalistic maneuvering, Lance got her a 24-hour release, with an ankle monitor, to take care of her personal affairs before her prison sentence began. Half of that time was gone, leaving a few precious hours to pull off her scheme.

First, she considered choosing a gullible, unattached male as her victim, knowing how a touch of flirtation made men pliable. But after an hour of scrutiny, she began to doubt that approach. For one, all the guys seemed to have dates. And there was a risk that the jury hearing her appeal might treat one gender differently than the other. Without knowing if that would help or harm her case, Greta decided to play it safe. Her mark needed to be a woman, and as much like her as possible.

20

Her new strategy required another two hours of watching passersby while sipping her increasingly tepid drink. Just when Greta was about to give up, a young woman came alongside her and leaned against the bar, trying to catch the bartender's eye. She noticed Greta staring at her. They exchanged smiles.

"Not the most relaxing evening I've ever had," the woman shouted over the din.

Greta nodded. "I thought it would be less crazy here at the bar. I was wrong."

The woman laughed, a delightfully soft sound that managed to rise above the noise. "I need less crazy in my life." The woman stuck out a hand. "Rachyl. With a 'y.'"

"Pleased to meet you, Rachyl With a 'Y.' I'm Greta. You been here before?"

"Often enough to wonder why I keep coming back. After a long day, you'd think I'd try for something a bit less."

"Less … crazy? Crowded?"

"Loud."

Both women laughed. Then Greta turned and shouted for the bartender, who promptly shuffled over. Rachyl admired her command.

"Mango margarita?" asked Greta.

"If you recommend it."

"I do."

Greta placed the order. After the drink arrived, the two women abandoned the bar for an available table. There Greta channeled every ounce of her charm into building a new friendship. Rachyl was a talker, which served Greta well as a consummate listener—or someone good at faking it. She learned her new friend worked as a systems engineer for an IT group, shackling her with long office hours and few relationships. Greta responded with lots of sympathetic nods, arm patting and friendly smiles.

By the time Rachyl's second margarita arrived, she was Greta's BFF.

"Hey, aren't you having another drink?" asked Rachyl.

Greta hated to risk another margarita, but her hours-old libation had become a gag-inducing swill. She'd have to be careful; even a slight buzz could ruin the plan.

"Good idea. This one's lost its kick."

Rachyl stood as Greta waved at a server. "You get another drink while I get rid of the last one." She giggled and headed toward the restroom.

The moment she was out of sight, Greta pulled a small vial from her purse and dumped a thin, clear liquid into Rachyl's drink. She didn't know what it was; Lance had procured it from one of his sleazier clients, a complete reptile who said it was the best he'd ever used on an unsuspecting woman. The thought made Greta ill, so she pushed it from her mind.

Big picture, Greta. Focus on the big picture.

By the time Rachyl returned, Greta had her own margarita in hand. They clinked glasses and sipped. Rachyl made a face. "Not as good as the last one. The mango's a little bitter this time."

Uh oh. Greta swallowed a sting of panic. "Bait and switch, probably. This place does it all the time. They pull out the cheaper stuff as the night wears on."

"That sucks. Maybe I should complain."

Greta shook her head a bit too emphatically. "No, no. Let's not make things worse. For all you know, the bartender will spit in your replacement."

"Yeah, I suppose you're right." Rachyl took another sip. "It's not really that bad, I guess."

With that, Rachyl leaned her head back and drank the margarita in two massive swallows. When she lifted her head again, she wiped her mouth with her sleeve and laughed.

Greta smiled and waited.

Within minutes, the drug began taking effect. Rachyl gradually drooped over the table; when she tried to stand, she wobbled and nearly fell. Greta caught her and helped her back to her seat. As time passed, Rachyl became obnoxious, shouting lewd comments at passing men. Greta let her carry on for half an hour to cement her drunken reputation publicly.

Finally, Greta put aside her barely touched margarita and took Rachyl by the arm.

"Okay, my friend, it's time to go home."

Rachyl mumbled her assent as the two left the table and pushed their way through the crowd. As they reached the club's entrance, a bouncer stopped them. He scowled at Greta's stumbling burden.

"She's not driving, is she?" he growled.

"Absolutely not. We got a rideshare," Greta lied. "I thought we should wait outside till it got here. Rachyl was acting out in there. I didn't want her to be disruptive."

The bouncer relaxed. "Thanks, we appreciate that."

Another tactic done well. Rachyl was now known by name as the unbearable drunk, with Greta the sensitive friend and gracious customer. Smiling a farewell, Greta led Rachyl into the parking lot. She grabbed Rachyl's purse and fumbled around inside it, looking for her key fob. Once she found it, they walked among the rows of cars while Greta pressed the unlock button. Finally, one of the vehicles—a sporty Toyota—beeped and flashed its lights. With considerable effort, Greta opened the driver's door and stuffed Rachyl behind the wheel.

Now came the dangerous part. To make sure Rachyl bested Greta's crime, Greta would have to ride along.

She couldn't see a way around it. If someone wasn't there urging Rachyl to drive faster, there was no guarantee she would. Greta needed to make sure her new friend caused greater mayhem without killing them both.

Risky? Absolutely. But Greta must take the gamble to stay out of prison.

Suddenly, Rachyl realized she was in her car. She flung her head back and forth, studying the steering wheel as if it were the strangest thing she'd ever seen.

"I shouldn't drive," she slurred.

"But you promised to take me home!" said Greta. "I don't have a car. I was counting on you!"

Rachyl looked at her, a mix of worry and confusion on her face. "But I'm not ... can't ... "

Greta let her voice rise, ladling on the guilt. "You mean you won't! Some friend you turned out to be!"

She moved as if to get out of the Toyota. Rachyl reached over and flopped a hand on her arm. Her other hand gripped the steering wheel as she tried to center herself. She swallowed a couple of times.

"No. I'm sorr … sorr … *sorry*! I'll take you home."

Rachyl put one foot on the brake, searched the dashboard until she found the start button, then reached for it with a finger. She missed it twice. Finally, with a firm press, Rachyl summoned the car to life. She carefully put it in gear, strangled the steering wheel with both hands, and edged out of the parking space. With the fastidiousness of a nonagenarian, she coasted slowly down the center of the parking lot, made two wobbly turns, and ventured into the street. There she accelerated—if one could call it that—to a speed just above that of a preschooler on a tricycle.

Greta sighed. *At this rate, the only ticket she'll get is for obstructing traffic.* "Rachyl, you're going too slow."

"What? No," she argued. She nodded at a speed limit sign. "That's a '3.'" Then she pointed at a digit on her dash. "That's a '3,' too."

"The sign says 35. You're driving 23."

"Right. Both '3s.'" Rachyl snickered. "Anyway, I wanna be safe. I shouldn't be driving."

Time for a little drunk-driver logic, Greta thought. If it had worked for her last time, it ought to work on Rachyl.

"Listen to me. You're right, you had a little too much to drink. So, the less time you're out here driving, the less chance you'll get caught or cause an accident, right?"

"Yea-a-a-h … ?"

"If you go faster, you'll get us to my place sooner. And you can sleep there, okay? Everyone wins! All you've got to do is speed up a little."

Rachyl shrugged. "Okay."

She pushed on the gas pedal—hard. The Toyota accelerated rapidly. Greta watched the numbers climb: 45 … 60 … 75.

Not fast enough!

"Almost there. Just a little faster, girl."

Barely conscious, Rachyl shoved her foot downward. The digits on the speedometer crept upward, hitting 85 … then 95 … 110 … 115!

As if on cue, blue lights began flashing in the rearview mirror. A siren sliced the chill night air.

"That's it, Rachyl! Keep going!"

Rachyl shook her head. "The lights! Cops!"

"They're going somewhere else. We need to drive faster and get out of their way. Hurry up!"

She did. The speedometer crawled higher, flirting with 120 miles per hour. More police cars joined the chase. The Toyota's engine howled, spitting out RPMs it had never chewed on before.

Watching the landscape flash by, Greta felt the first touch of fear. They were barreling down a long, straight roadway. Because of the late hour, there wasn't any other traffic. But if they came upon another car, or even a slight curve, there was no way Rachyl could avoid a crash. At this speed, a crash would be fatal.

This has to be enough. Time to end it.

"Okay, maybe you'd better slow down," said Greta.

"No."

Greta looked at Rachyl in anxious surprise. "What do you mean, 'no'?"

"Not gonna let you down! Gonna get you home!"

And she pushed on the pedal with all her might.

Incredibly, the car reached 130 miles per hour. Even the police cars began to fall back, whether from lack of power or lack of moxie. All but one, that is. It stayed in the chase, far too closely for Greta's comfort. And Rachyl wouldn't back off.

"Rachyl, I really think you should slow down."

She ignored Greta, gripping the steering wheel and staring into the night.

"Dammit, Rachyl, *slow down*! You're going to get us killed!"

The Toyota flew on, engine screaming, trailing half a dozen police cars.

Greta was in a full-blown panic, pleading for Rachyl to stop. In reply, Rachyl started swiveling the steering wheel, causing the Toyota to wobble. Greta screamed, begged, cried, all for naught.

Then came the curve.

Thankfully, Rachyl saw it. She slammed on the brakes. Lights flashed as their nearest pursuer swerved to avoid a collision. The rear of the Toyota swung around, and for a moment Greta feared they were going to roll. At this speed, a roll would shred the car—and its occupants.

By some miracle, the car stayed upright as it left the road. Something big and darker than the night appeared in front of the careening car. Greta screamed and covered her face. The Toyota struck it, causing a screeching of metal and an explosion of leaves.

After what seemed like forever, the car came to a sharp, sudden stop.

Greta slowly looked from behind her hands. They were in a small park, a dozen feet away from a picnic table. Covering the car was an odd mix of steel wire, leaves and flowers. Greta realized they'd crashed through a sculpture garden. They were surrounded by the remains of a unicorn.

And, a moment later, five police cars.

"Driver! Open the door slowly and keep your hands where I can see them!"

Rachyl did neither. She simply sat there, staring at the dashboard.

"I let you down," she whispered. "I'm sorry. So, so sorry."

Greta ignored her. Instead, she slowly opened her own door and held her hands in front of her.

"I'm coming out, officers! Thank God you stopped her! I was *terrified!*"

Rachyl looked over, bleary eyed. "You ... what ... ?"

Several hours later, after she sobered up, it dawned on a pitiful Rachyl that her newest friend was her greatest enemy.

* * * *

This time, a very different Greta greeted Lance in the jailhouse visitors' room. This Greta was jovial, almost giddy.

"Have you seen the news?" she said. "Rachyl's everywhere! It's totally viral! I can't wait to hear how her trial went." She looked at him expectantly. "Here to take me home?"

"Uh … not exactly." His briefcase shielded him once again as the lawyer shifted his feet awkwardly.

"What do you mean? I'm the victim in this, right? Rachyl was supposed to drive me home. How was I to know she'd drive like a maniac and put people's lives at risk?"

Lance cleared his throat. "It's a bit more complicated than that."

Greta's bright demeanor began to melt. "I'm not interested in how complicated it is, Lance. Did she or did she not have her trial?"

"Oh yes, she had her trial," he replied, his face turning from pink to red. "The virtual jury had as much evidence as they had for yours. More, in fact. The lead police car swerved when Rachyl hit the brakes, and he crashed into a telephone pole. He survived, barely. He's partly to blame because he followed so closely, but the jury didn't really factor that in. Being a cop, there's a lot of sympathy there. Upshot is, your new pal got a life sentence, same as you did."

Greta beamed. "That's great news! Same sentence, worse crime. Now we can appeal! You've even got a new twist: me as the unwitting victim. That should earn me some sympathy, too, right?"

Lance said nothing. Greta's heart began to beat rapidly.

"Right?"

The lawyer took a deep, wavering breath.

"You forgot one thing, Greta: You were part of what happened. The cops did a blood test on Rachyl to find out what she was on. They figured she was way too erratic to just be drunk. They found whatever you put in her drink."

Greta waved it off, albeit with a slight catch in her voice. "I didn't put anything in her drink. That's my story. No one can prove otherwise."

"Except they can. The DA let Rachyl testify. They know you doped her."

Greta's legs began to tremble.

"It's her word against mine!"

"It usually is. Doesn't matter."

"But … but she was the driver!" Greta cried. "She broke the law! Where's their outrage at her?"

Lance sighed. "Ever hear the old proverb about pointing out a speck of sawdust in someone's eye while ignoring the plank in your own? That's what you've done, Greta. What's worse, you planted the speck. And the jury held you responsible."

"What … what's that mean?"

He looked at Greta in sorrow.

"It's the online community, remember? No quarter. No mercy." He hung his head.

"They sentenced you to death."

Lance winced, but he had the good grace not to cover his ears when she screamed.

ALL THE STAGE A WORLD

I wasn't surprised that the crowd at the Teatro Riviera could fit inside a Mini Cooper, but I was still disappointed. After all, it's not every night a century-old movie house closes its doors for the last time. But nostalgia, free popcorn and a scratchy print of Casablanca wasn't enough to draw people from their big-screen TVs and on-demand videos, where they could watch Casablanca from their couches in high definition.

I put on my game face as the solitary family of four trundled through the lobby toward the exit. They said nothing. The dad nodded, the mom offered a sad smile, and the kids looked relieved to escape.

In a way, I knew how they felt.

I did the usual clean-up patrol while pretending it wasn't final, pretending the red theater seats weren't worn pink, that the painted walls and ceiling weren't peeling in grimy sheets, that the varnish on the stage's oak flooring wasn't long gone. In happier days, the Teatro Riviera showcased vaudeville acts and a steady parade of Hollywood films, from silent Tom Mix shoot-'em-ups to Flash Gordon serials and, much later, the *Star Wars* trilogies.

That was all over now. The Riv was done in by multiplex theaters and internet cat videos. Time to lock the doors.

"Excuse me."

The unexpected voice nearly brought me out of my skin.

He was an old man, immensely so, a hundred if he was a day. Small and round-shouldered, he wore a black blazer, white turtleneck and khaki trousers. His upper lip sported a pencil moustache, and a few strands of stringy hair splayed across his age-spotted scalp. Cheeks pink with embarrassment, he apologized profusely for scaring me.

"Robinson Vidal," he said, extending a trembling, knob-knuckled hand.

"Darren Starr. You missed the movie."

"I love Bogie, but that's not why I'm here. I came to save the theater."

Somehow I thrust aside an incredible urge to laugh. "You're way too late, Mr. Vidal. Unless you brought a few hundred thousand bucks to pay the overdue bills and renovate the place, we're closed for good."

The old man's bushy eyebrows lifted. Maybe he hadn't realized the Riv was in that deep.

"I'm afraid I don't have any money," said Vidal. He leaned close and lowered his voice. "I have something much better: a way to make money."

I made no effort to hide my skepticism. "I see. And is this way legal?"

Vidal looked insulted. "Of course! It's just that ... well, I haven't done it in a long time. A very long time." His rheumy eyes roamed the sad-looking auditorium. "It only happened here, you know. Never could do it anywhere else."

"What are you talking about?"

In response, Vidal lifted a heavy object from a nearby seat. I needed a moment to recognize it: a vintage Underwood portable typewriter, from the mid-1930s. While the keys were well loved, the unit itself was in remarkable shape. A sheet of paper hugged the platen, waving at me as Vidal struggled to hold the contraption.

"Life, Mr. Starr! We can bring life back to the Riv!"

By now I'd decided Robinson Vidal was a kook. But he was on a mission. He brushed past me and marched to the chest-high stage, where he plopped the heavy Underwood. Then Vidal placed withered fingers on the typewriter's home row and began to type with surprising speed, filling the air with a mechanical clatter.

"Look, I think you should leave now."

He shook his head firmly. "Not before you see what happens."

As annoyed as I felt, I didn't think I should drag a frail old man to the street. Best leave that to the cops. I'd already taken a dozen steps toward the phone in the back when Vidal cried out, "Done!"

I stopped. "With what?"

He yanked the page from the Underwood and scuttled toward me, waving the paper excitedly. "Go ahead, read it!"

Sighing, I took the paper and squinted at the dull gray text spattered on the page:

```
BeeGo laughed and danced. The sun was shining. The
birds were singing. BeeGo was going to have fun!
Today was a Happy Day! Every day was a Happy Day!
And that meant BeeGo wanted to dance!
```

"What kind of garbage is this?"

Well, that's what I *meant* to say. But I choked on the words as I beheld an incredible sight on the stage.

The best way to describe the creature is that it looked like the love child of a platypus and a bumblebee. It was six feet tall and twice that around, with slick fur, translucent wings and a broad beaver tail. Its immense torso was a stack of black and yellow stripes. A duckbill mouth split in an almost human grin as the beast gyrated across the stage, serenaded by songbirds flitting among towering trees.

A forest! On my stage! And a dancing thing straight out of a Maurice Sendak book!

"What the bloody—?"

The creature froze in mid-dance, as if God had pressed a cosmic pause button.

"That's all I wrote," Vidal said apologetically.

Trembling, I climbed onto the stage, keeping a wary eye on the beast. It remained motionless. I walked around it, poked it a couple of times, then summoned the courage to run my fingers through its warm fur. Even then, the creature didn't move.

"What is it?" I finally gasped.

"It's BeeGo. That's his name, anyway. Never bothered to describe his species. Kids don't care about that stuff."

"But the trees! The birds! They're all *real*! How is that possible?"

Vidal's gaze was full of pity. "You don't know the history of the Teatro Riviera? About the Saturday children's shows, before the war?"

I dug deep into my memory.

"I recall a few old newspaper articles. Back in the day, the Riv put on live plays. A local guy wrote these fantasy stories about magical forest animals. Kids came from all over to see the shows. The reviewers would marvel over the costumes and how the sets seemed so realistic. But I guess folks got bored with it, especially when the Saturday movie serials got big."

Then the penny dropped.

"You're the one who wrote those plays?"

Vidal indulged in a modest smile. "As you can see, they're not ordinary plays. You must understand, Mr. Starr, every writer is a world builder." He spread his arms, taking in the forest where I stood. "There's something magical about the Riv, something that made my worlds real. My plays opened doors to other lands, fantastic places filled with creatures like BeeGo. All I had to do was write about them, here in this place, and there they were."

He fixed me with his watery eyes.

"Now I'm opening those doors again to save this theater."

* * * *

Vidal was as good as his word. Many trees were slain over the next four years as he and his Underwood wove fantastic tales on paper, tales that came to life on my stage. BeeGo was just the first creature he summoned. Soon came Laifly, with her white bunny tail and bulbous, iridescent eyes; Fragnormous, a lumbering satire of an elephant; and the scary but harmless Sabre-Chomp, heroine to generations of hamsters.

Best of all, the Teatro Riviera came alive again. Children filled the reupholstered seats every Saturday, laughing at the misadventures of Vidal's amazing beasts. Parents who grew up on Pokémon, grandparents nostalgic for Narnia, even a few great-grandparents who recalled the Riv's old magic joined the kids in their revelry.

At the end of every show, once the theater was cleared, Vidal destroyed the pages of his magical script, and his creatures vanished. The stage stood empty, ready for the next fantastic tale to spill from his typewriter.

And the best part? We made a bunch of money.

I put a lot of it into refurbishing the theater. It took a year, even with work crews laboring around the clock, but the results were worth every dime. The Teatro Riviera exceeded its former glory. The ornate woodwork was stripped of decades' worth of grunge, then carefully repainted in the vibrant green, gold and magenta of its birth. The stage was sanded and varnished, the carpet replaced, and the loges—the private boxes—made fit for royalty, of which we had a few now and then.

With the renovations done, the money kept rolling in. I paid Vidal, who was terrible with numbers, the monthly stipend we'd agreed upon. The substantial balance was mine. That was only fair; I deserved the extra shekels for keeping the Riv going for so long.

And then those extra shekels became fewer.

Consumers are a fickle lot. They'll camp outside a store in frigid weather for a shot at the latest smartphone, then jump to a different brand within weeks for some new feature. Vidal's stories were quaint, his creatures beyond imagination, but the old man only had so many happy tales to tell. The audience became jaded.

"You're trying too hard to be chipper," I groused one night as we sat in my office, tallying up that day's disappointing receipts. "People don't like bright, happy stories anymore. The world is darker. Death. Mayhem. Betrayal. They want their entertainment to reflect that."

Vidal stared with wounded-puppy eyes. "But I've always believed people came to the theater to escape the darkness of life."

"Not anymore. Now they want to see someone else suffer. It makes their lives seem a little less depressing."

With a furious frown, Vidal declared, "I don't like those stories. My creatures might look scary, and sometimes sad things happen to them. But they're never cruel, and they're never sad for long."

"And that's why you didn't succeed years ago," I scoffed. "This is a business, Robinson. It's about supply and demand, not art. You've got to write what the audience wants."

I couldn't believe Vidal missed this all-important point. Being true to his muse was blatantly selfish. People demanded a product. It was our job to give it to them, lest we wind up with no job at all.

"We need a new angle. Shake things up a bit." I drummed my fingers on the desk.

"Well, what if we had BeeGo and Laifly get married?"

"Dammit, Robinson, that's more of the same happy crap! You know the definition of insanity? Keep doing the same thing while expecting a different result. Do us both a favor and stop being crazy!"

That shut him up. He dropped his head and stared at his kneecaps while I kept spouting ideas. "Sabre-Chomp is pretty scary-looking. What if we made her a vampire? A sparkly one? Nah, no one will buy it, not after the whole Dance of the Fireflies escapade. We need something really, really different."

And then it hit me.

"Forget the creatures. Forget the magic forest. Let's go for something full-on adult!"

"Like what?"

"Like a murder mystery!"

That snapped Vidal fully upright. "You want me to write about people getting killed?"

"Yes! It's worked on Broadway, off Broadway, in every good and bad theater across the country. It'll do spectacularly well here. Why should the kids have all the fun?"

"But I've never done a story where someone got hurt." His hands quivered at the thought. "I don't think I could do that. I'm not even sure it would work."

"Why not? Words are words. All you do is write about people instead of … whatever those things are. Instead of a happy dance, someone gets shot. I don't see why that's a big deal."

Robinson was shaking so much that he seemed on the cusp of a full-on convulsion.

"The worlds I've summoned through my writing have always been happy ones, Darren," he said. "You're asking me to open a door to a dark and scary place. That's not who I am."

I felt utter contempt for this old man. What kind of writer never explores the darkness these days? A failed one, that's what! And his failure was about to take a big Sabre-Chomp out of my financial plan.

I leaned over my desk, grabbed him by the collar and lifted him out of his chair.

"You better find a way to do it, you sniveling coward!" I shouted. "Fact is, those happy-peppy pets of yours aren't bringing in the bacon! I'm not going broke because of your quirky ethos!"

I released his collar, and he fell back so hard he nearly toppled over. His eyes blazed with hurt, anger and fear.

A perfect foundation for a tale about killing.

"Now," I said, wrestling my voice back under control, "write the damned story."

And he did.

For a guy who had only penned children's fantasies, Robinson Vidal pecked out a better-than-passable murder tale. I'd read plenty of them over the years, from Christie to Cornwall, so I knew the genre, but even I didn't guess that the victim's teenage niece was the murderer. The entire story played out around the murdered man's body as suspect after suspect was presented, scrutinized and shuffled off until the real culprit was discovered and taken away. The last scene was simply the body, serving as a silent, poignant reminder of the real tragedy.

It was bloody. It was lewd. It was going to be a hit!

I blew a ton on advertising, nearly draining my account. But the math said we'd double that investment with a six-month run.

The only trick was figuring out how we'd recreate the show every night. To clear the stage after each performance, Vidal had to destroy the script. After much pressure from me, he decided a few notes in shorthand would give him what he needed to retype the story on the Underwood and summon those dark characters night after night.

To say the premiere was a sellout hardly does it justice. People lined up a dozen wide and blocks long, gladly shivering in a bitter winter wind to see Vidal's magic played out as an adult tale. Tickets went for two grand a pop. I could have sold them for double that, but I didn't want to get greedy. Not yet, anyway.

When the performance began, I stood in the back of the theater, happily counting heads. A full house, 500 people at $2,000 a ticket, a million bucks from one show! By the time Robinson shuffled to my side, I was giddy enough for a BeeGo happy dance.

"Isn't this incredible?" I asked, waving a hand at the crowd.

Robinson shook his head. In the dim light, I didn't notice he was pale and sweating.

"This isn't right, Darren," he whispered.

"Are you nuts? This is what the people want! Tonight's receipts prove it. We're going to be the richest guys on the planet, you and me!"

"No!" His voice was a thick wheeze now, loud enough to distract the patrons in the back row. "I never wanted to be rich. This ... this *ugliness* ... this isn't the world I wanted to build. And I won't do it again. I hid the script, and when this nightmare is over, I'm going to destroy it. My notes, too. You can't make me write this travesty ever again!"

"What the hell are you ... hey, are you okay?"

Vidal grabbed my arm with remarkable strength, but it wasn't enough to keep him upright. His legs gave out, and he slipped to the carpeted floor.

A gunshot startled the crowd. The victim on the stage fell, his body soon outlined in a growing puddle of blood. Just as Robinson Vidal wrote it.

The last story he would ever write, it seemed.

I admit it was heartless to wait until after the show, when the audience had ceased its thunderous applause and melted into the wintry night, to summon an ambulance for Vidal. But he was already dead, his ancient heart finally giving out. Why ruin things for everybody?

Of course, I conveniently left that delay out of the events I described to the police.

"That explains the old man," said the detective as the paramedics wheeled Vidal's body out of the theater. "Now what about the dead guy on the stage?"

A perfectly logical question—one that sucked the air from my lungs.

"Dead guy? Wh-what dead guy?"

"You're kidding me, right? The gunshot victim up there."

Visibly shaking now, I leaned against a meticulously painted wall for support.

"Oh, *that* guy. He ... uh ... heh ... that's not real."

The detective was incredulous. "What the hell are you talking about? That's a real body with a real bullet hole in his head and lots of real blood on the floor. Now, are you going to tell me what happened?"

"No! You're wrong, sir. All that's just a fantasy! Robinson Vidal created it! The dead guy's just a character in a story! It isn't real!"

The cop stared at me for a long time. Then he pulled a set of handcuffs from his pocket.

"Better turn around, Mr. Starr. I'm detaining you till I sort things out."

My heart pounded wildly, and the blood roared through my eardrums like a hurricane.

"No, dammit, you've got it all wrong! I'm not a murderer! It's … wait! The script! Just find the script! Find it, tear it up, and you'll see! There's been no murder here! *I can prove it!*"

I shouted those words all the way through booking, through the arraignment, through the entire trial. And I've screamed them every day I've been on death row.

Yeah, I could prove it—if I knew where Robinson hid the script.

WHAT MIGHT HAVE BEEN

"You're kidding, right?"

The Rodge family stood beneath the dry-rotted sign at the entrance to the amusement park. They saw no activity inside—no rides moving, no squealing children running about, no carnies hawking corn dogs or games of chance. The only thing moving was a small tumbleweed that bounced by their feet on a breath of hot Florida breeze.

It was Jina, recently transformed from sweet princess to belligerent preteen, who voiced the first objection. Nelia followed up with a sharp jab at her husband.

"Really, Ted? We left Michigan two days early for *this*?"

Even the normally upbeat Ted appeared crestfallen. "When I was growing up in Deland, my family came to Wakefield Family Fun Park every year. It was quaint and magical." He paused. "Back then."

Looking up from his handheld video game, nine-year-old Ethan spoke for only the third time since their road trip began.

"Can't we just go to Disney World now?"

Nelia shook her head. "We can't get into the resort until tomorrow, sweetie. We left early so Daddy could bring us to this … special place." She flashed a scowl at Ted.

Ethan sighed and returned to his epic digital battle. Only little Katie, asleep in her stroller, failed to offer any opinion.

Nelia chided herself again for letting Ted plan their vacation. Leaving the office for two weeks was itself a huge risk; Nelia's marketing career was on the rise, and she was on track to make partner at the agency within the year. To that end, she'd spent the drive from Michigan glued to her smartphone, directing four campaigns and landing two new accounts.

Even so, Nelia carried the usual insecurity of successful executives: fear that a lengthy absence would cost her vital momentum. She didn't need that. Nor did she need one more disappointment from her husband.

Sure, Ted was a nice guy; everyone said Nelia was lucky to have him. But he puttered away his days as the manager of a grocery store. That wasn't what embarrassed her. Honest work was noble work. She simply resented his lack of ambition. While Nelia reached for the future, Ted lived happily in the present.

This discontinuity had made their marriage more volatile as the years passed.

At the gate to the creepy, seemingly abandoned park, the unflappable Ted tried to make the best of things. He led the family along the crumbling sidewalk to a tiny ticket booth, its lemon paint seared to a faint cream by the brutal Florida sun. Inside, blue hair waving wildly in the blast of a desktop fan, was an old woman. She was slumped in a lawn chair, eyes closed, mouth wide open, a trail of drool running along her fuzzy chin.

"Is she dead?" asked Ethan.

"Stop that! She isn't dead!" Ted tapped lightly on the dirty glass. The woman merely snorted.

"Excuse me? Ma'am?" He thumped the glass harder this time. With an explosion of arms and legs, the old woman jerked awake.

"Dear Lord! You trying to give me a heart attack?" she shouted.

"I'm … I'm very sorry. I didn't mean to startle you."

The woman took several deep breaths to compose herself. She put a hand to her chest and silently counted a few beats.

"Whew. Guess the ol' ticker isn't done yet." Slightly less annoyed, she turned her attention to the family. "Whatchya need?"

"Uh … you're open?"

"Every day 'cept the Lord's Day, Christmas and Bike Week."

Ted's crooked smile telegraphed a mix of relief and uncertainty. "Good to hear. We'd like five tickets, please. Two adults, three children."

The woman reached for a roll of red tickets and, after a brief struggle hampered by trembling, arthritic hands, ripped off four stubs. "The little one is free," she explained, "but she can only go on the carousel. That'll be $30."

While Ted peeled off the bills, the old woman opened the rear door of the booth and let out a shout that pierced the family's ears and prompted a fearful cry from Katie.

"OH-WWENNNN! We got customers!"

A wrinkled, balding head poked from behind an old ring toss game booth. "What say?"

"Customers, you deaf old coot! You gas up the rides lately?"

Owen scratched his scalp. "Been what, two weeks since the last group come through? Reckon it's still fresh enough. Come on in, folks!"

The family said goodbye to the old woman and walked into Wakefield Family Fun Park.

The place was a disaster. Rides were few—the carousel, a set of bumper cars, a miniature Ferris wheel, and three mini-boats of dubious seaworthiness in an algae-choked circular pool. Peeling paint, cracked fiberglass and rusted metal were everywhere. Ankle-high weeds choked the gravel walkways between attractions, which also included three games of chance: dart throw, baseball throw, and ring toss, each adorned with mildewed stuffed animals hung on racks like slaughterhouse meat. Beyond the games was a single tent promising some mystery attraction. The food booth was empty except for two vending machines, neither of which appeared to be working.

Nelia struggled to contain her fury.

"Well," she said in a clipped tone, "we're not wasting our thirty bucks. Get on the rides."

"Aw, Mom, do we—"

"Yes, Ethan, you do. Every. Last. One. And you're going to have a good time, understand? No, a *great* time."

Arms folded, her face a no-nonsense glower, Nelia watched as her husband and children dispersed.

She didn't share any of the rides with her kids, and certainly not with Ted, who remained the target of her frustration. She needed space. Nelia waded through the weeds, making her way past the game booths toward the mystery tent. Owen, clad in worn coveralls, slipped a John Deere cap over his bare head and met her at the entry flap.

"Sorry, ma'am, you'll have to wait a few minutes while I get the rides started for your youngsters," he said.

"I don't need to see the show. I just need to … get out of the sun."

Owen gave a sympathetic sigh. "Sorry you're frettin'. I know the park ain't what she used to be. Everyone goes to Disney and SeaWorld these days. But Mamie and I can't bring ourselves to shut it down."

Nelia nodded politely. Dedication to one's career was something she could understand.

"Besides," Owen continued, "we got an attraction that none of the fancy places got. Right here, in fact."

He waved a hand at the tent before them. Nelia looked at the worn canvas and the faded letters over the entrance:

Make Your Wish In
The World Of Might-Have-Beens

"What is it? A game of some sort?" asked Nelia.

Owen wagged his eyebrows. "Not exactly. Look, you stay here while I get the rides a-goin' and then I'll come back and show you."

Nelia watched as Owen trotted off toward the carousel where Katie, astride a peeling white unicorn, grumpily wagged her legs, urging the steed to begin its circular journey. Ted stood next to her, a protective hand at her waist. Jina and Ethan were over at the bumper cars, ready to carry their sibling rivalry into true battle.

Nelia's eyes drifted back to Ted. In years past, watching him interact with the children would spark a warm glow within her. But now all she felt was resentment.

I let him plan this trip, and we end up in this dump! Do I have to do everything myself? It's not like I don't have enough on my plate. I've got a career, one that isn't helped by wasting my time at this rundown carnival! If Ted had any kind of smarts, any ambition at all, he would have checked this place out before we left.

The more she mulled over her husband's latest failing, the angrier she became. She couldn't even stand to look at him. And the sun was so blasted hot! In disgust, she turned her back to him and threw open the tent flap, hiding herself in The World of Might-Have-Beens.

The light inside was dim. A single, bare incandescent bulb clung to ancient wiring that snaked along a tent pole. Dots of sunlight pricked through the weathered canvas, piercing the musty, dust-filled air. A small pedestal, waist high, stood in the center of the tent. It held a metal box, coated with patina, that looked a lot like an antique cash register with a hand crank on the side. About a dozen feet beyond the display were three threadbare curtains of dark-red velvet, each hanging beneath a large wooden sign. The marker on the left said *Yes.* The one in the middle said *No.* And the sign on the right said *Your Way.*

"Weird," she said aloud. "It must be some sort of game after all."

Nelia approached the metal contraption, looking for instructions on how to play. Owen had asked her to wait, but Nelia wasn't the patient type. Soon enough she found words printed on the top of the pedestal. She squinted to read them in the dim light:

Make your wish and turn the crank.
Accept your fate? The curtain waits.
But turn from destiny's say,
There lies the peril of choosing Your Way.

"What kind of nonsense is that?" Nelia was no fatalist. She believed in owning her destiny, making it work for her, allowing nothing to stand in her way.

Including Ted.

There it was. In the silence of a half-rotted tent in the heart of steamy Florida, she finally admitted it.

Her marriage was a joke. Meaningless. Stifling. Sure, lots of women succeeded brilliantly in personal and professional worlds, but those women weren't married to Ted Rodge, the poster child for inertia.

It was time for a change.

Make your wish …

Silly. Childish. But what the hell?

"Okay," she said to the strange metal box. "I wish I was married to the man of my dreams—ambitious, powerful and successful."

She turned the crank once and heard metallic clacking noises from inside the box. But nothing happened. She turned the crank again, then again, until it locked. There was a clanging sound, and a card popped into view beneath a small glass window.

It said "No."

The answer came entirely at random, of course, the result of gears and levers and slides moving within the metal box. It bore no true meaning, no impact on reality. Nonetheless, the response infuriated Nelia. She slapped the side of the device in frustration just as Owen came into the tent.

"I really wish you'd waited," he said.

Unfairly but unrepentant, Nelia turned her fury toward the old man.

"Why? So you can explain your elaborate take on the Magic 8 Ball? That's all this is—a giant fortune cookie without the cookie! And this is what you've got over Disney World?"

Owen shook his head. "Ma'am, you don't understand."

"Oh, I understand plenty!" Nelia seethed. "I've been in business long enough to know a scam when I see one. You had the gall to charge us thirty bucks to tour this flea trap? Well, guess what? Screw your wishing game! Screw your whole sad excuse for a park! I'm going to walk out of this tent, get my family and get the hell out of here!"

Refusing to go anywhere near this pitiful old man, Nelia spun around and stormed toward one of the curtains, the one labeled *Your Way*.

"No, wait!" Owen cried.

Ignoring him, Nelia threw the flap aside.

And stepped into a walk-in closet.

She froze, stunned by the sudden change of scenery. Unlike the dark, stifling tent, the closet was long and brightly lit. It even had a small window at the far end, framing an azure sky. On either side of Nelia were rows of expensive clothing, men's on her left, women's on her right.

Her mind began to spin, and she held tightly to the velvet curtain in her hand to keep her balance. That's when she noticed that the curtain wasn't a curtain anymore. She was clutching the massive sleeve of a luxurious velvet robe.

Nelia shoved the robe aside, ready to storm back into the tent and demand an explanation from the old park owner.

Except there was no tent. There was only a blank wall.

Something a lot like terror stabbed Nelia's heart.

"What's going on?" she whispered, trembling. She touched the wall, then tapped it lightly. It was real and solid. A hook above her held the velvet robe, which she released as if it were on fire. She suddenly noticed that the stifling Florida heat and humidity was gone, replaced by almost chilly conditioned air.

Turning again, Nelia walked the length of the closet. Surely this was just one of those carnival mazes. A labyrinth of some sort. She'd find the exit soon enough—and, moments later, she came upon a door next to the small window.

As Nelia reached for the doorknob, she glanced out the window.

And gasped.

Rather than the tumble-down structures of Wakefield Family Fun Park, Nelia saw the familiar skyline of Manhattan pasted against a postcard-perfect sky. Looking down, she could see Central Park, rolling out like a long, green carpet 40 stories below her.

This can't be happening!

It was a trick, an illusion. That was the only explanation for suddenly finding herself a thousand miles away from the amusement park.

Then she heard a noise beyond the door: the sound of rustling bedsheets and a murmur of conversation, voices she didn't recognize.

As impossible as it seemed, Nelia had to accept that she was hiding in the closet of somebody's high-rise apartment, with the residents right outside the closet door.

Keep your grip, Nelia! Releasing the scream now bubbling in her throat would surely worsen matters. Yet a confrontation seemed inevitable. She couldn't hide in the closet forever. Sooner or later, someone would want to get dressed. Better to seize the initiative, surprise the occupants and maybe get out of the building before the cops arrived.

As unlikely as that sounded, Nelia thought it more promising than phoning her husband in Florida and convincing him to bail her out of jail in New York City.

With a deep breath, Nelia seized the doorknob, turned it and stepped forward.

The bedroom was massive and ornate, filled with expensive wall hangings, bronze sculptures and a wall mirror the size of a small car. To Nelia's right was a bed so big that it made her king-size bed at home look like a camp cot. Atop the disheveled sheets sat a man and a woman, each clad in blue satin robes, sipping golden mimosas.

That is, until Nelia's entrance caused them to spill their drinks.

"Whoops!" said Nelia with exaggerated good cheer as the two cursed and scrambled away from the vanishing puddles on the bed. "Sorry about that. Seems I got myself turned around. I'm looking to rent, and the landlord must have given me the wrong key. Please, don't mind me, I'll just—"

The man acted as if he hadn't heard a word. He stared at Nelia, his expression a mixture of annoyance and alarm—mostly the latter.

"Nelia!" he stammered.

She froze. *How did he know who she was?*

"I … I thought you were in Dubai until Saturday, babe," he continued. "I got back early from Beijing after nailing the joint venture, and I was going to, uh, surprise you."

"Dubai? What … wait a minute. Did you just call me 'babe'?" She despised that term, banning it from Ted's vocabulary years ago.

The man didn't seem to hear. He shrugged awkwardly. "I know what this must look like."

Nelia put her hands on her hips. "I assume it's exactly what it looks like. Which means it's none of my business. I'll just be on my way."

The man's anxiety faded, replaced by sudden fury.

"Fine, you little bitch! It's what you've wanted all along anyway. Just make sure you and that lawyer you're screwing don't forget about our prenup. I worked hard for all this, and you're not going to take it away from me!"

Prenup?

All of Nelia's confusion, all of her anger and embarrassment, faded in a cold deluge of dread.

"Who ... who are you?" she asked, her voice soft and ragged.

The man seemed genuinely astonished. "Who am I? You been drinking again? I'm Geoff, your husband."

"My ... my *what?*"

"Come on, babe, we've been married for 15 years. Let's not play this game."

No! It can't be!

"Are ... are you okay?"

It was the woman who spoke. Nelia looked at her, really looked at her. She was young, beautiful. Stunning, really. Emerald eyes gleamed from her perfect face, which was framed in natural, golden blonde. She was maybe a few years older than Jina—

Jina!

Evan!

Katie!

"Dear God, where are my children!"

Geoff stared at Nelia in genuine confusion. "Children? What's wrong with you? Don't start on that again! We both agreed—no kids. Didn't want to mess up our careers."

Nelia finally screamed. From deep within her terrified soul came a shriek as loud and pitiful as any ever heard. Geoff and his mistress flung themselves off the bed and backed away from the raving woman. Then Geoff reached for the bedside phone.

Nelia turned and fled back into the closet, still screaming. The corridor seemed to go on forever, pressing in on her from the sides like a collapsing cave. Desperately she grabbed the velvet robe and flung it aside.

There was only the blank wall.

"No, no, *no!*" she cried, slapping the wall with her hands until they went numb. She clutched the robe and buried her face in the sleeve, weeping uncontrollably.

"Oh God! Oh God, please! Not Ted! Not my children! I'm sorry! Please, please don't take them away! Please ..."

A powerful hand grasped her shoulder. Nelia whirled around, ready to fight, to rage against Geoff and the bizarre world she'd been dropped into.

Only it wasn't Geoff standing before her.

It was Owen.

The closet had vanished. There was only the dark tent, the smell of hot canvas, and the corner of a velvet curtain clutched in her hand.

"Like I was sayin'," Owen said, shaking his head as he released the trembling woman, "you shoulda waited for me."

Nelia looked around slowly, fearful that the nightmare might return. It didn't.

"What happened?" she finally asked, her voice small and quavering.

"What never should, but often does," said Owen softly. "Seen it happen here a thousand times."

"But it ... it wasn't real, was it? It couldn't be!" Owen sighed. "It was, in a manner of speakin'. See, ma'am, everybody's got wishes, hopes, prayers. Sometimes they're granted, sometimes not. Sometimes they come after a lot of work. And that's all good. But then there's folks who don't see the precious thing they got right in front of 'em. They keep wishing for something else, maybe something that ain't good for them in the long run. But they won't pay attention."

Nelia shook her head. "I don't understand."

Smiling, his eyes alight with a wisdom that belied his humble image, Owen gently patted her shoulder.

"A wise man once said that some people say to God, 'Thy will be done,' and some to whom God says, 'All right, have it your way.'"

He nodded at the sign over head. Then he gave a quick wink.

Still trembling, Nelia stared up at the sign for a long time. Then she fled, bursting from the tent in a wild, tearful rush to embrace her family. Her present, and her future.

HAVE NOT

"We have a big problem."

I finished sipping my Château d'Yquem—the 1811 vintage, of course—and suppressed the urge to roll my eyes.

"What is it this week, Bernard? What crisis of epic proportions do we face?"

Bernard made a face. "Sarcasm doesn't become you, Philip."

"Just as paranoia doesn't you. Have you any notion how tiresome it is? Remember last month? You warned of an imminent economic collapse. Never mind that the systems in place at Hăven make that impossible. All you accomplished was getting yourself disinvited from the Economic Forum on the Davos Level."

"I was talking about a global collapse outside of Hăven."

"And how would that matter to us?"

That Bernard, or anyone, cared what happened outside Hăven was the only surprise. For more than a century, none of the six million residents of our secure, towering city-state, erupting from what was once the American heartland, had ventured into the empty prairie. There was no reason to do so. Inside Hăven, every necessity was met: generous living space, a rich and vibrant cultural life, every nutritional and material need served through technology. Indeed, the name of our great society, Hăven—with a short "a," as in "apple"— carried the moniker deliberately. Here we had everything we needed. Time for every worthwhile pursuit. No violence. No worries. Except for those Bernard imagined.

I took another sip of wine. "If you're searching for a crisis, consider that this is my last bottle of the 1811. The last one anywhere, in fact. Sad."

Bernard leaned forward in the guest chair in my study. Only the faintest sound of vicuna-swaddled rump on leather emanated from beneath him, so supple was the chair's full grain covering and soft were his woolen pants.

"What matters, my friend, is that we've run out of Have Nots."

I lowered my wine glass. "Beg pardon?"

"Have Nots. They're gone. All of them."

Have Nots. I hadn't heard the term in many years. It bore too much baggage even now, long after our society had purged outdated notions of political correctness. After all, the people of means—the Haves, if one must—had fashioned a free society where anyone could succeed if they worked hard enough. Those who didn't ... well, they made their choice and bore the consequences. Life really was that simple: Achieve, or don't. Anything else was charity in the worst sense, and charity coddled the lazy. Tolerance, diversity, equity, all those politically correct ideas—and the people they once represented—did nothing to build our social and economic success. It startled me to hear Bernard bring up Have Nots with such fret.

"Isn't that a good thing?" I asked, puzzled. "The Have Nots were greedy and resentful. They drove much of the turmoil throughout history. If we've all succeeded, and the Have Nots are no more, doesn't that prove our point?"

Bernard shook his head so hard I feared self-induced whiplash.

"'When a nation is filled with strife, then do patriots flourish.' Lao Tzu."

I snorted. "Taoist nonsense!"

"Dismiss it if you want. You can't blame the Taoists anymore."

"Fine by me. Less philosophical twaddle to waste my time on. See? There's a bright side after all." I lifted my wine glass, tipped it toward him, then drained the last of its ancient nectar.

"You don't get it, Philip. We can't condemn the Taoists for anything because there aren't any. We can't blame the Buddhists, either. Nor the Hindus or the Jains or the Sikhs. They're all gone."

His doom-and-gloom gibber still made no sense. "What are you talking about? Blame them for what?"

Bernard wheezed like an exasperated parent.

"Let's try this again," he said slowly.

I tried not to react to his patronizing tone.

"Our entire society in Hăven is built on objectivism—the belief that we are a heroic race, that our happiness serves as our moral purpose, and productive achievement is our noblest pursuit. We're motivated by rational and ethical self-interest."

"Thank you, Bernard. I'm up on my Rand."

He ignored my snark. "Objectivism demands a baseline. We must know what is *not* in our self-interest if we're to pursue what *is*. How can we strive for happiness without comparing it to what constitutes unhappiness?"

I still wasn't getting his point. "I'm reasonably certain I know what makes me unhappy. Running out of my favorite wine, for example. Or listening to paranoid delusions—no offense. My goal in life is to overcome such things."

"But," said Bernard, "what if you fail?"

Shrugging, I replied, "I've always believed failure is a temporary state for the true objectivist. If I fail, it's because I haven't tried hard enough."

"Or?"

"Or," I pondered, then offered, "something prevents me from reaching my goal."

Bernard smiled and poked at the air. "Correct. Something. Or someone."

Thinking hard, I leaned forward, edging closer to Bernard. A light went on in my head, fell into my gut and began to smolder. I was beginning to understand his concern. Worse, I was starting to share it.

"You're suggesting I need a scapegoat to explain my failures?"

"We all do," said Bernard. "It's vital to our sense of accomplishment and self-worth."

He went on. "You finished second in a race because another runner cut you off. You didn't get that promotion because the guy who did sucked up to the boss. Or the reverse: You won because you trained harder than the other runners, or you did more for the company than your peers. The Have Nots served that role for centuries. They've been the gauge for our success.

"So what happens when we lose the measure of how far we've risen? How do we know we've succeeded without a meaningful metric?"

I squirmed in my chair, increasingly troubled by Bernard's train of thought. "Can't we measure productive achievement by circumstances? Why limit it to people?"

"Because people either create circumstances or exacerbate their consequences," he replied. "Either way, people tend to anthropomorphize the challenge, and then demonize it. Think back on history. When did the United States truly thrive? When it had enemies to fight—living, breathing enemies who embodied the threat. We even gave them horrid names. 'Savage redskins,' 'damned Japs,' 'godless Commies.' You get the idea. Those terms became too offensive for polite society, and we banished them to locker rooms and dark corners of the bar. But the sentiment remains. It's how winners distinguish themselves. We need people to blame for our troubles, people to overcome in our fight to be better, to prove we accomplished the task.

"Problem is," Bernard continued, "we've run out of them."

"Ridiculous! There are plenty of other groups out there."

"Such as?"

Foolishly, I hadn't anticipated his question. How many times had I talked about the ambiguous "them," the faceless "they" who posed some offense or threat? Everyone knew who "they" were, right? Except, at this moment, I struggled to conjure a name. But I wasn't about to back away from Bernard's challenge.

"Illegal trespassers in Hăven," I declared.

He shook his head. "None, not since we built our wall of security systems. It's impenetrable."

"But what about those who got in earlier?"

"Purged years ago. Try again."

"There must be those whose social pedigree isn't up to the highest standards."

Bernard's tongue *tsk-tsked* a negative. "It took decades, but we've eliminated the social strata. Every resident of Hăven is highly educated and cultured."

"Even the economic lower classes?"

"We're all quintillionaires."

"But surely we still have lower-class ethnic groups around!"

"None. Everyone is of European descent. Hăven barred the rest long ago. Or deported them." He paused. "For all we know, my worry about a global economic collapse was years too late. We haven't had a genuine sighting of a human being outside Hăven since the famines a decade ago."

I ignored that last. For some reason, the notion that Hăven might hold the last of humankind unsettled me.

"What about servants? I mean, sure, I have a robotic butler—"

"So does everyone else."

I was running out of groups to suggest, much to my growing annoyance.

"Political extremists?"

"Everyone's a Rand acolyte."

"Altruists?"

"For whom?" he chuckled. "Thoroughly rejected."

"Impressionable youth?"

"Fully indoctrinated."

"Religious extremists?"

"Gone. Only the Prosperity Christians remain."

"The elderly?"

"Our medical systems keep even the oldest person healthy and strong. No chronically sick people, either."

I flung my hands in the air. "You win. I'm out of ideas."

Bernard took no satisfaction in his victory.

"See the dilemma? We lack an enemy. Sure, we'll always have individual differences. You like wine, I prefer scotch. But those differences don't constitute a big enough challenge to fuel society's growth."

I leaned back again, deeply troubled by my old friend's prophecy.

"I get your point. If we can't grow, if we can't achieve more, then we die."

I fiddled with my empty wine glass. "You're talking about the end of Hăven itself."

Bernard nodded. "Over time, we'll lose all ability to make Hăven greater than it is." Then he made his final, most damning statement:

"We're the Haves. And if we're to survive, we need the Have Nots."

* * * *

Hăven possessed a minimal government, being largely unnecessary because of our sophisticated technology and success over want. Still, we weren't anarchists. We had a small council that met now and then, managing the mundane, needle-and-thread functions that kept our city-state running smoothly.

Thanks to Bernard's newly identified crisis, things had suddenly become less smooth.

"Why must the Have Nots be a specific group? Why can't they be ambiguous?" asked Reggie, brushing the crumbs of his seventh *kouign-amann* from his Dourmeuil suit. "In the old days, societies created scapegoats from thin air all the time. A threat didn't have to be identifiable to be accepted as real."

Victoria, a wrinkled, blue-haired council member of uncertain age, shot him down.

"That's not entirely true," she said in a gravelly voice. "In the old days, even broadly defined enemies had a cultural or geographic link. 'Terrorists' typically referred to Middle Easterners. 'Illegal immigrants' usually meant Hispanics. 'Lazy poor people' was a label placed on low-income blacks and whites. Not accurate labels, perhaps, but that wasn't the intent. The Haves needed a reference point. I see what Bernard is getting at."

The conversation spiraled from there, with Reggie insisting a vague menace would suffice while the rest dismissed his idea and argued over what the peril should be. As the council's chair, I listened for a while, lamenting my long-gone Château d'Yquem as I quaffed a disappointing grapefruit-infused spritzer.

Finally, I could stand the sniping no longer.

"Let's come to order," I said loudly. After a pause for the group to settle down, I continued.

"I think we all agree with the basic principle Bernard raised: Haves only exist when there are Have Nots to compare against. The question is, to what or whom do we assign the role of Have Nots?"

Ideas flew like gnats; all were batted away. The most promising involved making a threat out of the population beyond Hăven, but while people almost certainly lived somewhere beyond the prairie, they remained scarce at best, unseen for years.

I ended the debate after three fruitless hours. We agreed to reassemble in a week's time, with each council member preparing a list of potential Have Nots.

Back in my condominium, I slid onto my Peugeot Onyx sofa, careful not to spill my drink—a sunny Ritz-Paris Sidecar—and heaved a weary sigh. I resented my old friend immensely. As I studied the night through my window, the good life in Hăven carried on as it always had, a product of our hard, centuries-long work. The Have Nots didn't vanish overnight; why must we surrender to Bernard's anxieties with such urgency?

Enough. I should go to bed, I thought. Instead, I reached for my interface on the table beside me, unrolled it and asked it to start a list of potential Have Nots.

When the door chime sounded an hour later, I hadn't come up with a single candidate.

Hobson, my robotic servant, sought permission to usher in the visitor. I granted it. Moments later, Bernard shuffled in, looking ill at ease. He took up residence in my Foretti Bergere armchair.

"You look haggard," I said, concerned. "Hobson, bring Bernard a scotch. Neat."

Bernard shook his head. "That won't be necessary." He swallowed, as if steeling himself. I didn't like it.

"I'll get right to the point," he said. "We've solved the problem."

"You mean, the Have Nots?"

He nodded. "The council agreed unanimously." My blood pressure rose quickly. "The council met? Why wasn't I told? I'm the chair!"

"Because you're the reason why."

I frowned and shook my head slightly. "I don't understand."

Bernard took a deep breath. "I'll put it simply: You and your kind are the Have Nots."

I tried to stand, but my legs failed to lift me.

"What the devil are you talking about?" I demanded.

Bernard shoved himself back into his seat, putting a few more centimeters of space between himself and my growing rage.

"It was your idea, actually. From when we met earlier. You suggested the economic lower class. They've served perfectly as Have Nots for millennia. Rand herself said money is the barometer of a society's virtue. It stands to reason, then, that as we gain wealth individually, we gain virtue collectively."

Bernard's logic resonated, but his point remained elusive.

"You said it yourself, every person in Hăven is a quintillionaire," I said, wagging a finger at him. "That's a hell of a lot of virtue!"

"But far from the ceiling," replied my so-called friend. "Philip, what's your net worth?"

My eyebrows lifted, not from offense at a personal question, but because it took me a moment to do the math. And because his question shifted my anger to deep dread.

"Seven quintillion, give or take a trillion," I said at last.

Bernard nodded. "You and roughly 15 percent of the population of Hăven fall below the decaquintillion level," he explained. "You're placing undue burden on the system."

Had Hobson fallen into my jacuzzi, he wouldn't have sputtered as violently as I did.

"How in God's name am I a burden? I'm part of the wealthiest population in the history of humanity!"

"And yet you don't drive our society forward at the same rate as the rest of us. Compared to me, you're not achieving productively."

Bernard moved beyond his nervousness as he gave himself to his twisted logic.

"You are a drain, Philip. You and the rest of your people. It's too bad, really. If only you'd apply yourself, build upon your individual potential. But you don't. You've become complacent, perhaps even lazy. Hăven can't abide this."

My voice broke in rage. "I dare you to name one thing I do—one thing!—that poses a threat to Hăven!"

Bernard gestured at my living room. "Your home, for starters. The trappings of productive achievement, but none of the substance. Indeed, as I look around, this place hardly reflects housing that aspires to be something better. But we'll fix that."

"Fix it? How?"

Bernard lowered his arms. "I bought this entire level. Well, a small group of investors and I. But I'm the principal shareholder. We're going to renovate the level completely, create all-new, high-quality housing designed to appeal to a—" he paused, retaining just enough grace to smile sheepishly, "—a certain clientele, at a certain income level. I'm afraid, old friend, your kind won't qualify."

My fists balled, pressing manicured nails into my uncalloused palms. "This is outrageous! Where will I live?"

Bernard shrugged. "That's not any of my business, is it? I'm sure you'll figure out something. You've got the same opportunities as the rest of us. And if you choose not to apply yourself … well, the outside world awaits. The prairie and all."

Fury finally lifted me to my feet.

"Get the hell out of here!" I shouted.

Bernard rose slowly, deliberately. He studied me with a mix of regret and resolve.

"We have to look after our interests. Ours and our community's. I'm sure you understand," Bernard said quietly.

He turned and headed toward the door while I continued to stand, speechless and trembling with rage.

Then he looked back at me, a glimmer of sadness in his eyes.

"You do see it, right? Hăven can't bear your mortgage on our labor. The Haves cannot tolerate the Have Nots. Our individual futures depend on it."

Then he was gone, pursued by Hobson's preprogrammed farewell.

I said nothing. All I could think about was the prairie.

LOCUM TENENS

"I ... I have some bad news, dear."

Bing Hedwig grunted from behind a wall of newsprint. He was deep into his Saturday ritual: coffee, the old-fashioned morning edition, and ignoring his wife. Her rusted-hinge voice, made loathsome by the years, barely penetrated his fortress of mind and paper.

"Same old stuff," he muttered at the soy ink. "Crime rate's down again. The Middle East issue's finally settled. Even the politicians are behaving." He shook his head. "Hardly worth buying the paper anymore. Used to be twice as thick as this, and they still couldn't get all the bad news in it. All since—"

"Funny you should mention bad news."

Uh oh. Bing slowly lowered one corner of the paper. Willa Hedwig's nervous gaze drifted down to the ragged gray carpet beneath her house slippers.

"You broke something, didn't you? What was it this time?"

"The ... uh ... the Mark 3."

Bing convulsed. Beefy hands mangled the half-read paper.

"You broke our Ersetzen?" Willa nodded pitifully.

"How?"

"It wasn't my fault! This telemarketer called and hounded me about life insurance, and I was just so angry I almost slammed down the phone, but I didn't want to break it, so I—"

"Took it out on the Ersetzen!"

"But isn't that what—"

Bing flung the wadded newspaper across the living room. "Didn't you read the owner's manual? Those things aren't indestructible, you know!"

"I know! Well, *now* I know."

She lifted her head and offered a tentative look, weak hope glimmering in her eyes. "Couldn't we just buy a new one?"

"Oh sure!" Bing roared. "We'll zip down to Postiche's Superstore and buy a fancy new Ersetzen with our slush fund!" He snapped his fingers, as if something suddenly occurred to him. "Oh, by the way, *sweetheart*, how much have we managed to squirrel away?"

Willa didn't answer. They both knew there was no slush fund. The Hedwigs rode life atop the wheels of consumerism. There was no other way to keep pace with their middle-class neighbors. But this, *this* put the brakes to the wheel.

Bing raged through the house like a small typhoon, howling at his quivering wife. Willa knew only one way to calm that storm, and she employed it in earnest.

"Now don't start bawling!" Bing moaned. Sniveling he could stand, but Willa's hysteria twisted his tender gut. In recent years, he'd had an option for dealing with it. But now the Ersetzen was gone, Willa blubbered uncontrollably, and Bing's stomach hurt.

"You don't love me anymore!" Willa yowled.

"And don't be bringing love into it, either!" Despite his anger, Bing was desperate to calm her down. Swallowing bile, he took a deep breath and summoned a soothing tone. "Hey, listen … maybe it was already broken."

Willa's despair took an abrupt and optimistic turn. "Do you really think so?"

"Sure. It was, what, 30 years old? Anything could have broken it. We'll just go down to Postiche's today and check out the new Ersetzens. Maybe there's a sale. Just don't start crying again, okay? *Please?*"

Willa's grief vanished. A yellow smile appeared from beneath the twin waterfalls of her cheap mascara.

* * * *

Jefferson P. Maxwell was the best salesman at Postiche's Superstore.

In the past five years, Maxwell had been Sales Associate of the Month a whopping 28 times. His secret—rumors ranged from magic spells (unlikely) to sex appeal (even less likely)—was, in fact, just a carefully nurtured instinct for sizing up customers.

So when Maxwell saw the middle-aged couple stroll into the store, he recognized the classic portrait of a sure sale. The woman, thin and puffy-eyed, scurried about like a child clutching her allowance and turned loose in a toy store. Meanwhile, her husband wore the stern mask of a man determined not to leave with so much as a business card. It didn't matter. Jefferson knew the right words, the right tone of voice, the no-fail process to make the deal. Maxwell smiled broadly, awash in confidence. Today he would add a few more bucks to the store's bottom line—and to his own pocket.

"Afternoon, folks!" He spoke cheerfully, standing just far enough away to make his presence felt without violating their personal space. He clasped his hands in front of him and kept his shoulders slightly rounded, all sending a message of subservience. "Anything I can help you find?"

"Yes!" the woman chattered. "We—"

"No!" The man impaled his wife with a dagger look, then turned dulled eyes to Maxwell. "We're just looking."

Maxwell nodded easily. "No problem. Browse all you like. You'll notice a few floor models on sale. Great deals."

"Oh. Uh, thanks." The man paused. Maxwell watched him closely. *One ... two ... three—*

"Are they damaged at all? The floor models, I mean."

Gotcha! But Jefferson betrayed no sense of victory. "Nope. These Mark 10s are good as new. And the prices are rock-bottom because the new 12s are due next month." Jefferson leaned casually against a convenient beam. "You folks ever own one?"

The man laughed heartily at the joke. "Have we ever owned an Ersetzen? Of course! But Willa broke ours today."

"Bing!" The woman was mortified. Maxwell moved quickly, holding out his hands in a gesture of comfort. He didn't want to lose the sale to a domestic squabble.

"Not to worry, ma'am. They all wear out eventually. How old was your unit, anyway?"

"At least 30 years old. It was a Mark 3."

Jefferson whistled, genuinely impressed. "A Mark 3! I haven't seen a decent Mark 3 in almost a decade. Can't get replacement parts, you know. Never could, in fact."

"I know," replied Bing, still not realizing he'd tipped his hand. "Parts aren't available on any Ersetzens older than five years. That's when they started lab production."

"You're absolutely right, sir. The Mark 7, first from the lab and probably the most popular unit ever made. Very durable. Took lots of abuse."

"Oh dear," Willa fretted. "Does that mean the newer models aren't as good?"

Whoops! "Not at all, ma'am. The 7s were great, but the manufacturers got even better at building later ones. The 8s and 9s weren't bad. The 10s are extremely well built, with lots of extras." *Nice save, Maxwell!*

"Take this one over here." Maxwell ushered them across the showroom to an Ersetzen standing atop a squat, circular platform. Blue and red neon lights cast a violet halo, and a cardboard display nearby explained its many features.

"Here's a Mark 10-SE, an upscale version. It features rapid self-repair, improved autonomic response and a mute option. It's built from a strong recombinant template, guaranteed to withstand up to eight major reprisals per day. Five-year warranty, all parts and labor."

Bing walked slowly around the platform, carefully studying the Mark 10-SE, searching for any fault that he could use to his advantage. But its solid construction and clean bronze surface were flawless.

"It's a beauty," he admitted.

"Care to try it?"

Bing glanced at the salesman in surprise. "Can I?"

"Sure! Like I said, the self-repair on the 10-SE is highly accelerated. If you bang it up, it'll be unmarked in no time."

"Unbelievable!" Willa breathed. "Our old Ersetzen sometimes took days." She jabbed her husband with a bony elbow. "Go ahead, dear."

Bing was eager to do so. After all, he'd been without an Ersetzen for several hours. He was still upset at Willa, and the salesman's careful manipulations had finally dawned on him. That annoyed him deeply, churning his aching stomach. He simply had to release that stress!

Bing focused on his tension and anger, directing it into his right arm. He clenched his fist, drew back, then let loose with a blow that lifted the Ersetzen clean off the platform. The unit flew backwards, smashing through the cardboard display and slamming to the floor.

Half a minute passed. Bing and Willa turned blue waiting. Then, slowly, the Ersetzen lifted itself from the showroom floor. Swaying slightly, it reassumed its upright position. The wobble soon faded. There was a dark splotch where Bing's fist had struck, but as they watched they could see the mark begin to fade.

"That's incredible!" cried Bing.

"We'll take it!" whooped Willa.

Maxwell needed little time to explain and complete the paperwork. It didn't matter; the Hedwigs blissfully ignored all references to interest rates, payments and finance charges. Their minds floated in the joy of their new purchase. "All I have to do now is phone in your credit application." Maxwell reached for the grimy receiver at his desk. "Won't take a minute."

"That's fine," said Bing. "We'll just go and have another look at our new Ersetzen."

Like giddy newlyweds, they glided hand in hand across the showroom until they stood before the 10-SE. The dark splotch that Bing left on its surface had vanished. The Ersetzen was as clean now as it had been when the Hedwigs first saw it.

"Isn't technology amazing?" Bing marveled. "A pop like that on our old unit would have shut it down for hours."

"That's the way of things nowadays, isn't it?"

Bing's crinkled brow asked for more.

"Well, when people need to improve something or make their lives easier, they just go out and do it," Willa remarked.

"Remember when there used to be so much crime and killing and war, like you said when you were reading the paper? Terrible! And whose fault was it? Certainly not ours! It's not fair to make good people suffer all that blame and guilt and stress. It's unhealthy. We needed the Ersetzens to make things right. Otherwise, where would we be?"

Bing had to smile. Dear Willa! She was a dolt, but now and then she surprised him with a precious insight. She was quite right. Little stress marred the Hedwigs' lives—or anyone else's, for that matter. They knew no guilt, for no one was guilty. The Ersetzens had seen to that.

A nervous cough interrupted his thoughts.

"Excuse me." Maxwell spoke in a low, apologetic tone. He stood behind them, his left hand clutching the Hedwigs' sales agreement.

"All set?" Bing asked the salesman.

Maxwell rubbed his forehead. "I'm afraid not, Mr. Hedwig. There's a small problem with your line of credit."

"Problem? What kind of problem?"

"Uh, you don't have one."

Willa's gasp came like a small scream. "We can't get financed? Why not?"

"Excuse me for asking, but did you two declare bankruptcy last year?"

"Well, yes," Willa replied. "But we had no choice! We were eight months behind on our mortgage, the car was repossessed, and the power company cut us off. But my nephew—he's an accountant—he said going bankrupt wouldn't cause a long-term problem."

"That's often true, Mrs. Hedwig. After enough time has passed."

"But it's been more than a year!"

Maxwell shuffled his feet uncomfortably. "Your credit score takes a long time to bounce back after bankruptcy, Mrs. Hedwig. Several years, in fact. I could try every trick I know—check with every bank, every credit union, every financial wizard. Pull strings. Call in favors. But they'll all tell me the same thing."

"What are you saying?" Bing's voice rose straight out of a tomb. "We can't get the new Ersetzen?"

"I'm very sorry, Mr. Hedwig."

"But ... what about a cheaper model?"

"Cheap, expensive, it doesn't matter. Not unless you pay in cash."

Bing's temper flared again. "If I had the cash, I wouldn't be trying to get financed!"

Without thinking, he whirled on the Ersetzen he'd nearly owned, fists clenched. Maxwell quickly grabbed his arm.

"Mr. Hedwig, I can't let you use this unit!"

"But it's *mine*!" Bing roared.

"It's not yours! Not until the sale is final!"

Bing struggled to free himself, so desperate was he to take out his ire on the Ersetzen. That's what they were for, weren't they? Why spend all the time and money growing human clones in thousands of goo-filled labs if they were just going to stand around in showrooms? Use them as they were meant to be used, as billions of people did every day: as scapegoats for their weaknesses, their disagreements, their accidents. As sacrificial lambs in warfare, dying so that mothers' sons could go on living. As pawns to shoulder all the world's anger and blame, relieving humanity of the unfairness of guilt, the injustice of responsibility.

Financing be damned! *He had a right!*

"Is there a problem here?"

A security guard, tall and menacing, appeared from nowhere. Bing's anger chilled in a sudden, frigid wave of fear and embarrassment.

"I think you and your wife were just leaving," the guard observed.

Bing could only nod silently. Nod—and leave. The Hedwigs scampered toward the exit.

"I'll keep trying, Mr. Hedwig," Maxwell called lamely. "When I figure things out, I'll give you a call. Honest!"

Bing risked a quick look back. Not at the glowering security guard. Not at the despondent salesman. Instead, he gazed at the Ersetzen—a six-foot wall of thickly muscled human flesh. Its chiseled face was expressionless, its eyes vacant. It was simply a lab-cultured human clone, bereft of independent thought. It didn't care who bought it or when. It was society's whipping boy. That's all it would ever be.

So why did it seem to be laughing at him?

The glass door closed behind the Hedwigs, flashing a gaudy sign cruelly inviting them to "Come Back Soon!"

They made it halfway across the parking lot before Willa lost it.

"What'll we *do*? We can't live without an Ersetzen! How will I get through the day? And you, you can't handle all your stress! You'll get sick! Your ulcer will come back! You'll have a heart attack! And you don't have life insurance! It's just like that telemarketer said—"

"Relax, will ya?" Bing hissed, still walking toward the car. "What do you think we'll do? What choice do we have?" He took a deep breath, willing it not to become a sob of frustration. "We'll have to ... get along without one. We'll just have to be accountable."

That shocked Willa Hedwig to a standstill.

"Dear God, not *that*!" she wailed. "Nobody can do that! Even poor people have Ersetzens—welfare loaners, or community units, or *something*! But we can't go on welfare! We just can't! Oh Bing, what will the *neighbors* think?"

Bing whirled, his face twisted in fury. "Would you shut up? Just shut up! It's bad enough that we can't replace the Ersetzen that you broke! I don't need to hear you yowl about it! Just ... shut ... UP!"

Willa shut up. But her eyes pleaded silently, her emotions swirling in a maelstrom of grief, fear and guilt. For the first time in many years, she had no way to unload them.

Bing Hedwig simply stared, hating her. Did she really expect him to comfort her now? He could barely contend with his own anger and helplessness.

Like Willa, he had no Ersetzen to blame.

And he had to blame *someone*.

THICKER THAN

The waning sunset dribbled crimson onto the surface of Lake Michigan. Autumn stars winked on above, drawing Brooks to thoughts more comforting than how he might have to kill someone shortly.

"Hey, you with me?"

Brooks shook off his indulgence. From the gloom gathering around the drab-gray boathouse, Calder scowled at him. Both men wore black body armor. Brooks barely discerned the five white letters on his partner's outfit: DWARP. As usual, his brain interpreted it as a word, "dee-warp."

"I'm here." Brooks pumped his squat Pelter rifle and waited as it cycled. Then he pressed his ear to the boathouse door. He heard voices and the labored *chug-chug-chug* of an old pump.

"Sounds like a pair," he whispered.

Calder nodded. "Easy peasy."

"Meaning we're not going to kill anyone, right?"

Calder pouted. "Party pooper." He switched his Pelter to ES mode.

"On three, then," Brooks breathed. "One—"

"Three!" Calder kicked in the door. Brooks cursed him and followed.

"*DEE-WARP!* Hands where we can see them!"

Calder's command startled the two men inside. They lurched from a crouch next to a fat yellow hose connected to a small tanker truck. One man lifted his hands in surrender. The other pulled a Glock from his belt.

"Gun!" Brooks cried.

The guy fired and missed. Calder didn't miss.

The deed done, he touched his left ear to key his comlink. "Suspects in custody. Scene secure."

"Copy that," a voice replied.

Brooks lowered his rifle, annoyed. "There's three hours of paperwork," he sighed.

The remaining suspect erupted. "You bastards!"

Calder shot him, too.

"Dammit, Calder!"

Calder shrugged. "He had the right to remain silent. I helped."

At least they weren't dead, Brooks consoled himself. The Pelter's ES mode merely scrambled certain brain functions, leaving the target unconscious. Still, it wasn't fun; having been ES'd during academy training, Brooks recalled the noxious hangover now awaiting these suspects.

Grumbling, he ambled over to the tanker and disconnected the hose. A few ounces of clear liquid dribbled from the tanker's valve onto the floor. Brooks held his finger under one of the drips, then stuck it in his mouth. He knew that taste.

"Lake water."

Calder shook his head. "They never learn."

* * * *

Brooks came in late the next day, having enjoyed a rare breakfast with Dayla. As usual, his little daughter asked why he couldn't eat breakfast with her every day. Brooks never had a good response. *Because my workday starts early, sweetheart. Because I must make money so we can live here. Because your mother ran off with some biker dude and said it was my fault for working so much.* Given those options, Dayla's question went unanswered.

By the time Brooks reached the South Haven precinct, Calder was at his desk, scowling over the previous night's report.

"I sound like a bystander," he whined.

"That's payback for making me fill out Form I-4-Got-Not-To-Shoot."

"Very funny, partner." Calder wasn't known for taking a joke. "Narayan interrogated them. They claim they're stealing water for some small town in Arizona. Strictly amateurs. Not Wet Market material."

Brooks cursed. They had hoped this bust would yield some key Market insiders running the Great Lakes ring. Not so.

"The Wet Market set them up, maybe to see how good our intel was," said Captain Narayan, sauntering into the office. He was a big man, gruff and gray, with a face like a granite cliff. On a fat finger swung a coffee mug declaring him *World's Greatest Mom.*

"If the Market knows we're onto them, they'll go quiet, cut every illegal water tap from New Buffalo to Ludington," Calder grumped. "We'll never catch them."

"Worst of it is, the Lansing District will taunt us for weeks." Narayan shuffled off, moping.

Brooks felt for him. The rivalry between the Lakeshore and Lansing districts of the Department of Water Asset & Reserve Protection was legendary. DWARP officers—known colloquially, and somewhat amusingly, as "AquaMarines"—had been chasing the Wet Market for thirty years, since before the midcentury Water War caused by the Great Drought.

The desiccated United States testified to the planet's increasingly ravaged climate. Water proved scarce west of the no-longer-mighty Mississippi. True, some coastal towns had enough, their desalinization plants sipping from the Pacific Ocean. Others managed to get by with shrinking aquifers and diminished mountain snowfalls. But the American Southwest and the Great Plains had largely withered.

Things were better in the Great Lakes. While bad weather leaned toward extremes—from brutal winters to raging summer storms—the regional climate trended moderate. For its 60 million residents, this helped preserve a bounty of fresh water.

Few experts thought the trend would last. Drought had been creeping east for decades. But panic hadn't set in, at least not yet. Thus, true to form, people worried about today without planning for tomorrow. This allowed the Wet Market to thrive as they stole water from lakes, rivers and aquifers and sold it to drought-stricken towns for outrageous sums.

It wasn't enough to fret the Great Lakes region, but it posed a thorny and persistent challenge for DWARP.

"Seems to me," Brooks mused, "if the Great Lakes Water Alliance loosened restrictions on water exports, you'd cut the demand that keeps the Market afloat. Send more water west, the Wet Market might dry up." He punched the air. "Puns intended."

Calder winced. "Bad humor aside, we can't be the water tap for a whole country. Let's take care of our own first." He picked up a pen and started doodling on a scratch pad. "Besides, last night proved how desperate people are getting. That rickety heap of tanker holds, what, three thousand gallons? Take a town of 300 people, that's two weeks of drinking water. Maybe three, if they ration hard."

Brooks kept up his dogged search for a silver lining. "Maybe the Wet Market will go after the Marshall Aquifer again. That'll give the Lansing office something to do."

"Not likely. Besides, you really want to live with Narayan if Lansing makes a bust?" Calder gave up on his doodle, crumpled the paper and tossed it at a wastebasket. It bounced off the rim and landed on the floor.

He stared at the wadded ball for a long time. Then his eyes lit up.

"You said it, partner—a different approach!" Calder swiveled his chair to face Brooks. "After last night, we're thinking the Market will back off. But what if they don't?"

Narayan drifted back into the office, clutching his now-full coffee mug. He'd overheard Calder.

"Talk to me," he said.

"The Market steals water from around the Lakes. Once we catch wind, they move on. We know their pattern. And they *know* we know it."

Brooks whistled, getting it. "Change the strategy. Don't run, at least not right away."

Narayan chewed on the idea. "Maybe. But why now?"

"Because they know we've tapped their communications," Calder replied. "They fed us intel about the Arizona boys, and we took the bait. Now's the time to change things up."

Narayan gave a thoughtful nod. "If they do, they won't go to their usual haunts."

Calder rose and walked over to an old, yellowed county map hanging on the wall. He stabbed a finger at a ragged line between land and water.

"Vacation homes," he said. "It's off-season. Empty houses and condos, mostly in shoreline plats. They'll target the most secluded ones, drive tankers to the beaches and top off."

"Only we'll be waiting," Narayan said, his eyes aglow. "We'll get 'em for sure!"

"The Wet Market, you mean?"

"No. The Lansing District." He drained most of his coffee in a single, victorious gulp.

* * * *

"*Daaad-DEEE!*"

Brooks leaped from deep sleep to his feet in an instant. Padding quickly to Dayla's bedroom, he caught the sweet, clean smell of his little girl. It was the most calming scent he knew.

"What's the matter, sweetie?"

"I'm thirsty. I want a drink of water."

A minor crisis, then. Brooks relaxed. "Okay, I'll get you some water."

In the kitchen, he turned on the tap while fishing for Dayla's favorite princess cup in the dish drainer. She was an enigma, his Dayla: a swirl of pink unicorns, sparkly tiaras and brutal rugby. Some moms scolded him for allowing his seven-year-old to scrum with boys twice her size. Brooks merely smiled and watched those judgmental moms grow silent as Dayla tore through beefy props with glee.

He found the cup and stuck it under the stream. The water's chill seeped through the plastic to cool his fingertips. He shut off the flow. Bubbles popped and faded in the cup until there was only clear water.

Water. Simple and clean, more precious now than gold. For the dehydrated people of western America, it was life. When it was denied, they'd launched the Water War. The AquaMarines made short, brutal work of them.

Brooks struggled to understand such despair. How did water provoke people to take up arms? After defeat, how did it compel two men to journey from the Sonoran Desert to the shores of *Mishigami* to steal a few days' worth?

"Daddy, hurry up!"

Her cry tugged at his heart. It also answered his question.

The law sought to protect Great Lakes water from theft. Following the law is easy when breaking it isn't your only option. But what if things were different? What if, say, your little girl's life was at stake? What then?

There were those like Calder who blamed the drought victims for their plight. They'd squandered their own veritable ocean of fresh water, the underground Ogallala aquifer, in little more than a century. But that opinion ignored how entire generations fueled climate change. There was plenty of blame to go around. Placing it now seemed rather pointless.

Brooks moved his wrist and watched the water swirl inside the pink cup. In years to come, how would Dayla remember him? As a protector of a vital resource? Or as a heartless fiend who turned his back on the thirsting masses?

Long-forgotten words drifted into his mind, words once given to him as a call to something greater, as a measure of one's integrity. Words about suffering, about having compassion: *I was thirsty, and you gave me something to drink.*

"*DAAAD-DEEE!*"

Brooks snapped out of his dark revelry.

"Coming, sweetie. Daddy's coming."

* * * *

Calder's tinny whisper crackled in Brooks' ear. "Told you they'd be here."

Lying prone in the tall dune grass above the beach, Brooks tapped his comlink. "As I recall, scouting this plat was my idea."

"Jealousy doesn't become you, partner."

Brooks peered at the tanker through night vision goggles. It was a big one, nearly 12,000 gallons. Its rear end pointed toward the dark waves of Lake Michigan as the diesel engine idled erratically. How the driver managed to back this monster down the narrow, sandy ravine that snaked from the street to the shoreline was beyond him.

"How many?" Calder asked.

"Three. Two running the pump, plus the driver. The guys outside are armed." Brooks studied their gear. "That's a high-volume fire pump, maybe 500 gallons a minute. No amateurs this time."

"Wet Marketers. Better call for backup."

"That pump will top off their tanker in the next ten minutes. Narayan's up with Harbour and Marsh in Saugatuck. They'll never get here in time." Brooks sighed. "Two against three. Bad odds. We lose this one."

"We aren't losing anything," Calder insisted. "I'm fifty yards up shore. I can get close enough to hit the two outside with my Pelter. You cut off the driver."

"You're nuts! If that driver is armed, he'll take you down."

"Got a better idea? I'm waiting."

Brooks didn't. "Fine. Give me thirty."

"Copy that."

Brooks slid back through the grass and down the dune. Once out of sight of the beach, he stood and began to run through the black forest, using his goggles to discern the path.

"Calder, status."

The comlink stayed silent. Probably too close to them, Brooks reasoned. Moments later, he burst out of the forest and into the ravine. He paused long enough to cycle his Pelter, then he moved toward the idling tanker.

A staccato of automatic gunfire ripped the night.

"Calder! What's happening?"

No answer.

Brooks was sprinting now. He heard the truck's engine rev, slide into gear and roar in his direction.

He reached the beach just as the huge vehicle pulled into the ravine. With the truck nearly upon him, Brooks eyed the cab and saw only the driver. Then he leaped aside, rolling across the sand as the truck barreled past. He came up quickly, his Pelter ready to fire at the two men he was sure must be clinging to the tanker's rear.

But no one was there.

He snapped left. Three bodies sprawled on the beach. One of them, face down, had "DWARP" emblazoned on his back.

Though worried for his partner, Brooks stuck to his training and secured the threat first. He approached the two Wet Marketers, his weapon ready, and kicked aside their bullpup Tavor rifles. The suspects didn't flinch. Both ES'd. Relieved, Brooks moved quickly to his friend and turned him over.

"Calder, are you—." He stopped.

A Tavor at close range does awful things to a person's face.

His horror didn't last long. It quickly collapsed into sorrow and rage that consumed him. Without a thought to law or procedure or anything but his fury, Brooks slung his Pelter across his back and ran after the tanker.

The soft sand between shoreline and roadway hindered the truck. Brooks found good purchase along the forest's edge and pressed the advantage. As the truck finally bounded onto the street, Brooks reached it. He leaped, arms outstretched, and locked his hands onto the rungs of the tanker's access ladder. Drawing his legs up, Brooks clung for dear life as the vehicle gathered speed.

He needed just two minutes to climb the ladder, crawl the length of the tank along a narrow metal shelf and reach the gap between cab and tanker. The truck lacked a sleeper unit, meaning the driver was almost within reach. Brooks slithered down to the coupling unit, grabbing a handhold on the back of the cab. Peering around the passenger side, he saw the truck's fuel tank had a steel grate over it capable of supporting his weight.

The tanker truck turned onto a deserted country road. Soon it would accelerate to highway speeds. If Brooks was going to act, it had to be now.

He slipped the Pelter from his back and hefted it with his right arm, using his chin to switch the weapon from ES mode to regular ammo. Then, firmly gripping the handhold, Brooks leaned over the road, taking the full force of cold autumn air. He lifted the Pelter and squeezed the trigger. Bullets shattered the passenger window and blasted through the windshield. Startled by the explosion of glass, the driver nearly lost control. The truck careened so violently that Brooks almost lost his grip. He flung his body backwards and hung on.

The driver slammed on the brakes, bringing the tanker to a squealing halt. Brooks knew if the guy had a weapon, he'd be reaching for it now. Without hesitation, Brooks leaped onto the grate, took hold of the windowless passenger door and shoved his Pelter inside the cabin.

"Stand down or I'll end you, you son of a bitch!"

The driver complied. He slowly released his grip on the steering wheel and spread his fingers in a sign of surrender.

"I don't want to die," he said, his voice quavering.

"Neither did my partner!"

"That wasn't the plan, I swear! I didn't sign up to kill people."

"Like hell!" Brooks seethed. "Did you forget the Water War? Did you forget all the people your Wet Market has killed? Well, this time someone's going to pay." He pumped the Pelter. "Might as well be you."

Panicked, the driver faced him, hands outstretched, his voice pleading.

"Please, no! You can't do that to her!"

Brooks paused, not sure what he meant.

"She doesn't know I'm with the Market. You kill me, she'll have no one left!"

Brooks shook his head, still angry but increasingly confused.

Then he saw the photograph taped to the dashboard.

She could have been Dayla. The age was about right, the hair similar, though shorter and unkempt. She beamed at him from a playground of sorts, with rusting swings and a lopsided roundabout, baking under a desert sun. It wasn't a professional shot by any means. It didn't have to be.

Daddy, I'm thirsty.

He could hear her voice. She sounded like Dayla. But there was something more to her cry. A little bit strained, a touch more desperate.

Desperate enough to send her father fleeing across a hard-baked country in a stolen tanker.

Daddy? DAAAD-DEEE!

Brooks shook his head, banishing the voice. In its place: clarity. As clear as cold, life-giving water in a pink princess cup.

Brooks slowly lowered the Pelter. "Go. Get the hell out of here."

The man was stunned. "I ... I don't understand."

Neither did Brooks the AquaMarine. But Brooks the father understood perfectly. Some things are thicker than water. He jumped away from the cab and made a sharp, choleric motion. A moment later, the giant truck lumbered off.

Brooks stood there for hours—long after the truck's taillights vanished and the smell of diesel faded, until the first pink tendrils of dawn tickled the sky. In twilight he began walking back to the beach. Explanations would be difficult. He'd have to concoct a convincing tale, one that salvaged his career, preserved his dead partner's honor and waved away a tanker full of stolen lake water.

Maybe that last one wasn't a big deal. After all, it was one small act. What difference could it make?

I was thirsty ...

Maybe all the difference for one little town. Maybe everything for one little girl.

He could live with that.

MOKSHA

If the bus hadn't swerved to miss the dog, maybe things would have gone differently. But that's not how it happened.

The driver threw the steering wheel hard to the right, narrowly missing the dog and barreling straight for its pursuing owner: a little boy, desperate to save his beloved pooch. Headlight beams bounced off the kid's terror-stricken eyes.

Then a flash of movement, a shadow dimming the light, grasping the boy, tossing him from onrushing death.

Squealing brakes, shrieking tires and the smell of seared rubber. The screams of panicked passengers. The sickening thud of bus and body colliding.

Then Amit Chiranjeevi woke up.

Again.

* * * *

He hadn't seen the sun in over a year, but that's not what bothered him.

He wasn't perplexed that his day, every day, began at dusk, when he awoke on a faded, splintered park bench. Nor did he fret that the bench was whitewashed in dried pigeon droppings, some speckling his neat clothes.

But knowing, with each awakening, he would die less than three hours later … yeah, Amit found that just a little irritating.

Even so, the urge to get moving overwhelmed his annoyance. Amit wasn't surprised; he'd tried exactly 187 times to resist the force that drew him each evening to the intersection of Ninth and Main. But he couldn't. It called as powerfully as the Sirens of myth, with none of the promise and all of the outcome.

77

Brushing the pigeon poop from his jeans, he rose and began his journey toward the crossroads, about half a mile away. He managed a side trip, however; Amit could resist the intense urge long enough to drop in at the local coffee shop for a cup of decaf and a lemon poppy seed muffin.

Once served, he snagged a newspaper and plopped onto a stool near the door. These few minutes were the only moments of joy he'd have that night.

The front page revealed little about this new world. Here, America had built its global might and influence upon an agrarian economy, rivaling its industrial muscle in Amit's. Most worlds varied only slightly; sometimes, with so little time to glean what he could, Amit found no discrepancies at all.

"Excuse me. Is this seat taken?"

Amit turned to behold the bright smile and ginger-ringleted hair of a young woman, nicely filling out a tight, colorful blouse and microskirt. Her face bore not one freckle, which made the hair color suspect, and she'd gone overboard with the eye shadow and rouge. Still, she was prettier than most hookers.

Waving to the adjoining stool, Amit said, "It's empty." Except for the two of them and the barista, the coffee shop was deserted.

"You look lonely." She slithered onto the stool and hiked her skirt half an inch from a misdemeanor. "I can do something about that."

Amit shook his head. He had no time and little desire for such commerce.

"You sure?" she pressed. Carefully polished nails, a vibrant red, scratched lightly at his arm. "My name's Candy."

"Of course it is," said Amit, bored stiff. "But unless you're a genius in quantum mechanics, there's nothing you can do for me."

The woman leaned back slowly. "You like them smart, do you? The librarian, naughty boy, time-to-pay-your-fine type?"

"That's not exactly what I meant."

Candy folded her arms and scowled, abandoning all attempts at seduction.

"I'm not an idiot, you know," she said, her tone changing from syrup to steel. "I went to college. I even took physics. So you can shove your holier-than-thou attitude up your quantum mechanical ass!"

Amit held out his hands as a sign of repentance. "Whoa! I apologize. I wasn't demeaning you or your, um, profession. I'm just … distracted, that's all."

Candy nearly left anyway. Oddly, now that she'd given up on him, Amit found her intriguing. She seemed both comfortable in her streetwalker role and way out of her element. It summed up his own dilemma nicely.

"Forgive me for asking, but if you went to college, why—"

"Turn tricks? Because I want to finish school, and it pays a whole lot better than waiting tables."

"I wish I could help you," he said, and meant it.

Candy summoned a small smile. "You can. Just give me a few minutes of normal, polite, we're-not-doing-business conversation."

Her body language softened. Without asking, and without objection from Amit, she began picking apart his muffin and nibbling the crumbs.

"So," she continued, "what's your story?"

Early on, Amit had tried sharing his experience with other people. Most called him insane. Those who didn't usually lived off-kilter themselves. No one believed him, and that eventually drove him to silence. Still, Candy seemed genuinely interested. Amit wondered how long that would last.

"Well, the first time I died—"

She coughed up a bit of muffin. "The first time you what?"

"Died. You know, heart stops beating, brain stops waving?"

Candy looked at him, incredulous. Amit knew that look all too well.

"So … you think you're dead?"

"Depends on how you define death, I suppose."

"Oh wait, I get it," Candy said, nodding. "You're from India, so you must believe in reincarnation, right?"

Amit sighed. "No, I'm from Terre Haute. My parents were teachers at Indiana State, and I attended Catholic school. Shall we dispense with the stereotypes?"

He shifted nervously in his chair and sloshed his coffee. The inner call had returned, growing insistent.

"Look, you're not going to believe any of this, and I really need to get going."

Candy patted his arm. "Come on, I want to know. What did you mean about the first time you … you died?"

"I mean," Amit said, taking a deep breath, "I was hit by a speeding passenger bus while trying to save a child's life."

He waited. The hooker looked him up and down, one eyebrow raised.

"You've recovered well," she said at last. The twinkle in her eye was unmistakable.

"Let's skip the sarcasm, too. The truth is, I didn't recover at all. I was killed. Expired. Shuffled off this mortal coil. You get it. And afterwards, I woke up on a park bench."

"It was a dream, then."

"No. It really happened." Amit drew another deep breath, this one ragged and edgy. "At first I thought maybe my grandparents were right. Maybe I was passing through samsara, the cycle of lives each soul is said to encounter. But that didn't seem to fit. You break that cycle through self-realization, which is called *moksha*. But how is that possible to achieve when each of my new lives lasts only three hours?"

"Wait a minute. Are you saying this has happened to you more than once?"

Amit nodded. "By my count, nearly two hundred times. Once I realized this wasn't a delusion, I spent a couple of cycles going to the library instead of the coffee shop, looking for a rational explanation. That's where I learned about the multiverse."

To Amit's surprise, Candy understood. "Of course. I remember this from my physics class—the idea that this is just one of a gazillion different universes bundled together."

"And I'm living proof it's no theory. Not that it matters to me anymore."

Candy ate the last of Amit's muffin, licking sticky crumbs from her fingers and patting her painted lips with a napkin.

"You're telling me," she said, "that you keep going from Earth to Earth, universe to universe, always to save a child from a careening bus, dying in the process and landing on the next Earth to do it all over again?"

"Yeah, that's pretty much it."

"Incredible!"

"I call it a living hell."

"Why don't you just stop?" asked Candy. "I mean, it sounds awful, but what if you didn't save the kid? He dies, and you go on living."

Amit stifled a laugh. Hers was a perfectly logical suggestion, one he'd attempted to follow dozens of times. It seemed cruel at first, condemning a child to the agonizing death he'd experienced over and over: the crushing force of 12 tons of moving steel shattering bones and bursting internal organs. It hurt—a lot!

But after a few deaths, his sympathy for the boy soon withered like a vine in the desert sun. Like the biblical Jonah, whose reluctant prophesies saved an entire city, Amit felt only resentment now. He couldn't even run away as Candy suggested, or as Jonah had tried. That powerful force wouldn't let him. No matter how hard he resisted, no matter how determined his will, Amit always ended up at Ninth and Main to face his death again. And again. And again.

His legs jittered nervously on the lower rails of the stool. *Time to go.*

"That option's not open to me, I'm afraid," Amit replied at last. He stood up and gave Candy a small, sad smile.

"Thanks for listening. It's nice to talk to someone about this for once. Too bad I won't have the chance again."

This puzzled Candy. "But if you're moving through parallel Earths, you'll meet another me again, won't you? Haven't you already?"

Amit shook his head. "I've never seen another version of you before today. You're unique, Miss Candy, at least to the worlds I've visited."

He turned away and moved toward the coffee shop's glass door.

Until Candy's next question froze him in his tracks.

"What if you could save the kid in a way that didn't require you to die?"

* * * *

The bus was parked next to a small, lighted shelter, idling roughly and spewing diesel fumes into the sticky night sky. Half a dozen passengers were aboard, scattered across the stained vinyl seats, dutifully ignoring one another while the driver studied his paperwork before embarking on his route for the umpteenth time.

In the shadow of a nearby building, Amit was trembling badly. He wasn't sure if it came from that insistent, mystical call, or because he was holding a gun and preparing to hijack the bus.

"This doesn't feel right," he muttered.

"Why do you say that?" asked Candy. "You're saving the kid. Isn't that what matters?"

"I don't know. It feels like I'm second-guessing God." He shook his head. "I can't do this."

Candy snorted. "Even if I believed in God, which I don't, I'd say you've got the right to get off his hamster wheel." She patted his arm. "You'll be fine. Besides, it's not like you're really going to shoot somebody."

Amit studied the pistol. He knew a little bit about firearms. This one strongly resembled the Smith & Wesson Model 637 on his world—a compact, .38-caliber handgun. Light. Easy to use. Deadly.

And, in this case, pink.

"You really think they'll take me seriously when I aim a pink gun at them?"

Candy made a rude noise. "It's not pink. It's cerise."

"That means pink."

"Trust me, all they're going to see is a huge gun barrel."

"I hope you're right." Amit's shaking made him vulnerable. If the driver and his passengers didn't cower before his dainty firearm, he'd be easy to overpower.

"Should I kick everyone off the bus before I hijack it?" he wondered.

"I thought about that. The driver and passengers were on the bus in every other world, right? It might be best to keep things the same as much as you can."

"Good point," Amit said, swallowing hard. "Okay, time to go. Wish me luck."

He held the gun behind his back and stepped out of the shadows. Candy followed close behind him.

Amit stopped. "What are you doing?"

"What does it look like I'm doing? I'm coming with you."

"Absolutely not! Candy, you have a life on this world. You're going back to college, remember? Whatever happens, I'm sure the police will be involved."

"But—"

"Nothing doing. If you want to help, go to the intersection and keep an eye on things. If this doesn't work, we'll need a Plan B."

Candy reached up and stroked Amit's thick, black hair.

"You know what? That's the sweetest thing anyone has ever done for me."

She kissed him lightly on the cheek and, with a backward glance, walked off into the darkness.

Alone, Amit felt the turmoil rage within him. *This isn't right!* Every fiber of his being screamed it. But he'd chosen this path; now he was determined to see it to the end.

And so he sprinted through the shadows, leaped aboard the bus and landed beside the startled driver, brandishing the pink gun.

"Don't move!" he shouted. His voice cracked a little. "Nobody gets hurt if you do exactly as I say!"

The driver, a balding old man in a coffee-stained blue uniform, trembled so badly that he didn't notice Amit was doing the same thing.

"We don't have cash, just tokens!" cried the driver. He started fumbling for his wallet. "Here, take all I got! Just don't shoot me!"

The man was terrified, as were the passengers cowering behind him. Amit felt sick to his stomach. He wasn't this kind of person.

"I don't want your money," Amit said as calmly as he could. "I just need your bus for a few minutes."

The driver stared at him, astonished. "M-m-my bus?"

"Trust me, there's no point in trying to explain."

He sent the driver back to join his frightened fares. Clutching the pistol awkwardly, Amit familiarized himself with the bus. It seemed simple enough: automatic transmission, foot pedals where you'd expect them to be, and the engine was running. He checked his watch needlessly; he knew he had to get going now.

"That's quite the, uh, pink gun you've got there," the driver remarked.

"Really not in the mood."

Amit put the bus in gear and mashed the accelerator. The bus lurched forward. He'd never operated a vehicle this large before; it sure wasn't like driving a sports car.

A block away, he could see a familiar intersection: Ninth and Main.

Grateful for a green light and no oncoming traffic, Amit swung the bus to the left in a long arc and then pulled the steering wheel right, gracefully slipping onto Ninth without losing speed.

Any moment now—

Something fast and low to the ground bolted from an alley and into the path of the bus.

Amit rejoiced. *This is it! Hit the dog, save the boy, and the nightmare ends!*

So why was Amit, entirely against his will, throwing the wheel hard to the right?

The bus tilted as it swung sharply, throwing half its screaming passengers from their seats. Amit lost his grip on the steering wheel. The bus was out of control.

He caught sight of the boy, riveted to the pavement directly in front of the bus. Headlight beams gleamed in his terror-stricken eyes.

Something moved, a shadow dimming the light. The boy? The dog? Amit wasn't sure.

He stomped on the brake pedal. The pads squealed as they locked the wheels in place. Tires skidded across the asphalt and howled louder, filling the air with the smell of burning rubber. Panicked passengers shrieked louder still.

But none of it covered the sickening thud of bus and body colliding.

The bus finally came to an abrupt stop at the curb, throwing everyone forward. Amit felt the steering wheel press hard against his ribs, forcing the air from his lungs. It took several moments of gasping before he caught his breath again.

That's when Amit realized he was still in this world. And alive.

Everything was oddly silent, including the cosmic call. Whatever demanded his sacrifice time after time, in world after world, was gone.

Before the passengers could regain their wits, Amit opened the bus door and leaped into the night. He knew he should flee, but there was one question that needed answering:

What happened to the boy?

Amit rounded the front of the bus, which bore a dent from the collision. Twenty yards back, at the end of a slick of blood, was the crumpled form. Beyond that, under the orange glow of a streetlamp, the boy clutched his clueless dog and sobbed uncontrollably. Both were alive.

"Are you okay?" Amit called to him.

The boy nodded, but he couldn't take his eyes off the body in the street. Neither could Amit. A new feeling grew within him, becoming every bit as consuming as the obsession he'd outwitted.

That feeling was deep, soul-crushing dread.

It grew worse when he saw the ginger hair cascading in pretty ringlets onto the asphalt.

The pink pistol slipped from his grasp, clattering on the street. Behind him, the passengers fled the bus, and the old driver was on his cell phone, urging the police to hurry—which they did.

In the days that followed, alone in a stark jail cell, two things settled into the mind of Amit Chiranjeevi, the man who had achieved *moksha* of a sort.

First was an old French proverb: "One often meets his destiny on the road he takes to avoid it."

The other was a mental image more horrifying than what he'd seen on the street:

That of Candy rising from a faded, splintered park bench.

ENMITY

From his perch on a damp log, Phelan Herpet carefully flicked *ochroma lagopus* seeds into a row of crape myrtle. With any luck, the seeds would sprout their huge, balsa-like trees and choke the life out of that flowering bush.

Herpet wasn't in the best of moods.

The day was comfortably warm—not that it mattered. Herpet's flight suit, a dazzling silver modeled on those of yesteryear's test pilots, could handle a wide range of temperatures with ease. His scarlet face reflected his annoyance rather than the sun's heat. Being stranded in a rainforest was bad enough; being stranded in the past was intolerable.

That he was marooned rather than dead was no consolation. Amazingly, he'd survived the crash of his one-man Photon-6 spacecraft with little more than a bruised ego. The ship, unfortunately, was a total loss, leaving Herpet with little more than unanswered questions.

At first, he simply wasn't sure where he was. During re-entry, Herpet thought he was headed toward the Middle East, possibly near the Shatt al-Arab River, which flowed from the confluence of the Tigris and Euphrates along the Iran-Iraq border. But his surroundings didn't fit that geography. There hadn't been anything like this lush foliage and rich loam in the region for thousands of years.

That's when he realized his dilemma wasn't just one of where, but when. This part of the world had been a cradle of civilization for millennia; yet he'd found not one sign of human activity. Given the phenomenon he'd experienced during his spaceflight, Herpet faced the unsettling thought he was stuck in the far distant past.

Unsettling, and patently unfair.

Who in this ancient land would understand his breakthrough in spacecraft design? Who would give him the honor he was due for defying Einstein's universe and going beyond the speed of light?

Sadly, Herpet had only a vague memory of that glorious moment. He barely regained consciousness before Photon-6 fell from orbit. But what little data he squeezed from his ship's dying computer confirmed the feat, and other things: no cities, no ships on the ocean, no satellites in space, nothing but static on the radio.

If exceeding the speed of light had sent him backward in time, it did so with cruel irony. Herpet's genius had been proven in a time and place where no one could celebrate it.

A sudden flash of color pierced his dark mood. Glancing up at a branch, Herpet saw a vividly painted tropical bird studying him with intense curiosity, oddly at ease with this human interloper. A moment later, its scrutiny complete, the bird burst into glorious song. Herpet's pride resurged a little. For the moment, he would settle for the praise of this bird over the praise of men.

He stared at the bird as it flitted from branch to branch above him. It was a quetzal, a long-tailed, stunningly plumed bird native to Latin America. Herpet was surprised to find it in a jungle on the other side of the world. He marveled at its singing, so beautiful that it nearly brought him to tears.

And then he remembered: Quetzals couldn't sing.

Herpet soon dismissed the thought. He was stuck in the past. Who knows what quetzals could do in this era? The world itself was malleable. Continents drift, oceans rage, rivers reshape the landscape, species adapt or go extinct. Humans themselves had wrought tremendous change over the centuries, and not always for the best. Environmental havoc, clashing ideologies and religious fanaticism were among the thorny issues of Herpet's time. The latter he found especially destructive, and he wished all people would rise above such fairy tales.

A brilliant notion struck him. Maybe there was an alternative to his lost legacy in the future. Maybe he could establish a far more powerful one here, in the past.

History's slate was before him, blank and pristine. With his great intellect and vast skills, he could write a new narrative. Perhaps he, Phelan Herpet, could singlehandedly create a new and better human race, one that celebrated its own greatness, its own vast potential.

Its own godhood, as it were.

The jungle instantly went silent, as if shocked by his blasphemous thoughts. The quetzal, oddly spooked, choked on its song and flew away.

Herpet barely noticed. Alone once more, he returned to his trek through the jungle, studying his surroundings with an appreciative eye. The beauty of the rainforest was astonishing. Herpet had never seen such a diverse and vibrant ecosystem. Maple trees grew alongside palms. A Colorado Blue Spruce brushed its needles against sunset-colored oranges. A grapevine, laden with fruit, snaked around a clump of bamboo. It was like a botany experiment run amok.

A lot of what he saw was edible; in fact, Herpet could find no poisonous plants at all. Nor did he see any nuisance flora—no hiptage, no devil's hair, no weed of any kind. Another curious fact was that infectious bacteria, a scourge in any jungle, seemed impotent here. None of the scratches he'd endured had turned septic. In fact, they were healing with remarkable speed.

While intriguing, these little mysteries gradually drifted away as Herpet found his thoughts drawn to a more immediate concern. It was midday, judging by the vertical rays of sunlight filtering through the trees, and he was hungry.

Herpet relieved a vine of a massive bunch of concord grapes and sat down in a small clearing, his back against a large, twisted tree. He didn't recognize the species, but it was enormous and appeared to be quite old. Sunlight danced among its broad leaves and caressed his face. When he'd finished the grapes, he leaned back, content to watch the leaves shiver in a tiny breeze.

His mind returned to his vision for this younger world. Recasting the human race—what a challenge! Doing away with base tendencies would be the toughest task.

Take religion; it was rooted in the natural human search for truth and understanding. But rarely did Herpet find its followers eager to tackle pain and suffering, wars and famine, death and disease. Many blamed those tragedies on "sin," a corruption spawned by foolish humans in a farcical Eden. Those same zealots imagined a redemptive God who vowed enmity against sin's purveyors. But in Herpet's view, enmity was a double-edged sword. Some people used it as an excuse to oppress others, while some confessed their fallibility and spoke of compassion and grace.

Herpet saw the latter as the exception to the rule. His solution, then, would be to change the rule. And he would serve as the perfect example—

The snap of a twig was like a rifle shot.

Herpet leaped to his feet, his chest tight with fear. Something was moving in the bushes nearby. Since the crash, Herpet had seen little animal life, mostly birds and small mammals. But this was a jungle, after all. That meant there were other creatures lurking about.

Lions? Tigers? Bears?

Oh my!

From the bushes emerged the most beautiful woman he had ever seen. Her skin was bronze, lightly kissed by the sun, yet visibly soft and supple, without blemish. Long black hair framed her narrow face and spilled over her shoulders, totally unkempt yet perfect for her. She had a body that was lean and strong, without a hint of malnutrition or exposure to the elements. Although the flare of her hips disappeared in the waist-high brush, Herpet could tell that she wore no clothing at all.

She seemed as startled as he was. For a minute, both were speechless.

Finally, she spoke to him. Herpet found the language vaguely familiar—something from the Middle East, but an unusual dialect. Herpet had been stationed in the Persian Gulf during a stint in the Navy, so he managed to pick out a few words.

The woman pointed at him, waving her hands up and down and chattering excitedly. She seemed to be intensely curious about his silver flight suit, its anti-radiation coating aglow in the sunlight. Never before, she said—as far as Herpet could translate—had she seen such a beautiful creature in the garden.

Herpet smiled paternally. The woman had a quaint, if naïve, way of describing a natural rainforest. It told him all he needed to know about her. She was as primitive as the world Herpet was trapped in.

Maybe now was the time to start building that perfect world.

But first he needed to build a relationship. And for that, he needed a peace offering.

Looking around, his eyes fell on the old, gnarled tree that had been his leaning post. Among the leaves he saw, for the first time, its brilliant gold-and-red fruit. Almost too heavy for their narrow stems, the colorful orbs seemed to shine on their own, shimmering as drops of juice caught the light and flung it around the clearing. The nearest one was nearly too big for Herpet to pluck with one hand.

He pulled it free with a snap of wet wood. Its aroma was powerful, a sweet smell unlike anything he'd experienced before. It spawned an odd, almost reverent feeling in Herpet. Cradling it in both hands, he held it out to the woman.

Right here, right now, is where my new world begins.

So engrossed was he in the thrill of the moment that he didn't notice the strange glimmer in the woman's eyes. Apprehension. Fear. And maybe, just maybe, a hint of desire.

The jungle fell silent once again. Ominously so.

Herpet cleared his throat.

"Have an apple?" he asked.

THE GOOD PERSON

Harold P. Noblis was, in most people's view, a good person. Not perfect, of course; Harold himself would concede that fact. But he loved his wife and worked hard at his job. He didn't drink, smoke or speak ill of others. He never cut drivers off in traffic or throw colorful language to those who did it to him. He made it to church on Sundays, cheerfully dropping one-tenth of his wages in the offering plate. If he had any vice, it was the time he spent daily on the internet. Even then, Harold surfed his way to websites that improved his grasp of history, politics and social issues.

No doubt about it: Harold Noblis was a good person. He had no reason to doubt that fact.

Until one particular Tuesday.

That Tuesday was the same as every other Tuesday, or any day of the work week. He came home precisely at 5:40 p.m., enjoyed a home-cooked meal with his wife (whose culinary skills he praised as usual) and then, settling into his favorite chair, fired up his laptop and began working through his browser's list of favorites. He spent the next four hours online, pausing at 10:25 to return his wife cheerful "good night." After another 30 minutes to wrap up his virtual studies, he'd join her for a full eight hours' sleep.

But on this night, with 15 minutes left in his routine, Harold ran out of websites to visit. He clicked idly on a few random links, yet nothing drew his interest.

Oh well, nothing wrong with crawling into bed a few minutes early, he told himself. Harold slid a finger across the laptop's touchpad, watching the arrow on the screen move toward the "X" in the upper right corner that, once clicked, would close his browser.

But Harold didn't move the arrow quite far enough. It stopped in a blank white space on the screen. To his surprise, the arrow turned into a small cartoon hand, its index finger extended.

Harold was puzzled. The image was familiar to him, of course; it meant his cursor had found a link to a webpage. But there was nothing else to indicate a link should exist—no underlined text, no icon, nothing but the cartoon hand.

He hesitated. Curiosity tempted him to click on the invisible link. But he worried this was a lure to a site where a computer virus was poised to strike. On the other hand, such tricks were usually designed to get one's attention, promising money or fame or some other deceit. Harold found this link by accident.

Should I or shouldn't I?

He made his decision and clicked.

His browser window turned white for several seconds. Then it reformed into a simple group of frames, including a blank video field with on-screen controls and an empty box near a button that said "Send."

A webcam site with instant messaging? he wondered. That alone wasn't so strange. Harold was quite familiar with webcams. Like most laptops, his had one embedded above the screen. He usually kept tape over it, though now and then he freed it to chat with his brother in Ireland. This website's stark, utilitarian design gave no hint of source or intent.

    HPN66: HPN77, are you online?

Harold blinked as the words appeared in the instant-message field. He knew it was meant for him; HPN77 was his online moniker. But only his friends knew that. None of them had a handle so close to his own. How did this person, whoever it was, know Harold had stumbled onto this website? Was he being monitored?

    HPN66: I know you're there. Turn on your webcam.

What Harold should have done was turn off his laptop. But this was a mystery, and Harold Noblis couldn't resist a good mystery. Tentatively, he tapped out a response.

    HPN77: Who are you? How do you know me?

A moment later, the reply appeared.

HPN66: You'll figure it out once you're on webcam.

Red flags popped up in Harold's mind, and every one of them bore the word "scam." Harold mentally kicked himself for being misled this far. "Try it on your next sucker," he said aloud as he typed. "I'm signing off."

The response appeared almost instantly.

HPN66: This is not a scam. I have nothing to gain by contacting you, and you have nothing to lose.

"Nothing?" typed Harold, still skeptical.

HPN66: Nothing except a lot of misconceptions.

Once again, curiosity got the best of him. After another moment's thought, he peeled back the tape, turned on his webcam and clicked the on-screen controls to activate his video and microphone feeds.

HPN66: Ah, there you are. Stand by, I'll be onscreen in a sec.

The wait was brief. The miniature video screen on Harold's laptop display soon came to life, quickly resolving into the face of a haggard man. His hair was scraggly, his chin and cheeks stubbled. Beneath his eyes were dark circles framed by lines of weariness. This was the face of an angry, melancholy, troubled man.

It was also, to Harold's astonishment, a shopworn version of his own.

"What the hell is this?" Harold sputtered, both furious he'd been had and afraid he hadn't.

The man on the screen chuckled. "Mind your tongue, Mister Noblis," he said in Harold's own voice, made slightly tinny by the cheap speakers of the laptop. "Mother would have washed your mouth out with soap for using that word."

"Who are you? What kind of deepfake trick are you pulling?"

"Oh, it's no trick. Who you see is who you get."

Harold shook his head. "That's not possible. I see myself."

"True. And not quite you, am I right? A few more lines than those on the face you shave each morning."

"I'm still waiting for an explanation," Harold said coldly, crossing his arms.

The duplicate Harold leaned back and crossed his arms in precisely the same manner. "Interesting. The line between your side and mine isn't so sharp, is it?"

"You're not making any sense. My side? My side of what?"

"Of our existence."

Harold shivered violently, as if someone had just poured ice water down his back. His head spun and his words slurred, as if his lips didn't know how to function.

"This can't be real!"

Mirror-Harold gave a lopsided smile. "A poet once wrote, 'Between uncertainty and what is real, lies never exactly knowing how I feel.' I'm sure you can relate right now."

Harold said nothing. Mirror-Harold chuckled again and continued.

"Fine. I'm here to teach you a little something about yourself."

"Such as?"

"The truth. That's all. The simple, unadulterated truth. The full picture, without any of your misconceptions."

"You seem to think you know a lot about me," Harold growled.

"I do indeed," replied his doppelganger. "Better than you know yourself. But let's start with a simple question. Do you think of yourself as a good person?"

"Wha-what are you talking about?"

"Are you a good person? Do you treat people with respect, give to charity, show up to work on time, that sort of thing?"

"Well … yes. I guess I am, all things considered."

"All things, eh? You've never done anything wrong? Nothing that would, say, earn you a one-way ticket to the Bad Place?"

"Of course not! Hell is for evil people."

Mirror-Harold uncrossed his arms and leaned forward. "I see. Tell me, who gets to decide who is good and who is bad?"

"Well … God, I suppose."

Harold's twin rolled his eyes. "A nice Sunday school answer," he said sarcastically. "If that's true, why do people like you think they know what God has decided?"

"The evidence. It's not exactly rocket science, telling good people from bad."

"All right, then let's turn my first question around to me. For the record, I've shaved a few dollars off my income taxes. I've looked at internet porn. I've even slapped my wife in the heat of an argument. I'm everything you say you're not. Does that make me a bad person?"

Harold wasn't sure how to respond, so he merely shrugged.

"You'd rather not answer," Mirror-Harold observed. "Alright then, let's say, just for argument's sake, that you're 'good' and I'm 'bad.' Yet we share the same name, the same house, the same lives. How is that possible?"

Harold shook his head. *The same lives? What's he talking about?* The whole thing was bizarre, like a Jekyll-Hyde tale come to life. If it was a joke, it was the most elaborate and disturbing one Harold had ever seen.

And if it wasn't? Harold pushed that thought from his mind.

He needed to think logically. What could explain this webcam conversation with a duplicate of himself? An unknown twin who'd tracked him down? Or maybe it something way, way out there—a clone, a parallel universe, something even wackier?

He bounced these thoughts off Mirror-Harold, prompting a burst of derisive laughter.

"Oh, that would make things quite easy for you, wouldn't it? A parallel universe where a 'bad' Harold Noblis could violate every sacred law, revel in every sin, while you walk the straight and narrow. Best of both worlds, eh? All the evil, none of the consequences—for you, anyway."

The mocking smile vanished from Mirror-Harold's lips, replaced by an ugly grimace of barely suppressed rage.

"You read too many fables! The truth is much simpler. Answer me this: Have you ever told a lie? Even a little one?"

Harold started to shake his head, then thought better of it.

"Well … yeah, I suppose so. A white lie here and there. Who hasn't done that?"

"And have you ever taken something that wasn't yours? Maybe you were undercharged at a restaurant and didn't tell the server? Or you helped yourself to a few pencils and paper clips at work?"

Harold frowned. A feeling of dread was creeping over on him. Once again he considered closing his browser and shutting off the computer, but he couldn't bring himself to do it.

"Yes, I guess so," he answered at last.

"And what about women, Harold? Have you ever looked at a woman who wasn't your wife and wondered what it would be like to be with her?"

Harold fought the urge to squirm. "Who hasn't? Just because I got married doesn't mean I went blind."

Mirror-Harold nodded. "On the surface, it all seems so trivial, doesn't it? It's not like you're a murderer or anything, right? You're no Hitler or Stalin."

"Exactly! Have a little perspective."

Harold could see the simmering rage in his duplicate start to boil.

"Perspective?" Mirror-Harold snapped. "I'll give you perspective! You're no different than any other human being. You've partitioned your life. You've carved it into bits and pieces, pushing the so-called 'good' things to the front and hiding the rest. And I am the rest! I'm your whipping boy, your psychic scapegoat. I'm all the things about yourself that you're desperate to hide. And today that lie is exposed! The sham isn't mine, it's yours. *I am Harold P. Noblis!*"

"That's not true!" Harold shouted.

"Oh no? Think about it. By your own admission, you've lied, you've taken things that aren't yours, and you've mentally slept with other women. That makes you a lying, stealing adulterer! The 'good' Harold Noblis isn't so good after all, is he?

"And that's the problem," he raged on. "Your so-called perspective doesn't matter. Reality says you're tainted, and you can't wash that stain away. You're just as condemned as I am. Because I ... am ... *you*!"

Harold screamed, slammed his laptop shut—

And sat up.

He was alone in the den. The clock on his desk said 12:03 a.m. His laptop sat on the table beside him, dark and cold, as if it had been shut off hours earlier. Harold stared at it fearfully, afraid it would suddenly spring to life and drag him back into the web chat with a creature full of malice and evil. A creature claiming to be him. The laptop remained dormant. Gradually, Harold felt the tension and fear drain away.

A dream. That's all it was. A trick of the mind. There is no alter ego. His accusations are all false. I'm still a good person.

"Harold?"

He turned. His wife, clad in a long flannel bathrobe, stood in the doorway of the den, looking tired and concerned.

"I heard you cry out. What's wrong?"

Harold shook his head. "Nothing, dear. A bad dream, that's all. I must have fallen asleep after I shut down my laptop." He stood and walked toward her, intent on giving her a reassuring hug.

She shrunk from his touch, with a sharp intake of breath. Harold froze, stunned by her reaction.

Then he noticed the bruise under her left eye.

Pièce de Résistance

The president of the United States was talking on the big white telephone. It was not a pleasant conversation.

Just when he felt sure that nothing could cause his taffy-twisted gut to heave again, someone else stepped into the bathroom and spoke.

"Sir! Was it the squid?"

Well, so much for that assumption.

Long afterward, Martin J. Grimes, leader of the free world, uncoiled himself from around the commode. The intruder offered him a damp washcloth and a bottle of lemon cream antacid.

"I'm tempted to think you did that on purpose," Grimes groused, his voice thin. That's when he noticed that Judson Cariotte, his normally dapper Secretary of State, wore a frilly mauve apron over his neatly pressed Italian suit.

Cariotte caught the look. He shrugged. "I was in the kitchen, and ... well, this is an Armani."

"Cute. Never mind that now. How are our guests?"

"They're eating peanuts, sir. Without shelling them."

Grimes forced himself to his feet. "Uh oh. They're getting impatient. We'll have to move fast."

He reached for the phone on the bathroom wall—a real one this time—and punched in the kitchen speed-dial code.

"This is the president. Serve those garlic potato knishes immediately. Heavy on the garlic. Then the cinnamon apple spoonbread. Move!" He hung up.

"The knishes will taste good but have some, uh, unfortunate aftereffects," Grimes told Cariotte. "That should send a message of regret that I was unavoidably detained. Meanwhile, the smell of the spoonbread should create an air of expectation, meaning I'll return soon."

"Makes sense, I guess," said Judson. "Sorry about the pickled calamari. The Breadbreakers were stressing their distrust of Western society. You know, distasteful, a bit slimy—"

Grimes felt his stomach gurgle. "Do you mind?"

Cariotte bit his lip, trying to look mortified and failing completely. Grimes managed a lopsided smile. "Distasteful and slimy, eh? Couldn't have said it better myself."

"Actually, Mr. President," said Cariotte, wrinkling his nose, "I think you did."

"Amusing. Can we continue this banter somewhere el—?"

"Sir," Judson interrupted, "I came to report that we've defined your key messages and linked them to several prepared dishes. I'm supervising. Watching the cooks, checking translations, that sort of thing." Cariotte smiled with little sincerity. "Who'd have guessed your two years in cooking school would pay off here?"

Turning to a wall mirror, Grimes began fiddling with his tie. "History is all about timing, Judson. Only someone with degrees in sociology, political science and gourmet cooking could pull off this treaty. Turns out that's me. And to think my mother accused me of being a 'professional student.'" He paused for a swig of antacid, wiping away the yellow moustache.

"What's amazing," Grimes went on, "is how these loons got hold of a hundred nuclear missiles."

Cariotte shrugged. "It slipped by everyone, sir. The Russians lost a few, the Chinese stole a few—that's what we thought. No one suspected the Breadbreakers."

"Thank you, Judson. I did read the report." In fact, Grimes had written much of it. His culinary knowledge had been vital in understanding the Breadbreakers.

An odd cult, and oddly well financed, the Breadbreakers believed that sharing food—literally "breaking bread"—formed the cornerstone for peace. To make their point, they communicated solely through the act of eating. Certain foods sent certain messages, from formal greetings (ritually breaking a loaf of Italian bread) to a casual exchange about good weather (fried eggs, sunny side up).

Their approach to language wasn't the Breadbreakers' most bizarre trait. To preserve their custom, they surgically removed their own vocal cords.

The Breadbreakers' strange ways gained global attention after they began quietly purchasing nuclear missiles from every nation. They were convinced they could literally buy the way to global disarmament—and with it, world peace.

Then came their sudden, urgent plea to the United Nations: a karidopita, a Greek walnut cake. Without walnuts.

A karidopita is, of course, a disaster without walnuts. Likewise, the Breadbreakers were gripped in a smoldering crisis. Only one man had the knowledge and skill to resolve the impasse. And he knew it.

"Scrambled eggs with chorizo and pepper strips," Grimes recalled. "Two factions and a spicy conflict among the Breadbreakers. The younger cultists want a more visible role in world affairs. So said their tossed salad with fresh carrot slices on top. But the older Breadbreakers want to preserve their isolationism—salmon tartare, with a smooth, refreshing taste that is purposely savored. Each group came to the table soured on the other—a California lemon, strongly sucked."

"You certainly figured it out long before anyone else." Cariotte paused, apprehensive. "Sir, do you realize that this treaty could be the defining moment of your presidency?"

Grimes lost the battle not to look annoyed. "Your tact underwhelms me. It may surprise you to know that I'm sick of being called 'the ho-hum president.' No international conflicts. No sweeping reforms. Not even a good, old-fashioned sex scandal."

"That's not quite what I meant."

"Well, it's not for lack of trying!" Grimes whined on. "I searched out every possible emergency. Even tried to make up a few. All for nothing."

His tirade faltered. Grimes' uneventful term was an emotional garrote strangling his considerable pride. Whatever his strengths, conceit was the president's greatest flaw. It was also another of his mother's frequent criticisms.

"'When pride comes, then comes disgrace,'" she'd warn in her irritating squawk. "'But with humility comes wisdom.'" A well-read, slightly eccentric woman, Grimes' mother rarely spoke in anything other than dusty proverbs and obscure quotations, most from the Bible. He doubted she'd ever constructed an original sentence.

He'd ignored her, rebuked her, felt relief when death finally silenced her. Martin Grimes had long ago, and happily, made Pride his mistress. And Pride whispered—no, *demanded*—that he not pass into insignificance.

Cariotte was right. The Breadbreakers' conflict was indeed a defining moment. Such moments invariably made great men. And Martin J. Grimes was poised to become great.

"Mr. President, we should reconsider negotiating with the Breadbreakers."

Grimes thought he heard a pair of hands shred his half-written page of history.

"Reconsider?" he cried. "I'm four or five courses away from a treaty!"

"Sir, I don't buy their 'eat-bread-make-peace' drivel, and neither should you," said Cariotte. "What sort of peace lovers secretly stash a hundred nukes?"

"I thought we'd figured that out."

"Mr. President, they aren't after world peace. More like world domination." Cariotte clutched the president's sleeve. "Call their bluff, sir! Don't talk peace until they give up their nukes!"

"Judson, you're crazy! Even with all their weapons, the Breadbreakers are no superpower."

"They don't need to be. Think about it! If they launch a first strike, we could never respond in time. One hundred missiles, sir! One hundred American cities wiped out!"

"That's enough!" Grimes roared. "I will not break off negotiations with the Breadbreakers! I will not lose this chance to stake my claim in history! Understood?"

The intensity slowly faded from Cariotte's blue eyes. He heaved a deep, almost mournful sigh.

"Very well, Mr. President," he said quietly. "I understand your position. I hope you understand mine."

The secretary of state finally walked out of the bathroom.

Several minutes passed before the president followed suit.

* * * *

Grimes glided into the White House dining room with a profuse apology to the Breadbreakers. He dismissed his Secret Service team and sat alone with the two emissaries, each representing a faction. The older one, portly and gray, wore a tweed jacket two sizes too small and, despite the mansion's no-smoking policy, puffed on a well-blackened pipe. The younger was a woman with jet-black hair and a smart red business suit. They were two clearly different people, yet they shared a common trait: a noticeable scar across their throats, the Breadbreakers' badge of honor.

Naturally, the president's apology wasn't spoken. He expressed his regrets with a wild dandelion salad, its bittersweet, nutty taste reflecting his contrition. The Breadbreakers eyed him as they ate—even they relied on body language and other cues to gauge sincerity. At last, they replied with épi and crown bread, its tough crust yielding to a sweet, chewy inside, and the bread's doughnut shape indicating a return to harmony. The crisis of etiquette had passed.

The older Breadbreaker launched negotiations with smoked eel pâté and eggplant marmalade, both splashed with a spicy-sweet, acidic sauce of raspberry purée and Balsamic vinegar. Grimes, acutely aware of his earlier grapple with seafood, kept his mind off his stomach and on the intended message. He guessed it was an expression of hope for success in the bargaining, though the older faction remained suspicious of the younger.

Not to be outdone, the female envoy waved for a Breadbreaker cook—an essential member of their diplomatic corps—and soon produced a baked Alaska ablaze in the dancing blue of flaming brandy. When the fire died, Grimes cut into the frigid sponge cake and ice cream lightly coated with meringue. This was easier to translate. The young Breadbreakers also wanted to end the conflict, but their anger would have to die down before there could be a lasting peace.

Grimes explained this to Cariotte, who had joined him *sans* apron.

"We can't wait until they cool off," the president insisted. "There's too much at stake."

"Besides your reputation?"

The president clenched his jaw. "Don't push me, Judson! If even one of these freaks has an itch to push a launch button, we could be facing a global holocaust!"

"Exactly my point, sir." Cariotte pulled a small spiral notebook from his suit pocket and slowly paged through it.

"The secret may be in a small measure of formal respect," he said through tightly drawn lips. "Not that of a full-fledged nation, of course, but a group representing a large population. Start by endorsing the principles all sides share. Global peace. Disarmament. But—"

"That works for me," said Grimes. "Just so it doesn't involve pickled squid."

"Mr. President, I must ask you again to reconsider! Recognizing the Breadbreakers this way, as a near-nation, might solve the immediate problem, but it sets a horrible precedent. If you do this, every wacko group with a bomb will demand the same treatment."

Exasperated, Grimes jabbed a finger in the diplomat's face. "That's enough!" he hissed. "I don't care about any other group! Just *this* one, at *this* time!"

Cariotte finally lost his tenuous composure. He grasped the president's wrist and forcefully moved his hand aside. In a low voice, he growled, "Don't ever talk to me like that again!"

Grimes' own rage outstripped his astonishment. "Are you threatening me? I'm the president of the United States!"

Realizing his error without regretting it, Judson released Grimes. "If you do this, you'll be the greatest fool in American history."

Grimes stared at Cariotte for a long time. Finally, he pulled a pen from his suit pocket and quickly wrote on a convenient napkin.

"By my best guess, here are the proper foods for granting the Breadbreakers near-nation status," he said, passing the napkin to his Secretary of State. "Tell the cooks to serve them. *Now*."

Stone-faced, Cariotte rose from the table and left the room.

Fortunately, Grimes had done his homework, calling upon every dim memory from cooking school. Many of the foods he'd expected to use were already in some state of preparation, meaning he and the Breadbreakers didn't wait long for the next round of negotiations.

The first dish served were cheese straws, puff pastries flavored with Parmesan cheese and paprika. At Grimes' suggestion, the chefs had carefully stacked them like Lincoln Logs, with a few extras haphazardly scattered on the plates. The message was that the talks had begun to form a solution.

The Breadbreakers carefully ate the cheese straws, which were served to each simultaneously. To Grimes' pleasure, the two diplomats looked at each other and smiled as they ate. Until now, they'd all but ignored one another. Serving them together underscored the United States' view that the Breadbreakers were seen, and respected, as one.

The dining room door opened again, and this time a nattily dressed waiter pranced in. On his platter were two plates of gingery chicken congee, a savory rice pudding considered a comfort food by the Chinese. It reassured the diplomats that peace was the ultimate goal of the new, evolving plan.

The president sat back, nervously watching his guests. The fate of these negotiations—and Grimes' place in history—now rested with them. He waited for some sign that they accepted his approach.

The two diplomats finished their congee and stared at each other for nearly an hour. Grimes nibbled a thumbnail—until it occurred to him that this, too, might send a message. He thrust his hands beneath his legs and waited.

Finally, the Breadbreakers summoned their cooks. Moments later, they exchanged black raspberry jam dartois—puff pastry sandwiches that they ate together.

No one needed a cookbook to translate that message.

Grimes looked around for Cariotte, but he had long since left. No matter. Soon the whole world would know about this historic pact and Martin Grimes' laudable role in making it happen.

Once again, the door to the dining room opened, and the waiter glided in, platter in hand.

"My friends, the *pièce de résistance*: chocolate goblets with espresso ice cream," he said. "Just as you ordered, Mr. President. Mr. Cariotte said now was the appropriate time."

Grimes studied the three desserts on the platter. Each was a three-petaled flower of chocolate filled with a hefty sphere of espresso ice cream. After a day of endless courses of food, plus one unpleasant reaction, Grimes was surprised to find his mouth watering.

"This should cement the deal," Grimes said. "Serve it. Quickly!"

The president beamed as the chocolate goblets were placed before the Breadbreakers. This was the moment he'd waited for. His presidential term would end on the highest note possible: a historic treaty with a group that, ironically, had threatened the very peace it so desperately sought. Martin Grimes' name might not be mentioned in the same breath as Washington's, Jefferson's or Lincoln's, but it would be said with respect. He could live with that. The president dipped his spoon into the hard ice cream and carefully placed a small portion in his waiting mouth.

"Excuse me, sir," the waiter whispered as he passed by. "Mr. Cariotte also had a message for you. I hope you understand it. I'm afraid it makes no sense to me."

"What did he say?"

"He said, 'When pride comes, then comes disgrace.'"

Grimes choked on his ice cream. He began to cough, his face turning red as the worried waiter thumped him on the back. The choking became severe, and a burning sensation erupted in his throat and mouth. His eyes watered and his nose dripped mercilessly. In his distress, Grimes didn't notice that the Breadbreakers were gasping and choking as well.

Finally, the president spit out the ice cream. That's when the horror of the moment became clear. Grimes saw the message that the Breadbreakers, now storming from the dining room in mutual rage, would take home to their people. And he knew what history, or whatever might be left of it, would say of Martin J. Grimes.

On all three plates, barely visible in the melting ice cream, were the half-chewed remains of *bhut jolokia*.

Ghost peppers.

RANDOM PRECISION

I died six years ago. Or a century back. Or today, a few minutes from now. It all depends on how you look at it.

I really thought I deserved a waiver, if there was such a thing. There isn't. Too risky. Temporal Staffing figured that out when they snatched 14 pilots from 1945, held on to them, and inadvertently rewrote the history of the Bermuda Triangle. Now they can't send them back; it would make an all-too-close encounter with the past a lot worse.

Anyway, back to my being dead. I always loved speed, and that's what cost me. I crashed my '51 Merc in a drag race. Lost control and rolled it. The fire was spectacular. My folks chose a nice cemetery plot for me near a gnarled oak tree in my hometown. The headstone says, "Lorelai Tanda, 1938-1961. Beloved Daughter—Racing Forever." A nice touch.

Except the body they buried isn't mine.

My Merc started to flip, I blinked—and opened my eyes in 2082. Awful place to be. The climate's shot, droughts are widespread, food shortages everywhere. Two nuclear wars since the 2020s killed three million people and sterilized a quarter of everyone else. Most of those who can have kids choose not to consign offspring to this hellhole. The birthrate's at rock bottom; it only took 20 years to run out of young, healthy workers.

Necessity being a mother, or something like that, it spawned twin inventions: time travel, and a scheme to kidnap workers from the past.

After I finished throwing up in the displacement chamber—time travel plays hell with your digestion—the folks from Temporal Staffing, LLC, explained it to me.

If they know precisely when and where you die in the past, they snatch you just before your fatal moment. Brought to the future, you have a choice: live a few more years there, with fair labor and a comfortable lifestyle, or go back immediately and die as fate decreed.

Not many people choose the second option.

That said, the deal isn't forever. The timeline is too fragile, as the Bermuda Triangle screwup proved. They avoid major historical events, like the Titanic or Pearl Harbor, for the same reason. For the rest of us, though, Temporal Staffing eventually sends you back to that nanosecond before your death. Three years is the usual tenure—stay too long, and the people of yesteryear get a dead loved one who is visibly and genetically older, raising timeline-altering questions.

Naturally, I took Temporal Staffing's offer. They implanted a small wristchron below my left palm and taught me to be a nursing attendant. I spent the next three years helping new arrivals recover from the pukes, savoring each day and trying not to think about how soon I'd run out of them.

I nearly did, until Dabria Morana came along. She fell off a cliff near Durango, Colorado, in 1997 while posing for a photograph. Snatching her was easy; the photo was time-stamped and, years later, posted on social media as a tribute. Temporal Staffing grabbed her 30 feet into her 100-foot fall. As I helped Dabria recover in the displacement chamber, I noticed she looked a lot like me.

So yeah, I swapped my identity for hers. Hacked our wristchrons, a surprisingly easy task that bespoke simple tech and poor security. Then I drugged her, like we always do for returns—who willingly goes back to the moment of their death?—and watched as the clueless technicians sent her to 1961 to die in my place, preserving the tragic tale of Lorelai Tanda.

Sure, I took Dabria's three years, but how does that matter? As far as history was concerned, she was already dead. After I became Dabria Morana, I had to find a new trade. Couldn't go back to Lorelai's job, after all.

With some luck, I got into Temporal Staffing's Records Division. Using the holocomp database, I had access to the background of every person brought from the past—photos, life story, arrival time, everything. As 2088 dawned and the clock ticked down on my second three-year term, I kept a close eye on incoming workers, watching for anyone who resembled me.

With nearly a thousand arriving daily, it didn't take long to find a promising match. Libitina Kritanta, Libby to her friends, was 29 and a researcher for a high-dollar private investigator in New York City at the turn of the century. She looked more like me than Dabria had. A smile of relief crossed my face. I could easily get to Libby in the recovery area, dope her, and arrange her exit as Dabria. An easy swap, and I'd nab three more years of life.

That's when I noticed a small note in Libby's file that made me gasp. Where her cause of death should be listed, only the words "retrieval error" appeared.

It took me forever to realize what happened. They'd snatched someone by mistake. Libby Kritanta wasn't supposed to die.

For Temporal Staffing, this had "PR nightmare" written all over it. The people of 2088 mostly ignored the ethical dilemma of using time travel to conscript workers, rationalizing it as a kindness to people who were already dead. But snatching someone who wasn't at the brink of death, that's a different issue. Send her back, and you risk her knowledge upsetting the timeline. Keep her a prisoner in the future, and now you're talking slavery—not to mention deleting her from history, along with any impact she was supposed to have.

There really was no choice. Temporal Staffing had to send her back, and soon. The longer they delayed, the more Libby was exposed to the future, and the bigger the risk to the timeline.

My decision was just as easy to make: I'd help them out, and myself along with it. I would take Libby's place in the past, living out her life while Libby closed out Dabria's.

Murder? Again, not true. I made my choice decades after both of us were dead. All I was doing was rearranging the deck chairs of history.

Getting into the medical center was no biggie. I had an employee badge, and I knew my way around as Lorelai. No risk of being recognized, either, since all my coworkers had been returned to their deaths years ago. I stopped by a locker room and borrowed some medical scrubs to blend in. Stuffing a small duffle with my clothes—rather, the ones Dabria wore the day she arrived—I headed deeper into the medical center.

To make this work, I'd need to dope Libby, which meant I needed a dose of dyneopropofol. Getting the sedative required a little patience and a lot of *chutzpah*. The pharmacy entrance was coded for pharmacists only. It emptied into a large courtyard where I loitered until one of the pharmacists stepped out for a vape break. With his back turned toward me, I slipped inside before the door latched. His partner was busy filling an order for a floor nurse, so I scanned the shelves until I found the dyneopropofol. I grabbed two vials and an air syringe, then exited before anyone noticed.

My badge got me into the Recovery Unit, but finding Libby proved difficult. As I said, Temporal Staffing pulls in nearly a thousand workers every day, and there were easily a hundred in Recovery when I got there. I grabbed a tablet and a handheld vitals scanner so I looked semi-official, then wandered around, peeking into the curtained cubicles as covertly as I could.

An hour of searching turned up nothing. Libitina Kritanta wasn't in Recovery.

I found a quiet corner to sulk. So close! I was on the cusp of forever escaping this time-hopping death sentence. But to pull it off, I had to find Libby.

Then it struck me. If she'd been retrieved accidentally, Temporal Staffing would put her somewhere secluded, a place where she wouldn't see too much of this era. That meant somewhere close to the displacement chamber, closer even than Recovery.

Of course! The Triage Room!

It sat between Temporal Retrieval and Recovery. Every now and then, a person from the past suffered a medical issue—a heart attack or something—and needed immediate medical care. The displacement techs probably put Libby there until their superiors came along to decide what to do with her. That meant my time was short.

As if to put a fine point on that fact, my wristchron suddenly buzzed and flashed red.

Dabria Morana's employment, and her extension on life, had ended.

I had an hour, at best, to swap places with Libby before Temporal Staffing's minions tracked me down. I could reboot my wristchron, but only by swapping the ID information with Libby's. I had to get to Triage fast!

Because my employee badge wasn't coded for that area either, I trolled Recovery again until I found a doctor's lab coat tossed carelessly on a chair, badge attached. I took it and moved quickly to the Triage access door. A quick wave of the new badge, and the door opened automatically.

The room was empty and dimly lit. A single stretcher, bearing a motionless human shape, stood at its center like a religious altar, a small light shining from overhead. The patient's arms were lashed to the stretcher's rails with restraints. Moving quickly to her side, I beheld the face of Libitina Kritanta.

Lightly sedated, she awoke at my approach. Bleary eyes held mine.

"Who are you?" she whispered, her voice groggy. "What's going on?"

"Don't worry, Libby," I answered. "Everything's going to be all right."

I put the air syringe to her neck and shot her with dyneopropofol. The drug would leave her conscious but largely unaware for about 30 minutes. That was all the time I needed.

I pulled a holocomp interface from my pocket and used my access privileges—thankfully, they hadn't been deleted yet—to call up Dabria's and Libby's files. Dabria's, of course, had my digital photo. I swapped it with Libby's and rebooted our wristchrons. Suddenly, the unit on Libby's arm buzzed and flashed red, as mine had done a few minutes before. Mine turned orange—a "hold" signal, reflecting Libby's current status. I'd soon fix that. A few more commands, and Libby's file had a new directive: "immediate return."

I needed a few minutes to strip Libby of her clothing—a smart-looking business suit, odd to my lingering 1960s taste—and dress her in Dabria's outfit from my duffle. I shed my scrubs, put on Libby's suit, then pulled another stretcher from storage and slipped under a blanket just as the door to Triage opened from both sides.

At the entrance from Recovery stood two security guards with handheld stunners. Opposite them, at the door to Temporal Retrieval, hovered a single technician.

"What are you guys doing here?" the tech demanded.

"Worker expiration. We're here to return—" the guard checked his pocket holocomp "—Dabria Morana. Her wristchron alert brought us here."

The tech waved at the two stretchers. "The one over there, I see her wristchron flashing red. Is she the one?"

The second guard looked at his own holocomp. "Yep. And it looks like she's already prepped. That makes things easy. You got it?"

"Sure. I'll send her first. Who's the other one?"

"No idea. Wait … isn't she the mistake?"

The first guard grunted. "I heard about that. Someone's gonna lose their job."

"He already did," replied the technician. "Why do you think I'm working solo today? They fired Del the moment it happened. Too hasty, if you ask me. No time for a proper follow-up." He sighed as he checked his holocomp again. "But I guess they got what they needed. The system says she's to be sent back immediately."

"Gutsy call," said the second guard. "What if she remembers what she's seen?"

"Doubtful. Del realized the mistake right after she got her wristchron, and he sedated her immediately. She might have vague memories of what she's seen, but it'll be hazy, like a dream. Besides, it's not like there's a choice."

I heard the guards grunt some more, then they helped the tech move Libby into the next room. I lay quietly for what seemed like an eternity, trying not to think about what was happening to her. Alone in the displacement chamber, all metal and blue light. Then a loud whine, an eye-searing flash, the leap across time … and the bright Colorado sunshine, the biting mountain air, the rush of rock from below—

Full stop.

I'd be lying if I said I didn't feel guilty. Mostly, though, I hoped the impact would shatter Dabria's body enough so her family didn't wonder why she looked different.

They came for me a moment later. I continued to play dead. A medic would tell immediately I wasn't sedated, but the tech neither noticed nor cared. He was overworked, striving to do two people's jobs alone. He just wanted to be done with the day. I shared the feeling.

He wheeled me into the displacement chamber, lifted me off the stretcher and gently laid me on the gleaming metal floor. I stayed there, eyes closed, until he wheeled the stretcher away and locked the chamber door. Then I sat up but stayed on the floor, knowing that it would make the transition to Libby's time easier.

Excitement grew within me. I was moments away from pulling it off! Still, I didn't relish the coming nausea. Should've popped a Dramamine.

Then came the hum, growing in intensity as the temporal displacement process began. I didn't understand the science, nor did I care to. The hum became an electronic scream, almost earsplitting, and the blue light around me fluctuated. A flash, and—

… nothingness …

—I rolled over onto a carpeted floor, my stomach heaving.
"Libby! Are you okay?"

Strong arms tried to lift me to my feet, but I waved them away, keeping my face turned. I needed a minute or two to recover. Finally, the nausea faded. I looked up and saw a middle-aged man, graying at the temples, in a pink button-down shirt and crisp tie. Around us was a maze of fabric-covered cubicle walls. I focused on the man's face. His eyes were locked on something else far across the room. He looked worried.

No, not worried. *Terrified.*

"We should get out of here," he said, his voice quavering. "I don't care if they think we're safe."

"Safe?" I was still a bit fuzzy from the time jump. Of course we're safe! *I'm* safe! Safe from dying in a car wreck in 1961. Safe from dying on a mountainside in 1997. Safe and alive here in—

What year was this again?

Still turning my face away from my scared companion, I slowly climbed to my feet and followed his fearful gaze. On the far side of the office area, a dozen people stood, their backs to me, their faces pressed to a wall of towering windows against a perfect blue sky. A few people were crying. Pushing back a wave of vertigo, I stumbled toward them.

"Libby! What are you doing?"

The man still hadn't noticed I wasn't Libitina Kritanta. But that didn't worry me. I needed to know what was happening outside.

I joined them at the window. We were in a skyscraper, the tallest I'd ever seen, towering far above Manhattan. To the north was another tower, a twin to mine. Several floors of the other tower were burning, spewing thick, black smoke into that cloudless sky. "You weren't supposed to be here today," the man wailed from behind me.

"You shouldn't have to see this! All of those people over there, dying!"

I shook my head. "What the hell is going on?"

He wasn't listening. "My fault. All my fault. You gave up your vacation to help me with that false-ID case. Right now, I don't care what that family thinks! I don't give a damn about Dabria Morana!"

I whirled to look at him, horrified to hear that name.

Just as the second plane hit.

TELEPHONE TAG

"Hello, this is the voicemail system. The party you have called is unavailable. Please leave a message at the tone."

beep

"Hi, Stell, it's Misha. Sorry we didn't connect. Hope Madge is feeling better. She was green in the gills yesterday morning! I wonder if it's a boy or a girl? Hey, I called because I may be a bit late for lunch. I'm deep into that budget review you asked for, and I'm meeting with a Dr. Westbury on something called the Postern Project. No idea what Postern is, so I'm already suspicious. Do your best to charm Norton till I get there. Fingers crossed!"

beep

"Madge, Stella Caine. Where in blazes are you? When my phone rings, I want a warm body there to answer it! I shouldn't have to retrieve my own voicemail —that's your job. I just got a message from some woman, no idea who she was, and voicemail can't ask, can it? We'll talk about this later. Bet on it! "If you can find a spare moment, call Fritz Arden in Legal. Have him contact Norton Odolf at the Odolf Group and tell him I've agreed to his terms. We'll finalize at lunch tomorrow. Then make noon reservations for four at Via Pompeii. And have Fritz find out if Norton's position on personnel remains the same. I'll call in again later, and I expect you to answer!"

beep

"Stell, Misha here. Aren't you ever at your desk? Look, I know you don't like to mix it up with the eggheads, but you'd better take a look at this Postern Project. You told me to dig up anything that could threaten the deal with Odolf, and this might qualify. Postern has cost upwards of $50 million so far, and there's nothing to show for it. Could be all the excuse Norton needs to kill the buyout.

"Let me know if I can help. Good luck at lunch today!"

beep

"Madge, this is Stella. It's been two hours since I called! Where are you? I need you to ask John Tracey in HR if he knows a female employee named Misha. I don't have a last name. This Misha left two messages on my voicemail, and she seemed to know about some, uh, confidential matters. She's a bit confused on the date, though; she's off at least a day. And she acts like she's my pal or something, but I've never heard of her. Have Tracey track her down.

"Also, I'm expecting a call from Norton Odolf. Be sure to pipe him through to my cell phone. I'll be back in the office at three."

beep

"Hello, Stella. Norton Odolf here. I'm sorry I got your voicemail. I was looking forward to chatting with you.

"I'm very pleased to hear that you've accepted the terms. I look forward to joining you for lunch tomorrow to sign the papers. Assuming regulatory approval, Odolf Group will legally acquire the Caine Research Institute within 90 days. That shouldn't be a problem because we both have friends in high places who can move things along.

"Also, I wanted to respond personally on the other issue you raised with Fritz Arden. Stella, I'm afraid my position is unchanged. You must understand, Caine Research is valuable to me for its assets, not for its employees. I suppose my conscience ought to prick me on that point, but this is business, and in business I echo Hamlet: 'Conscience does make cowards of us all.'

"Anyway, I'm sure you're looking forward to a comfortable early retirement once our deal is finalized. We'll see you at lunch tomorrow."

beep

"Yes, uh, Ms. Caine? This is Dr. Westbury. Nathan Westbury. We met at the employee picnic last year. I won the sack race. You handed out the trophy, remember? Did I ever tell you that I left it in the car all day, and it, uh, melted? What I mean is … I didn't think it was … well, I really liked it. The trophy. Before it melted. Boy, I hate voicemail.

Anyway, I need to talk to you about a project I'm working on. It's … well, it's fairly urgent. Please call me at extension 171."

beep

"Misha again, Stell. You're not playing fair in this game of telephone tag. Why aren't you returning my calls? I'm starting to take it personally.

"Did you talk to Westbury yet? He didn't keep our 10 o'clock, but he sent his Igor. Weird guy. Anyway, from what the assistant told me, I'm even more uncomfortable about this Postern thing. He kept talking about … oh, I don't know, inflation or something. It's all really technical. Smoke and mirrors, if you ask me. You'd better do something. And would you please call me back?"

beep

"Madge, Stella. Are you out sick today or something? Never mind. Did you talk to Tracey yet? Look, I need to find out about this Misha woman. She's ticked off because I'm not returning her calls. I don't even know who she is! And start picking up my phone, will you? This is giving me the creeps!"

beep

"Stell, Misha. What's going on? Look, I'm sorry I missed lunch with you and Odolf today. Give me a break—I got stuck in traffic. Would you please call and tell me how it shook out? Did you two sign? At least fill me in before the all-staff meeting this afternoon, will you?"

beep

"Norton, this is Stella Caine calling. I'm sorry you got my voicemail earlier. I guess Madge is out sick today.

"I just want to thank you for explaining your position on personnel. Rest assured, I fully support you. You're certainly under no obligation to retain anyone after the buyout. I'm just pleased that you recognize the value of Caine Research. You know how hard I've worked, and for how long. Thirty-two years! But I built one of the best independent research labs in the world. Your offer proves that.

"Maybe now, thanks to your generosity, I can kick back and enjoy life a little. As for the people, hey, the economy's good, jobs are plentiful. And I adore Hamlet!

"Now that we've cleared the air, let's put the wraps on a great business deal. I'll see you at Via Pompeii tomorrow at noon."

beep

"Stell, it's me, Misha. You know, Misha Navette, your best friend? Right now, I may be your only friend. What in the world are you thinking, letting all the employees go? Couldn't Norton use any of them? Unbelievable!

"Stell, you owe those people something. You didn't pull this off on your own. Your employees sacrificed a lot to build Caine Research. Some of them gave up better-paying jobs or university tenure to make the institute what it is today. How can you cut them off like that? And your attitude! I mean, I always knew you were ruthless, sometimes even cold-blooded. But I never thought you had no heart!

"Stella, why won't you return my calls? It's like you fell off the face of the Earth. Call me, day or night. Please!"

beep

"John, Stella Caine here. Another early day? Is this what I pay you for? Madge was supposed to call you, but she's been out ill. Something about a pregnancy test tomorrow. Just what I need, a giggling mom-to-be for a secretary!

"Anyway, I need information on a female employee named Misha Navette. I've never met her, but she keeps leaving me voicemail messages about certain confidential business. And if that's not strange enough, she talks about things that ... well, that haven't happened yet. Like Madge's pregnancy, and a lunch meeting that won't happen until tomorrow.

"I know that sounds strange. And no, I don't think she's psychic or something. She's probably playing some sort of mind game. I'll deal with her, but first I need to find out who the hell she is. Check the employee database and get back to me right away. At least this weirdo gave me a good idea. I need you to arrange an all-staff meeting in the auditorium for 3:30 tomorrow. Call me if there's a problem."

beep

"John Tracey calling, Ms. Caine. I'm very sorry I missed your call earlier. I was having dinner with my son. He leaves for college tomorrow. So I got your message late, and it took longer than expected to dig up the information. Our servers crashed. Some sort of electromagnetic event—a solar flare or something. I had to pull files manually. Haven't done that in 20 years!

"Anyway, I'm afraid my answer isn't very helpful. There's no record of a Misha Navette. Not as a full-timer, part-timer, co-op, intern or contractor. Not now, not ever. I'll keep checking, though. If the computers are back up in the morning, it'll make the search a lot easier.

"By the way, I set up the employee meeting for tomorrow in the auditorium. Can you tell me what it's about?"

beep

"Stell, I can't stand this! What's going on? Please call me!"

beep

"Ms. Caine, Dr. Westbury again. I hadn't heard from you yet, so I thought I'd follow up. Did you happen to hear about the computer problem? I think I can explain that. Please call me."

beep

"Well, now I know. I can't believe you did this, Stell! Not to me! After all I've done, you're firing me, too?

"If it wasn't for me, there'd be no deal with Odolf! I made the contact! I made you a rich woman! The only reason you're headed for early retirement with a bulging bank account is because of me! Where's your loyalty? Where's your honor? Why are you doing this to me?

"You think you've earned this, don't you? You think your future is secure. You don't even see the blood on your hands—the blood of all the loyal people you've betrayed! You've put your trust in the wrong things, and I swear someday you'll pay for it!"

beep

"Madge, Stella. Before you do anything this morning—anything!—I want you to get my phone extension changed! And shut off that damned voicemail! I hate it! I hate it!"

beep

"Ms. Caine, this is Dr. Westbury again. I'm sorry I couldn't reach you. You needn't bother calling me back. By the time you get this message, I won't be with the institute anymore. I just can't stay, not knowing what I've done. But I couldn't leave without telling you, either."

"You see, I've been spending institute money on an unauthorized project. Quite a bit of money, in fact. It started out as legitimate—a study of scalar fields. But it became so much more.

"Ms. Caine, when you were a kid, did you ever play with one of those soap bubble pipes? You know what I mean. You'd blow in the pipe and create an endless stream of bubbles, like rainbows all woven together. Remember? That's the secret of the universe. Self-inflation. Blow in the pipe—scalar field, breath of God, whatever. Bam! A new universe. Then another, and another.

"Doesn't that leave you wondering? What would it be like to actually push through the domain wall of our universe and into another? Into the next bubble, as it were? What would you find? Maybe a place where physical laws are entirely different. Or maybe a place just like ours, but with a different history. Maybe we'd discover our own future, or some variation of it. The possibilities are infinite!

"I had to know what was there. Couldn't help myself. Can you understand that? So I set up a new project. Even gave it a name so it would appear legitimate. 'Postern.' It means 'gateway.'

"And what do I have to show for my deception? A lot of fancy gear and a few electromagnetic anomalies. Crashed the servers and screwed up the phones. But I didn't find the proof! I've sacrificed everything for a gateway to nowhere.

"I ... I just can't face the consequences of that, Ms. Caine. I'm sorry. Goodbye."

beep

"Madge, hi, this is Misha Navette. I called your extension first, but you didn't pick up. So I'm leaving this on Stella's voicemail. I hope you'll check it.

"I heard what happened to Stell yesterday. Oh Madge, I'm so sorry! What a tragedy! She had everything. Success. A great business reputation. More money than either of us can imagine. The rest of her life should have been blue skies. Ease and luxury. She was ready to sit back and savor it all. Dear God, it's so awful!

"I didn't agree with what she did—especially to me! Yes, I was angry. Yes, I felt betrayed. But I never, ever would have wished this on her! I ... I just wanted to tell you. To tell someone."

beep

"Tracey, you're wrong, and I ought to fire you for it! There *is* a Misha Navette! She just left a message on my voicemail for Madge. John ... look, you've got to help me figure this out! This Misha woman keeps talking about future events like they've *already happened*! My business deal. The employee meeting. And now, God help me, she talks like I'm *dead*! It's crazy! It's like she's ... she's living a full day ahead of me. Isn't that weird? Just yesterday, some crackpot scientist tried to tell me such a thing is possible. But no, that's sheer lunacy! A delusional fantasy! I only believe in what's real! And do you want to know what's real? I'm on my cell phone, crossing Surcease Street right now, headed for lunch with Norton Odolf and the greatest business deal of my life. That's real! I don't believe in—

"*MY G—!*"

beep

"This voicemail message is for all Caine employees. This is John Tracey. I'm deeply sorry to tell you that our CEO, Stella Caine, was killed in an accident today. She was struck by a car as she walked to a lunch meeting. Ms. Caine was ... um ... an excellent leader and a ... a true humanitarian. Please join me in mourning the death of this ... this wonderful woman.

"One final note: The all-staff meeting this afternoon has been cancelled."

beep

"Hello. I'm trying to reach John Tracey. I'm a candidate for your CEO position, and your search firm suggested I contact you directly. Please call me at your earliest convenience.

"My name is Navette. Misha Navette."

beep

SUPERHERO

"We need to talk about Barry."

Suspended in his La-Z-Boy, Thomas Parker grunted at his wife from behind his smartphone, perusing the evening news. Martha snatched the phone away.

"I'm serious, Thomas. He's getting worse."

With a sigh, Thomas flipped down his glasses from atop his balding head—he refused to get bifocals for close-up reading—and fixed Martha with a bored look.

"What happened this time?"

"Those kids duct-taped him to the soccer goal during recess."

"Again? Third time this year. No originality."

"This isn't funny!" Martha snapped. "I can't leave work every time our son gets bullied. We need to do something!"

Thomas held up his hands. "What do you suggest? Take away his cape?"

That gave Martha pause. "Seems cruel," she admitted.

And there it was: the impasse. The Parkers had debated what to do about their son countless times. They always reached the same dead end.

In many ways, Barry Parker was a typical 10-year-old. Wiry, brown-haired and lightly freckled, he reveled in video games, comic books and outdoor adventures. Even his active imagination, as broad as the Kansas sky, hadn't put anyone off.

Until Barry imagined he was a superhero.

"The simple fact is our son is weird," said Thomas. "He wears that cape every day. I'm afraid to take him anywhere. Last week at the bank, he climbed on a table and shouted a warning to all potential bank robbers. Scared the customers half to death."

"'Weird' is a bit harsh …" Martha began.

125

"You think so? Remember last summer when he sunbathed nude for a whole day, seeking the 'powers' of a yellow sun? That burn put him in the hospital!"

"I know, but—"

"But nothing! Don't forget the $500 paint job on the Toyota after he superglued cardboard Batmobile fins to the fenders."

"Well … it *was* rather creative."

"Yeah, creative. Like microwaving a spider and trying to make it bite him so he can stick to walls." Thomas shook his head. "The kid's off his nut!"

A sudden shout of delight from upstairs paused their argument.

"Mom! Dad! *It worked!* I'm climbing up the—"

The sound of a dozen wooden-framed pictures crashing to the hardwood floor cut off the boy's joyful cry. An ominous silence followed, then: "Um … never mind."

Thomas took back his phone. "I rest my case."

"Maybe he just needs counseling," Martha sighed, shuffling off to survey the damage.

Thomas buried his nose in another news story.

"A superhero," he snorted. "That'll be the day."

* * * *

Barry Parker stepped onto the playground in his usual attire: a sky-blue T-shirt with long sleeves, a pair of faded jeans and scuffed yellow sneakers. His wardrobe rarely changed; only in the most frigid weather did he surrender to the cold and don a winter coat. On this steel-gray December day, his cape was enough to ward off the chill.

That cape! Red as a dwarf star, rippling in the breeze, it hugged his shoulders with cotton-polyester lightness, giving Barry a sense of comfort and strength. He stuck out his elbows, resting his small fists on his waist as he studied his snickering schoolmates.

"Greetings, citizens!" he cried. "I'm here to keep you safe. Never fear—"

"Doofusbrain is here!"

The kids guffawed as Alex, Barry's pimple-chinned archenemy, fired a barrage of insults.

"Hey Doofusbrain, what are you gonna do? Leap the swing set in a single bound?"

Another round of derisive laughter took its toll. Barry dropped his arms to his sides, lowered his eyes and chewed his bottom lip.

But Alex was just getting started. "Look! It's a bird! It's a plane! It's … oh wait, it is a bird. A dodo bird!"

The chortles reached kryptonite strength. Barry's shoulders sagged as he shrunk into his cape, trembling at his sudden weakness. He should be used to Alex's barbs by now, but he wasn't. It hurt the same every time.

"Get rid of that stupid cape!" Alex cried.

"Yeah!" the other kids shouted in unison.

But Barry wouldn't. He couldn't. Not today, not ever. Not if the whole world called him Doofusbrain.

Ms. Foster, the playground monitor, soon appeared. She placed a comforting arm around Barry's caped shoulders and scolded his tormentors. Still snickering, they disbanded.

"Did they hurt you?" Ms. Foster asked.

Barry shook his head, not looking at her. "No duct tape today. It's my only weakness."

"The only one?"

He said nothing. Ms. Foster hugged him and sent him on his way.

Barry trudged off, his shoes crunching on the last brittle leaves of autumn, until he reached the far corner of the playground. There stood a relic of the schoolyard's past: a giant concrete drainage pipe, six feet across and a dozen feet long, laid on its side. Once a plaything for kids of decades past, now supposedly off-limits, it served as Barry's fortress of solitude. There he could escape the schoolyard taunts, recharge his powers and strengthen his resolve. But it did nothing to salve his loneliness.

Recess ended, and he made it to class on time; no one lashed him to the soccer goal again. Being the last school day before winter break, most of his classmates were focused on Christmas and the gift-filled, school-less days ahead.

The final bell sparked a furious scramble as kids donned coats and backpacks, weary teachers waved farewell, and rivers of children streamed to waiting buses—or, in Barry's case, began a solo walk toward home.

Snow had begun to fall heavily that afternoon, with six inches predicted by midnight. Already the grass was snow-covered, and an icy wind had picked up, prompting Barry to slip on his winter coat and the far-too-big woolen hat and mittens Aunt May knitted for him.

Defiantly, Barry wore his cape outside of his jacket and over his backpack. It billowed in the stiffening breeze, tugging at his neck. Alex and his gang hooted at him from their bus. Barry didn't care. That's what he told himself, anyway.

Walking alone, Barry puzzled over his plight. Why didn't anyone understand? Even his parents failed to see what he was trying to do, and that hurt worst of all. He'd heard his mom worrying, his dad calling him "weird." That cut deeper than anything Alex spewed at him.

Of all people, his parents should get it. Grownups should know how bad things were. Kids were starving or getting shot. Families were getting kicked out of their homes. People were being robbed or hurt or both. Wherever he turned, people were angry. Or sad. Or afraid.

For Barry, it was crystal clear: The world needed to know things could get better. It needed hope. That's why the world loved Christmas so much. That's why it needed superheroes.

"Hey, kid."

Barry snapped out of his reverie. A stranger stood before him, blocking the sidewalk. He wore a tattered cloth jacket and oil-stained jeans. The falling snow clutched at his chaotic hair and dark, scruffy beard. He was old—not old like Papa Parker, who lived in a stark place that reeked of rubbing alcohol, but more like dad-age old. Maybe he had a son like Barry, too.

Still, he was a strange man loitering near an elementary school. Barry should have been frightened. Maybe he was, just a little. But he had the cape. He had the power. Dismissing any unease, Barry struck his superhero pose.

"How can I help you, citizen?" he said in his bravest voice.

The man smiled, genuinely amused. He didn't seem evil at all. Barry maintained his guard anyway.

"Halloween was six weeks ago, kid. What's with the cape?"

Barry puffed out his chest. "I'm a superhero."

"I see. What's your superhero name?"

The question caught Barry by surprise. It hadn't occurred to him to come up with a name.

"I'm … still working on one," he admitted.

"Fair enough," the man chuckled. "I won't ask for your real name, of course. Secret identity and stuff."

Barry grinned. Finally, someone who gets it!

"I do need your help, though. I haven't eaten since yesterday." He held up a battered piece of cardboard that Barry hadn't noticed until now. On it was a message scrawled in black marker: *Veteran. Out of work. Need help. God bless*!

"I usually ask for money, but I won't do that to you," he said. "Maybe you've got something left from lunch?"

Eager to help, Barry shed his backpack and unzipped it. Deep within, beneath a forest of crumpled homework papers, he found a chocolate peanut butter protein bar. It was at least a week old and, judging by its lopsided form, had been stepped on at least once. Sheepishly, he handed it over.

"Sorry it's a little squished."

The man took it gratefully. "No worries. Thanks!"

He made short work of the treat, then stuffed the wrapper in his jacket. Barry saw that the frosty air had gnawed his hands a dark, angry purple.

The stranger nodded at Barry. "Thanks again. You saved my life."

Even Barry knew he was exaggerating. Yet he spoke with sincerity. It felt good. Really, really good.

"S'cuse me, sir. Your sign … uh, are you homeless?"

The man shook his head. "Nah, I got a place. It isn't much. But till I get work, what money I have goes to rent. That's why I'm out here, hoping to snag a meal."

"Oh. It's just … you look homeless, I guess."

The man sighed. Bending low, he pulled his purple hands from his pockets and rested them on his knees, his face close to Barry's.

"People say I look like a lot of things. Homeless. A deadbeat. Someone too lazy to make his life better. They don't know me. For every good person who gives me a buck or a sandwich, a dozen people call me names or pretend I'm not here." He straightened and stuffed his stiff hands back in his pockets.

"Thanks for being one of the good ones."

Then he flashed his biggest smile yet. "You gave me more than a squished protein bar. You gave me a little hope. That might end up being my best Christmas present."

With a nod, the man turned to go. Barry grabbed his sleeve. Without a word, the boy removed his floppy hat and mittens and offered them to the stranger. The stranger opened his mouth to protest, but Barry pushed them at him with a stern look. While too large for the boy, the hat and mittens barely fit the man. Even so, they worked.

He studied his warming hands for a long time. Then he sniffed and used the left mitten to wipe his eyes.

"You know what real superpowers are, kid?" he asked. "Compassion. Mercy. Grace. Ever hear those words before?"

Barry nodded. "In Sunday School, and from Mom and Dad. But I don't know what they mean."

The man smiled. "Yeah, you do, kid. Yeah, you do."

He turned and walked away. Barry watched as the man slowly vanished into the thickening, swirling snow.

A noise from behind caused Barry to turn around. To his surprise, his father stood there, clutching his coat to his chest. He was sniffing and wiping his eyes, too, just like the stranger.

"I came to pick you up from school because of the snow," he said, his voice breaking. "I saw what you did."

Barry wondered what was wrong. Had he messed up again? Was he in trouble for giving away Aunt May's present? Had he been … weird?

It was none of those things. Thomas didn't scold him, didn't ground him. He embraced Barry instead, hugging him like he'd never let him go.

At last he understood. In the season of hope, as the falling snow painted a Christmas card all around them, Thomas knew what made Barry special. He knew that the world needed people like his son.

A superhero. That'll be the day.

Today, it was.

THE MARGIN

Charity Gritt's running shoe thumped across a manhole cover. The manhole cover thumped back.

Her workout screeched to a halt. Palming sweat from her stinging eyes, Charity jogged back, stopped short of the cover and, leaning forward, peered at it with a touch of unease. Unlike the round, rusted-iron lids of old, this one was a red square of composite metal, three-quarters of a meter per side and flush with the walkway. Two recessed handle-locks squared off at opposite ends, and a textured surface helped avoid slips and falls. Few people paid attention to these hatches. But then, to Charity's knowledge, one had never thumped of its own accord.

She read the white lettering on the cover:

WARNING! MARGIN ACCESS HATCH
AUTHORIZED PERSONNEL ONLY

As if to make the point, the cover gave another loud, threatening thud.

Charity lurched back. The sound could mean only one thing: Someone was trapped inside the Margin.

She brought her left wrist to her mouth and tapped the skin with a finger, activating the telelink beneath.

"Call Dad," she told her wrist. Not for the first time, Charity felt grateful for inserting the device in a conventional place. She'd seen others converse with less modest body parts.

A few moments later, her father's jovial voice replied.

"Hello, sweetheart. Interrupting my new life of leisure already?"

"It's not like you've had much time to settle in," Charity chuckled.

Former Captain Gerald Gritt had added "(Ret.)" to his name just six hours earlier. Live on video and with considerable ceremony, he'd turned over command of the starship *Estera* to his only daughter.

"At least you caught me after my nap." They both laughed at that ludicrous suggestion. Even at his advanced age, Gritt was the picture of endless, restless energy.

"Well, before you go back to sleep, I need to check with you on something. I'm on a run in the Habitat Ring, not far from Transit Tube Four. This'll sound crazy, but I think there's someone trapped inside the Margin."

A long, puzzling silence followed.

"Did you get that, Dad?"

Finally, "Yes. I'm just … trying to wrap my head around it. What makes you think someone's down there?"

"I heard banging from beneath an access hatch."

"Probably just a maintenance crew."

"None scheduled this month."

Another long pause. Charity frowned. It wasn't like her father to be so uncertain.

"I suppose it could be a problem with the temperature control system," he suggested. "If it's gotten cold down there, you might have heard metal contracting."

That seemed unlikely to Charity. On the other hand, she'd been captain of this generational starship for exactly one quarter of one day. Gerald Gritt had 50 years notched on his recently removed belt.

"Maybe you're right," she said. "Sorry to bother you."

"No bother. Glad you asked, in fact. I'm not quite ready to be forgotten."

"You'll never be that."

He chuckled. "'Never' is a long time. Anyway, I was going to the Command Center to clear out my office. You finish your run. I'll look into this for you and report back."

A reasonable offer, typical of her generous father. And he was right; it was probably nothing. Yet Charity couldn't shake the feeling that something strange was happening in the Margin beneath her feet.

She thanked her father and signed off. Her first crisis, deftly handled. Would the challenges yet to come be that easy to resolve? With 35 years left in their journey, it wasn't likely.

That journey was the most audacious in human history, begun decades earlier with the discovery of a planet orbiting Alpha Centauri B. Just over four light-years from Earth, Centauri B turned out to harbor three worlds. One of them, eventually named Qanturis, proved to be habitable—and soon thereafter, became a global obsession. Nations united to build and launch *Estera* with a thousand people aboard to establish the first extrasolar colony. Nearly five miles in length, most of *Estera* was nuclear fuel and supplies. The living area was a mile-wide ring spinning at its midpoint. There the colonists lived and worked, preparing for their new home once the 85-year voyage was complete.

Charity was a child of *Estera*, born nearly two decades after its launch. She knew life only inside the spinning Habitat Ring, where the horizon curved upward and a three-mile run took her all the way around her "world." Gerald Gritt raised Charity alone, her mother having died in childbirth. Despite this loss, Gerald commanded the mission with insightful, compassionate leadership. Charity hoped to be half as great as he had been.

Maybe that was why the mystery of the Margin gnawed at her. Rather than handling it as captain, she felt like she'd passed it off to Daddy. That set a bad precedent. As Gerald's successor, Charity needed his counsel, but she also needed to assert her authority.

Charity studied the handle-locks. They were biometric, keyed to respond to selected staff, including the ship's captain. She reached down and grabbed them. The handle-locks recognized her DNA signature, tripped the latches, and the lightweight cover lifted away. A blue light encircled the lip of the opening, casting a dim glow onto a rust-colored ladder that vanished into the deep, unsettling darkness.

The Margin.

Beyond the hatch was an 80-foot chasm between the two hulls of the habitat ring—the inner hull where the colonists lived, and the magnetically shielded outer hull that screened out deadly cosmic radiation.

For most people, the Margin was *navis incognita*, entirely unknown, a largely empty space with a scattering of control and monitoring systems. Though it had a slightly higher radiation count, the Margin wasn't especially dangerous, at least not in the short-term. It even maintained low-power life support for occasional maintenance work.

Nonetheless, it was pitch-dark. Exceptionally creepy.

And, apparently, occupied.

Far below, a shadowy form scurried down the ladder. Charity leaned into the hole, squinting to see who—or what—was fleeing from her.

"Hey! Who are you? What are you doing?"

The shape paused briefly, as if considering a reply. Then it continued on, vanishing into the darkness. Still puzzled, Charity felt a dash of anger. The lack of response spoke volumes. This wasn't someone trapped in the Margin; this was someone hiding there.

With a determination she didn't actually feel, Charity swung her feet through the hatchway and climbed down into the Margin.

The descent took two terrifying, seemingly endless minutes. Although there was air and minimal heat, the *Estera* wasted no energy on lighting the Margin. Charity felt as if she were sinking into La Brea tar, except it was cold, seeping into her damp running togs, into her flesh, down to her bones. An irrational dread squeezed her chest, summoning paranoid visions of what might be watching her from the darkness.

And then it was over. Her feet landed on the inside surface of the outer hull at the base of the ladder. No monsters awaited—at least none that chose to attack in that moment. There was only the blackness, the chilled air and a speck of light from the hatchway far above. Charity crouched and touched the floor. It was cool but not glacial. Made of nanoquirillium filaments, the hull kept the cold of space at bay.

As her eyes adjusted slightly to the dim surroundings, she noticed a small toolbox attached to the ladder. Inside she found a tiny hand torch. More relieved than she wanted to admit, she clicked the power switch and swept the sharp white beam across a few scattered control boxes, most about chest high. Other than these, the Margin was as empty as it should be.

The captain peeked in and around the consoles, looking for whatever caused the mysterious thumping on the hatch or the movement on the ladder. Intent on her search, Charity failed to notice what lay underfoot. A stride became a catch and a stumble. She toppled to the deck.

The pain was sharp but momentary. Charity groaned and rolled on her back, waiting for her breath to return. No permanent damage, it seemed. Still clutching the hand torch, she aimed it at her feet to see what had tripped her.

A gray corpse grinned back.

Somehow Charity managed to keep from screaming. Swallowing her fear, she rose and inspected the body. Hard to tell how long the woman—yes, definitely female—had been dead, but Charity suspected weeks, if not months. The body was rapier-thin, its leathery skin stretched taut, like a mummy's. The near-sterile environment of the Margin had preserved it.

Obviously not the person on the ladder, then. But who was she? What was she doing in the Margin?

As if to add to the growing list of questions, a little girl popped up from behind the nearest console and said, "Hi."

This time, the newly minted captain yelped. After a long moment spent regaining her composure, Charity mustered a smile and a shaky-voiced greeting. "Hey there. You gave me quite a start!"

The girl, blond and disheveled, perhaps all of nine years old, covered her mouth and giggled.

"Was that you banging on the hatch?" asked Charity.

The girl didn't answer. She moved from behind the control box. The light of the hand torch bathed her face, causing Charity to gasp.

She had the unmistakable features of Down syndrome.

Charity had never known a person with a genetic disorder. Such conditions were unheard of aboard *Estera*. The original colonists had been thoroughly screened to keep such conditions out of the mix—for them and their progeny. The birth of someone with Down syndrome would be shocking news. Yet Charity had never heard of this girl.

"Are you alone down here?"

The little girl giggled once again. She pointed at the hand torch.

"That's very bright," she said at last. Her voice was soft, her words slightly thick. "How can you stand it?"

"I can't see in the dark without it. What about you? How do you get around down here?"

"Easy! I'll show you."

She turned and fled into the darkness. Charity could hear her sandaled feet slapping on the deck in an all-out sprint, undaunted by the maze of consoles and cables. A pause, and then the slapping sound returned, moving closer as the girl emerged from the gloom.

"That's amazing," said Charity. "I'd fall down if I tried to do that."

The girl laughed. "Here, let me help you."

She reached for the hand torch and snapped it off. Then she took Charity's hand and tugged lightly. They began to move through the Margin, a bit too quickly for Gritt's comfort. But the girl appeared to thrive there, expertly guiding Charity around the obstacles scattered along the curved hull.

"Remarkable! How can you see so well in the dark?"

"I know how to get around in my head."

This revelation startled Charity. The little girl had memorized the layout of their surroundings. That meant she'd been there for a long time. She wasn't trapped, nor was she hiding.

She *lived* in the Margin.

As they continued their flight, Charity began to make out more of their environment. She caught sight of an odd, flickering glow ahead of them. The girl led her directly toward it.

When Charity realized what it was, she stopped in astonishment.

Fire, splashing orange-yellow-blue hues in the air, blazed from an old supply barrel. Charity had never seen fire before; indeed, *Estera* had countless safety systems aimed at preventing it. True, the environmental systems in the Habitat Ring could handle an occasional campfire, but her father had never allowed it.

As stunning as it was, the fire proved less shocking than the people who huddled around it.

There were dozens of them, all ages and races and genders. Most garbed themselves in worn clothing. They were silent, almost ghost-like. As Charity studied them, she saw each had some sort of affliction: cleft palates, malformed limbs, twisted spines. Others appeared lost in the mental fog of misfiring neurons and damaged psyches.

Yet all shared one thing: afflictions unknown aboard the colony ship.

A few took note of Charity and her young host. Most ignored her. Finally, a scruffy man, tall and disheveled, wearing a stained trench coat, approached her with open suspicion. The girl let go of Charity's hand and trotted over to the man, wrapping her arms around his waist. The man hugged back, then ushered the girl aside, scowling at Charity.

"You're not one of the maintenance crew. What are you doing here?"

He failed to intimidate her. She met his gaze with equal steel. "Inspecting my ship. I'm Captain Gritt, commanding the starship *Estera*."

The man snorted. "I know Captain Gritt. You're not him."

"Gerald Gritt is my father. He's retired. I'm in command now."

The man seemed unconvinced. He made a grand show of walking slowly around the newcomer, sizing her up, looking for weakness. She resolved to show none.

"You claim you're the new captain. When did this momentous transfer occur?"

"This morning. It was on the ship's video network."

The man's laugh dripped with derision. He swung his arms wide.

"As you can see, we don't have the luxury of video down here. Tell me, why would a new captain, on her very first day, take a stroll in the Margin?"

Charity was neither impressed nor frightened by this man. Neither were his companions, who pointedly ignored his bluster.

"I don't need to justify my actions to you," she said tersely. "I heard someone banging on an access hatch. Turned out to be that girl. I thought she might be in trouble. In any case, as captain of this ship, I can go wherever I want. And it's none of your damned business."

"You expect me to believe you had no idea who was banging on the hatch? That doesn't speak well of you as the new captain."

Charity shook her head, puzzled. "I don't know what you mean. How would anyone know there were people living in the Margin?"

Chortling once more, the man turned away from her, returning to the fire with an elaborate show of warming his hands over the flames. "You aren't wowing me with your deductive skills," he said. "The riddle is a simple one. Think it through."

Charity shrugged. "I suppose a maintenance team might have found you. But they rarely come down here, and the Margin is a very large space."

"Wrong, captain. Try again." He paused, then added, "Very well, then, a hint: Think hard about your mission."

Charity thought hard, then shook her head. The lines of contempt on the man's face grew deeper.

"Your mission, Captain Gritt, is to colonize another planet. To spread humanity's seed elsewhere in the cosmos. That's an enormous risk. To reduce that risk, the variables must be controlled."

"Such as?"

"Biological weakness, for one. You need healthy, vibrant humans to give birth to healthy, vibrant offspring. Say you find someone doesn't meet the standard. Only it's too late—you've already left Earth. Well, that's more than just an inconvenience, isn't it?"

The answer hit Charity like a physical blow. She staggered back, horrified by the thought.

"You mean to tell me you were *banished* here?"

The man turned toward her and offered slow, sarcastic applause. "Well done! A brilliant deduction!"

"But … that's not possible. You can't stay in the Margin. No one can."

"Careful, captain. Don't let your feelings get the better of you."

Charity shook her head, insistent. "The radiation—it's low level, sure, but with enough time and exposure, it will kill you."

"Quite true," the man answered, his voice losing its sarcastic tone. "Some of us are dying now. Some have died already." His eyes glistened. "My wife, for one. Cancer killed her a month ago, or so I assume. She wandered away, into the darkness, so we wouldn't have to watch her die."

140

He wiped his eyes. When he looked up again, they'd regained their fire. His voice, however, continued to shake.

"Perhaps you've seen her."

Noticing his pain, the girl took her father's hand, renewing him.

"But this is easier for your shipmates to handle, isn't it?" he continued, stronger now. "Not burdening your utopia. Anyway, your crew isn't entirely heartless. A precious few know the truth. They provide just enough food, air and heat for us to survive. Enough to clear their consciences, to let them sleep at night. And you know the old saying: 'Out of sight, out of mind.'"

His laughter echoed across the cavernous Margin.

Charity turned and ran.

The laughter pursued her, accused her. She stumbled, dropping the hand torch, but the taunts kept her running. How she reached the ladder without getting lost was a miracle. Charity scrambled upward, every step a push against the horror of what she'd learned, against the lie it must be.

She reached the hatchway at last, escaping the black grip of the Margin.

Her father and two security men were waiting for her.

"Dad! Dear God, I'm glad to see you! You won't believe what I found down there!"

Gerald Gritt stared at her. He didn't reach out, didn't try to comfort her. His eyes reflected a range of emotions. Anger. Guilt.

And sorrow. Especially sorrow.

"I'm afraid I would," he replied, his expression that of stone. It told her everything—and it shattered her heart.

"You *knew?*"

"Of course," he replied. "And before you go all self-righteous on me, think about it. Think about what's at stake. Think like the captain of a starship carrying humanity's last hope." He pointed at the open hatch. "Those people, they're beyond hope. We can't fix them. And we can't afford the problems they represent."

"Problems? That's all they are to you? Dad, they're human beings!"

Gerald shook his head. "No. They're threats. Threats to our survival."

"You call them threats, but you couldn't bring yourself to kill them outright!"

"I'm no murderer."

"No, you're something far worse!" Charity snarled. "You turned your back on them! You're giving them just enough to survive until they die on their own! And you think that absolves you? Absolves any of us?"

"Charity, if you'd just let me—"

She cut him off. "No, I don't have to let you do anything. I'm the captain now. And as captain, I order those people to be brought up here and cared for." She lifted her chin and glared at him. "I won't allow this crew to become the monster you are!"

Gerald Gritt wasn't surprised by her reaction. He knew his daughter all too well. That's why he'd never told her about the people living in the Margin.

All for naught. No choice then, no choice now. He turned sad eyes toward her.

"I'm sorry, my darling. So sorry."

He gave a curt nod to the guards and looked away.

Maybe it will hurt less if I don't watch. As they say, out of sight—

Charity screamed.

It was short-lived. Her cries faded quickly as the guards cast his only daughter into the Margin.

A SHEEP ONESELF

At two o'clock in the morning, even the most delicate door chime shreds your nerves.

The sight of three armed men at your door does nothing to soothe them. The tallest of the late-night visitors stepped into my foyer. "Father DiMarco?" he asked politely. I nodded, not yet trusting my voice.

"The name's Batson." He flashed an ID badge with a colorful holographic logo and a very bad photograph. "Quantex Security. I'm sorry to bother you, Father, but we have something of an emergency."

"What kind of emergency?" I was fully awake now.

Batson hesitated. "It, uh, has to do with a friend of yours. Dr. Taylor Wayne."

That was all I needed to hear. "I'll get dressed."

The men waited patiently as I raced back to my room and scrambled into my clothes. My mind whirled. Taylor Wayne! Gone two years, and now he'd popped into my life twice in one week. In fact, our last encounter began much like this one: in the wee hours, with the chirping of the cell phone at my bedside.

"Please, Padre, you've got to help them!" Wayne's voice had pleaded. "They're dying, and I can't stop it!"

"Take it easy, Taylor. Who is dying?"

His answer came wrapped in a heartrending sob.

"*My children!*"

* * * *

143

Wayne calmed down eventually, but it required half a box of tissues and two straight-up bourbons. The latter was easiest; I found Taylor slouched over a small, battered table in a gloomy Tucson bar. The half-lit neon sign outside called it The Missing Tooth. As I cautiously eyed the clientele, I could see why.

I slipped into a chair next to him and laid a hand on his shoulder. He'd stopped sobbing, but his sorrow hung over us like smoke from a bad cigar. I wasn't used to seeing him like this—Dr. Taylor Wayne, the world's hottest digital physicist, known for his self-confidence as much as for his technical genius. But right now he was just a little boy with a shattered heart, and I didn't know why.

"It all started ten years ago, when I first joined Quantex," Taylor began. His normally rich baritone voice, the one I coveted for my parish choir, was thin and strangled by grief.

"I was called to create a true Turing machine, a universal computer capable of nearly infinite calculations per second." He gave a sad smile. "Some people said it couldn't be done. You can guess how I responded to that. It took a new idea. *My* idea. Dynamic neoquantum processing. It's applying quantum supercomputing and AI capacity in ways never imagined before."

Now I'm no slouch when it comes to computers—my first task as a new priest was to train my septuagenarian secretary on a PC—but Taylor's babblings already left me slack-jawed.

"I'm afraid I don't understand. What does this have to do with people dying?"

His eyes suddenly glistened anew. I shoved a pile of tissues toward him, hoping he'd settle for that instead of another drink. "No, I'm okay." He sniffed, rubbed his face and pressed on.

"Think about how far we've come in computer technology, Padre. Your smartwatch is more powerful than most computers from a few decades ago. Quantex was part of that revolution, nabbing grant after grant like so many potato chips. But while everyone else focused on zettaflops, I dove deeper."

"Zetta-what?"

"Patience, Padre. I'm getting there. You see, most folks are playing around with quantum computing. It's a good start. But dynamic neoquantum processing is like opening a whole other realm. The quantum physics of quantum physics. And I built a computer that taps into it."

He said it casually, the way you describe fixing a door hinge or scrubbing grout. I sat in silence, dumbfounded.

Wayne picked up an empty bourbon glass and slowly twirled it in the dim light, carefully studying the distorted reflection of our surroundings.

"It was easy, really, once I worked out the basics," Taylor said. "And Quantex gave me free rein. Even set aside a whole building for me. Good thing, because I needed every square inch just for the front end. The guts of a neoquantum computer requires enormous space —and not all of it is in *our* space."

"I don't know what that means," I piped up. But Taylor didn't answer me. He continued his confusing tale.

"Funny thing is, Quantex had no idea what I was really up to. They probably would have stopped me if they did. I went far beyond the parameters of the grants. That's going to cause me trouble at some point. I knew from the beginning I'd have to prove the thing worked in a big way. No cheap parlor tricks."

Wayne put down the glass and fixed me with an icy glare. "Isn't it sad how we've stopped trusting our fellow man?"

"Tragic," I agreed, and meant it. But by then I would have confirmed that the sky was MacDuff tartan if Taylor said so. He was emotionally unstable, and an argument on any subject wouldn't help matters.

"Not to change the subject, Taylor, but how does all this—"

"You keep interrupting me," he said in a quiet and disconcertingly miffed tone.

"Don't take it personally. I'm just trying to help. When you called, you claimed people were dying. Your 'children,' I believe you said. But you don't have any kids."

Wayne laughed, a harsh noise in the paranoid silence of the bar. The nervous glance I threw over each shoulder was reflexive.

"No children, you say? Padre, I have more children than you can count! More than the grains of sand on a beach. More than the stars in the sky. And every last one of them is dying!"

The tears flowed anew. He scrabbled for a tissue.

"We need to go for a ride," Wayne said at last, dabbing at his eyes. I wasn't sure I wanted to go anywhere with him.

"Where?"

He put a finger to his lips and smiled slightly through wet cheeks. "It's a surprise."

I already regretted it, but I knew I had to go with him.

"All right, Taylor. But I'm driving."

Wayne made good on his bar tab—the total shocked me and affirmed the wisdom of my taking the wheel—and in minutes we were headed across town in my old Ford. By the time we left the city limits and merged with the inky desert, I knew our destination: Quantex Laboratories.

It was surprisingly easy to get past security. Except for the electronic badge reader outside his laboratory, Wayne never bothered to show his Quantex identification to gain entry. Guards merely waved as we strolled by, with little more than a cursory glance at me. Apparently, Dr. Taylor Wayne was a fixture to the late-night security team. I was considered a safe risk in his presence.

Taylor had said little since we'd left the bar. Once inside his lab building, I prompted him for more of his story.

"You said something about proving your neoquantum computer would work. A demonstration of some sort. What did you do?"

Wayne smiled broadly. "I figured I'd tap my other degrees— biology, geology, cosmology and sociology. That way I could pull off the whole scheme by myself. And to think my dad called me nuts when I went after a quintuple major! I needed every bit of that education to design it within a dynamic neoquantum framework."

"Design what?"

He didn't answer with words. Instead, he opened a door and ushered me into a large, frosty white room filled with car-sized black boxes, winking lights and an odd, pervasive hum.

There was a gray steel door on the far side of the room, next to a tiny, cluttered office space. The air itself sizzled with power—and something else. I find it hard to describe even now. A sense of otherness, of elsewhere and elsewhen. It flowed and bounced and pummeled me until I shivered uncontrollably.

I tried to distract myself, turning my attention to the technology around me.

"Oh sure, I had to make a few assumptions," Taylor continued, as if he didn't notice the room's effects on me. "There are lots of things we don't really understand about physics, biology, social dynamics. But it all seemed to fit. I fed everything into the neoquantum processor, the AI took over—and suddenly, there it was."

This "read my mind" routine was getting on my nerves, and I said so. Taylor looked at me quizzically. "Haven't you been listening, Padre? There's no mystery to it. I created a universe."

I felt as if I'd suddenly dropped into a different conversation. It must have shown on my face.

"It's true," Wayne confirmed. "An honest-to-goodness universe. From the tiniest particle to the biggest galaxy. Every physical law, every ecological and sociological interaction. Everything."

That's when all the uncertainty about my old friend turned into outright dread—or rather, dread with a twist of anger. Before my eyes, my quirky companion had gone from a computer genius to a B-movie lunatic. Or a twisted practical joker.

"You dragged me here in the middle of the night for this?" I demanded. "A computer simulation? Come on, Taylor, I've seen them before. They're like games. My nephew does them on his home PC."

This time Taylor's glare was sharp enough to draw blood. "We're not talking about a kiddie sim, Padre! This is something unique and glorious. An entirely new reality."

"Ridiculous! I don't care how powerful your computer is, or how real this 'reality' might appear. It's just a simulation. It's bits of data carefully arranged to mimic something."

My lack of faith didn't go over well.

"You think I'm lying?" he growled. "Or I'm crazy?"

"No," I replied softly. "But I do think you're too close to this. Taylor, I'm sure you've done something quite impressive, but it isn't real. It can't be. That's why they call it virtual reality.

"It's all just a graphic representation of math and logic and binary code. If you don't like the sim, delete it. Do a reboot or whatever."

With a cry of rage, Taylor leaped at me. Before I knew it, he had my left arm pinned behind my back. I squawked in pain, but he didn't care. He shoved me across the white-tiled floor toward the steel door. The door had no knob or hinges, just a small keypad on the adjoining wall.

"You say it isn't real?" Taylor snarled, punching three numbers into the keypad. "Then you tell me what it is!"

The door moved sideways into the wall, and Wayne tossed me through the opening.

Into thin air.

Azure sky and cottony clouds spun around me. My arms windmilled as I fell forward, plummeting into a deadly hundred-foot drop. Terrified, I shut my eyes and screamed.

The plunge stopped abruptly.

I'd landed on my knees. Eyes still squeezed shut, I could hear my heart beating, feel air filling my lungs. *Okay, so I'm not dead.*

I slowly opened my eyes—and gasped.

I hovered magically, as if kneeling on an invisible floor high in the sky. Fighting terror and vertigo, I forced myself to look down at what appeared to be a huge field. Rows of bean plants swayed in the breeze. Nestled among the plants, contrasting with the undulating shades of green, were thousands upon thousands of brightly dressed people. They, too, moved—not to the wind, but to a slow, melancholy sound that flowed from a large platform.

I rolled over cautiously, looking back the way I'd come. Taylor Wayne still stood there, grinning madly, framed by a doorway cut into the virtual sky. His lab with its blinking consoles spread out behind him.

"You simulated … Woodstock?" I asked dumbly.

Taylor rolled his eyes and sighed, as if challenged by a hopeless child. "I created the world you see around you. They," he pointed to the tiny people below, "did Woodstock."

My fear melted into incredulity. I knew enough about computers to be thoroughly astounded by the world before me. Taylor had written a stunningly complex program, including some sort of holographic projection that afforded the smallest peek at it. But it didn't stop at visuals. There were real sounds. Real smells. A real sense of *life*.

And that life was somehow at risk.

"You said these people are dying?" It didn't seem possible. I saw no apparent threat. There was just the music, created by unfamiliar instruments generating sounds that hinted at … what? Sadness? Despair? I wasn't sure. But there was no mistaking my friend's desperation.

"Let me show you." He stepped into the sky with me. I winced, for my mind insisted that he should fall to his death. He didn't, of course, and he chuckled at my reaction. As I climbed to my shaking feet, he pulled from his pocket a handheld device, about the size of a cell phone, and tapped at its glass surface.

"It's a wireless interface," he answered my unspoken question. "I use this to call up different parts of the program. Hang on."

Instantly, Woodstock vanished. We stood on a city sidewalk shrouded in neon and nightfall. A whiff of smog and sweat burned my nostrils. Traffic sounds tickled my ears. We might have been in some shady corner of L.A. or New York or any large city. There was no way to tell where, though; the text on the blazing signs around me was utterly foreign.

But there were *people*—living, breathing, vibrant! They hurried about their simulated existence, bustling past but, oddly, never seeing or touching us. When they spoke, I couldn't understand their tongue. But their emotional tones were inescapable. Joy, sadness, excitement, dread, all the things one would expect to overhear on a busy street corner.

A dizzying mix of the familiar and the alien assaulted my senses. And the familiar was painfully so.

A man lay huddled on a nearby steam grate, snatching elusive sleep. Shellac-faced prostitutes hovered on the street corners, hawking their services to passersby. Two grimy youths exchanged a small bag of white powder, nodded and vanished separately into the night.

Behind me, a man came out of an apartment building with an angry—maybe jilted?—woman in hot pursuit. Passersby ignored it all, their eyes locked on the concrete underfoot, or dulled by their own mental ruminations.

Then, as I glanced across the street, two young thugs jumped an elderly man and began to hit him with baseball bats.

"Hey!" I cried. "Leave him alone!"

They didn't hear me, or they didn't care. They kept beating him until blood flowed on the sidewalk. Taylor touched my arm, but I shrugged him off and ran toward the attackers.

"Stop it now!" I yelled, grabbing one of the boys—or rather, I tried to grab him. To my astonishment, my hands passed through him as if he didn't exist. I stood there, dazed and helpless, until a distant screeching sound, something like a siren, wailed through the night. The youths fled. They hadn't even robbed the old man; it was a meaningless assault. Their bloodied victim curled up and wept like a child.

"You couldn't have stopped them," Taylor explained, coming up behind me.

"Why not?" I demanded.

"Because this is all part of a holographic storage matrix. For us, the neoquantum computer can reproduce sights, sounds, even smells. But we can't directly interact it. We're not part of this reality."

The madness of it all left me speechless. Swirling around me were the suffering, the purveyors of suffering, and those who dismissed suffering as part of the décor. Why would anyone make such a nightmare?

"Taylor—"

"No, not yet. There's more you need to see." He raised the handheld device. And I saw ...

—*tap*—

... a family torn asunder, the father wallowing in a senseless affair ...

—*tap*—

... a teenager, whimpering in fear and loneliness, clutching a bottle of sleeping pills ...

—*tap*—

… a businessman relishing the demise of a rival …

—tap—

… a war erupting over ethnic disparity …

—tap—

… hatred …

—tap—

… jealousy …

—tap—

… rage …

—tap—

"Stop!" I was shaking, overwhelmed by this hideous virtual world. We stood in a small, barren park under an overcast winter sky. A keening wind brushed across the holographic snow. I stared accusingly at Taylor Wayne.

"You created this … this *obscenity*?"

That should have offended him, and I meant it to. But an agony deeper than any man should bear already entangled Taylor Wayne's soul. The worst I could do was remind him of it. "I created this world," he said hoarsely.

"I created these people. But this," he waved at the somber sky, as if encompassing all of the vileness we'd seen, "this came from somewhere else. Like a virus. It came through the neoquantum interface, and the program—my children—integrated it. Embraced it."

I shook my head. "How is that possible?"

"It's a heuristic program. It learns, grows. My children became self-aware. There were protections in place, but that didn't matter. They embraced the ugliness. They *chose* it. Then everything began to change. Love became hatred. Peace became strife. They made up their own truths, their own morality, their own right and wrong. You've seen the result."

He tapped his handheld again. Once more we floated in the summer sky above the bean field. Music filled the air, the words lost in a language I couldn't understand. And yet there remained that oddly familiar quality, something haunting and sad. There was a deep grief in this place, as if these people who clung to each other were drowning in the harshness of this reality, unable to escape its hopelessness.

They were right to mourn. I knew the ultimate outcome.

And I knew why Taylor Wayne was so desperate to save them.

He'd already left, stepping through the open door in the sky. I followed him reluctantly. The door slid closed behind me, cutting off the bittersweet music. In the lab, a weary Taylor leaned against one of the consoles, his back turned to me.

"You can't save them either, can you?" It wasn't really a question.

"I … I don't know how." I could barely speak through my own despair. "I'm so sorry, Taylor. But let's not give up. They're bright people. Maybe they'll see—"

He interrupted me. "You know that will never happen, Padre. They've gone too far, given up too much." Taylor turned around. His eyes were flooded with tears.

"You were right, you know," he said. "They aren't real. Not in the way we define reality. That's why we can't save them. Not unless we meet them *where they are*."

I frowned. "What are you suggesting? A new kind of interface? Changing the program somehow?"

He offered a ghost of a smile. "Actually, I've been thinking about something Albert Einstein once said. Maybe you can relate to it. 'In order to be an immaculate member of a flock of sheep, one must above all be a sheep oneself.'"

I frowned deeper, not comprehending. He saw my bewilderment and shamed me with a disappointed look.

"Thanks for coming, Padre. I'll walk you out."

The drive home took two hours, and I never figured out what my grieving friend meant.

* * * *

Now, days later, I was back at Quantex, standing among the winking lights of Taylor's neoquantum computer, as baffled as ever.

"You've been here before?" Batson asked.

"Yes, with Dr. Wayne." I looked around. "Where is Taylor? Is he all right?"

"I'm afraid not, Father DiMarco."

He took my arm and led me to the office space next to the sliding steel door. A man slouched over the cluttered desk. He faced a wall-sized computer screen filled with meaningless code and mathematical formulae. Wires flowed from beneath the desk to a headset that wrapped itself around his long, brown hair.

I recognized the hair.

"Taylor? What in the name of—"

Waxen face. Eyes empty and glazed. Chest stilled.

Thunderstruck, I turned to Batson. "What happened?"

Batson fished a scrap of paper from his uniform pocket. "We were hoping you could explain it to us. He left this note behind." He handed the slip to me. "You know, I was a cop for 20 years before I came to Quantex, and this isn't like any suicide note I've ever seen."

I opened the note with shaking hands. There were just six words scrawled on it:

Dear Padre,
I've become the sheep.

My heart slammed against my chest, and I dropped the note. Suddenly, I *knew*! Where the note had mystified Batson and his men, it made perfect sense to me. Perfect, frightening sense.

I turned and headed toward the steel door.

"Father DiMarco!"

They were too surprised to stop me. In a moment, I tapped out the numbers I'd seen Taylor punch and flung myself through the doorway as soon as I could.

This time I stood in a broad field of long bent grass, flat except for a hill at its center. On the hill brooded a large oak tree, bathed in the mandarin glow of the setting sun. There was no breeze. No singing birds. Indeed, this virtual world was oddly silent.

And I saw him in the tree—the bloodied remnant of a man, stripped of everything he had been.

The horrible thing had been done hours before, but a few spectators remained. Most mocked him with their eyes, amused by his foolishness. Then they moved on, content to pursue their doomed, pitiful lives.

Except for a handful of mourners.

In contrast to their sorrow, they wore brightly colored clothes, with flowers in their hair and mud on their feet. The mud gave them away; they'd come from the bean field concert. Somehow they had heard Taylor Wayne's plea. And in it, they had found the hope for which they sang.

Now they wept again. I joined them.

And I wondered what would happen on the third day.

A Throw of the Dice

Brunettes and bar bets: Trevor Gaine's two greatest weaknesses drifted into the pub on a desert breeze, sweeping a path through the ashen haze to the copper-clad table where Trevor swam solo in his third gin and tonic.

"Mind if I join you?"

Her voice cascaded like satin. Trevor rose politely, if a bit unsteadily, and gestured to an empty chair.

"Reserved just for you, my dear," he said. His proper British tone clashed with the bar's Mexican motif. He flagged the bored server and ordered his new friend her own gin and tonic, which she amended to just tonic.

"So," Trevor said after the drink appeared, "to what do I owe this incredible pleasure?"

"To a rare opportunity, Mr. Gaine."

Trevor's eyes swept across the woman's slim form, tightly wrapped in a black, short-skirted dress before settling on her unfamiliar face.

"I'm afraid you have me at a disadvantage, Miss—?"

"Marta will do. Yes, I know a great deal about you. Son of a Yorkshire factory worker and a South London prostitute. First arrest at age 12 for stealing a cab. Six more arrests over the next 20 years. You fled England to avoid an embezzlement charge. You eventually found yourself here in Arizona, running a profitable home cleaning business that, oddly enough, hasn't yet cleaned a single house. Does that cover it?"

This summary of Trevor's sordid life spoiled his mood. "What's your game, Marta?"

"A friendly wager, that's all."

Trevor laughed. "A wager?"

"Yes. Potentially quite lucrative. But be warned, it will require deep reflection on your life."

"What are you, my conscience?"

Marta smiled. "An interesting notion. You could do with a bit of Jiminy Cricket."

"Interesting, indeed. You know, in the original story—not the one peddled by Disney—Jiminy Cricket was squashed to death for meddling in Pinocchio's life."

"Point taken." Marta coolly sipped her drink. "Last chance, Mr. Gaine."

Trevor mulled over her offer. This gorgeous woman oozed sincerity, which gave him every reason to distrust her. On the other hand, a wager is a wager, an opportunity to get ahead. And she did use the word lucrative.

"What's the payoff?" he asked.

"That depends."

"Not especially enticing, my dear Marta."

"Very well. A one-time bet, no ante on your part. If you lose, you're out nothing. If you win—"

Trevor pounced. "I get the proceeds, plus you spend a week with me in Mexico."

Marta scowled at him, clearly annoyed by this turn of events. Trevor savored the moment.

"I don't suppose a lavish dinner will suffice?"

Trevor shook his head smugly. The woman sighed.

"Very well, Mr. Gaine. I accept your terms."

With that, Marta opened her hand to show two translucent red cubes with white dots on each side. Trevor saw they were dice, slightly larger than normal but otherwise unremarkable.

"Not exactly hard-core gambling," he pointed out.

Marta slowly twirled the dice between her fingers. Trevor noticed that they were not quite translucent after all. Their insides shimmered with random flickers of light.

"These aren't ordinary dice," Marta was saying. "They're quantum dice."

Trevor shrugged. The term meant nothing to him.

"Quantum dice," Marta explained, "follow the laws of quantum mechanics. Every time you roll one, it lands on all values at once."

"Ridiculous! Only one side can show up at a time."

"True—if you're thinking in one universe."

Trevor shook his head, mystified. Marta set the dice back on the table and framed them with her delicate hands.

"In physics, quantum mechanics predicts countless universes. If I roll a quantum die and it lands on a six in this universe, it will land on a three in another, a five in yet another, and so on."

Trevor burst out laughing. "That's the craziest thing I've ever heard! Multiple universes! Quantum silliness, if you ask me!"

Marta said nothing. She merely picked up the dice, shook them in her hand and tossed them onto the table. They clattered briefly on the copper surface and rolled to a stop.

"What do you see, Mr. Gaine?"

"A two and a four," he replied, still chuckling. "What else would I see?"

"Are you sure?"

A harsh retort bubbled up, then caught in Trevor's throat. Gripped by a sudden, unsettling chill, he stared at the glimmering dice. They inexplicably blurred. He blinked hard, then rubbed his eyes, but the distortion remained. He leaned to the right. Instead of clearing, the distortion grew worse. Just as he was about to panic, the image abruptly became sharp as crystal.

The dice showed three and five white dots.

"What the—"

Marta sat there as before, smiling at him. Wearing a blue dress.

"—*bloody hell*—"

He stopped. Something else caught his eye: his drink. Instead of gin and tonic, a dark brown liquid enveloped the melting ice cubes. Trevor cautiously picked up the sweating glass, sniffed it twice, then took a sip.

"Rum and Coke!" he gasped.

"Yeah? That's what you ordered."

Trevor turned, startled by the sharp voice. The server, now appearing miffed instead of bored, speared him with a scowl.

"I did no such thing," Trevor replied. "I haven't had a rum and Coke in years. What happened to my gin and tonic?"

The server rested beefy hands on his hips. "Look, limey, you haven't ordered that sissy drink once in all the months you've been in here. It's always rum and Coke. *Always.*"

Trevor started to protest, but Marta stopped him with a touch.

"You won't win this argument," she said softly.

"Why not? I know what I ordered!"

Marta smiled. "I'm afraid you don't. Not in this bar."

Trevor swung around to look at her, but her flawless face was lost in sudden grayness. Inexplicably, his eyes were drawn to the quantum dice, once again a hazy red mass. He hid his face with his hands. *Am I going blind?*

When Trevor dared to look again, he was relieved to find his vision clear. The dice, untouched since Marta first threw them, displayed their white dots.

A one and a six. And Marta's dress was now kelly green.

"Dear Lord!"

Then he noticed that Marta's eyes were not on him, but on the place where the server had been standing. Trevor slowly turned around.

There was no server. Indeed, the man standing there was barely a man. Seventeen at best. Trevor didn't recognize him. Or did he? There was something about his hazel eyes and dark curly hair, something hauntingly familiar.

Something like the face that greeted Trevor in the mirror each day.

"Who are you?" he rasped.

The boy seemed nervous. Hands clenched in front of him, he twisted slightly on his feet, ready to react with fist or flight.

"I think you know," said the youth in a thick northern England tone. "It took me a year to track you down. But I knew I'd find you." He glanced around the brooding bar. "I just never expected to find my father in a place like this."

Trevor's jaw fell, and his hands began to shake. "You're mistaken, young man," he stammered. "I don't have a son."

"That's not quite true, Mr. Gaine. Don't forget Leila."

Marta's soft voice snapped Trevor's head around again.

"But … but she chose not to have the child."

"Partly true," Marta said. "Leila did what you wanted. She ended the pregnancy to keep from losing you. And then you left her anyway."

Trevor waved his hands in protest. "She was too confining. I wanted to live my own life."

"And you've done that exquisitely well. In fact, you've made your life's choices without any thought to the people around you."

"Who are you to judge me?" demanded Trevor.

"I judge no one. The scales of your own life are judgment enough. Leila is one example. You treated her like property. You carelessly formed a new life without any thought of the consequences. Face it: Every decision in your life, every action you take, is based solely on your selfishness and pride."

Trevor lurched from his chair, intent on choking this beautiful she-devil. The boy behind him cried out, begging his father to stop.

As he reached for her, Trevor glanced down at the quantum dice.

They glittered, blurred, then cleared.

And became six and four.

Trevor froze over the table. Marta still sat there, still gave him that sexy smile.

But now her dress was red.

A cold wave of terror drowned his rage. "What is going on?" he gasped.

"It's what I warned you about," said Marta. "Our wager is forcing you to look at the choices you've made. You must face the consequences of your actions. *All of them.*"

Trevor shook his head. "This is some sort of trick! Hypnosis? Something in my drink?" He picked up his glass and swirled the ice with a finger.

Marta giggled and shook her head.

"Then how? And where did you get the boy?"

"What boy?"

"Are you insane? That boy!" Trevor turned to point to his self-proclaimed son.

But the young man was no longer there.

"Something wrong?" Marta asked, all beauty and innocence.

"You bloody well know what's wrong!" Trevor screamed at her. "Where is he?"

"He *isn't*, Mr. Gaine. Not in your universe. And not in this one."

Deflated, Trevor flopped back into his chair. His head whirling, he gripped the table for support. That's when he noticed that the table was no longer covered in copper. In fact, it didn't appear to be the same table at all. This one was a black square scarred by the mindless etchings of penknife-wielding drunks. And the chair he sat in was different, too. Even the air, still blue with burned tobacco, had a thicker, fuller aroma. Trevor recognized the rich smell of pricey cigars.

And the voices murmuring around him were clearly English.

"This isn't the same bar," he whispered. "This isn't even Arizona."

"Very perceptive. We're in your favorite London pub, The Norwegian Blue."

"But how—?"

Marta tapped a die with a scarlet fingernail. "All values, remember? Anything that can be, is. In this universe, you never left London. You arrogantly assumed you'd never be caught on that embezzlement charge."

She glanced across the pub as the door swung open, letting in two men and a hiccup of London fog.

"Those inspectors are about to prove you wrong."

The men peered at the faces of the people around them. Their gaze stopped on Trevor. Then they began moving toward him.

"Help me, Marta!" Trevor begged, grabbing her arm in sheer panic. "This universe—it isn't mine! It's a mistake! Please, I'll do anything! Just throw the dice again!"

Marta firmly removed Trevor's hand from her arm. "A poet once said, 'A throw of the dice will never abolish chance.' Or fate, in your case. The mistake isn't the universe's, Mr. Gaine. *You* made a choice. You broke the law. The responsibility is yours alone—in any universe."

Trevor backed away from Marta, from the table, from the approaching inspectors. But there was no place to run.

No choices left.

He'd had a lifetime of them, countless opportunities to make the right decisions for himself. For Leila. For the son he never had.

He looked at the quantum dice, willing them to change. Demanding it. Begging it.

His vision blurred.

Five and two white dots gazed up from the table. And Marta was gone.

But Trevor, terrified, saw that nothing else had changed. He was still in the London pub, still staring at the two inspectors.

Wait! Something *was* different: In this universe, he had a gun.

One more decision. One last chance to make things right, to take responsibility for his choices instead of running from them. If he had the courage.

The inspectors moved closer.

Would it be courage? Or cowardice?

Trevor stared at the gun. The universe blurred. One white dot stared up from each die.

But no one noticed.

GHOSTWRITER

The gentle fall of night and the wet whisper of the Orontes River gradually soothed the Apostle's anger.

Even the best of friends argue from time to time, but this fight had been especially heated. With tempers lost and hearts broken, he felt it best to step away from his companion for a bit. So he'd wandered away from the late-day bustle of Antioch, the Roman Empire's great eastern city, coming to a secluded bend of the Orontes just as the sun slipped into slumber.

On its face, the argument seemed silly. Its roots were three years old, after all, when they set out together on a preaching tour through Cyprus and southern Asia Minor. In the middle of the trip, the third member of their team, young John Mark, abruptly went home, without apology or explanation. Leaving two men to do the work of three made for tough times and hard feelings—feelings that finally erupted when the Apostle's friend suggested giving John Mark another chance.

The solution was practical if nothing else: The partners would go their separate ways, one back to Cyprus and the other to Asia Minor. Each would choose a new companion.

Practical, perhaps. But no less painful.

At the riverbank, wrapped in cooling air and fading light, the Apostle prayed for peace in his heart, the release of his resentment and, most important of all, the restoration of a friendship that meant the world to him.

He finished his prayer—and opened his eyes to a vision.

A strange, blue mist swirled a short distance away. It hovered near a slope above the river, twisting like a desert whirlwind cast upon its side. Though seemingly ablaze, the mist added no heat to the chilly air. There was a sound, however. Small but strange, like a breeze made of iron.

163

Could it be?

No. That answer came with conviction. He felt amazement, and a tickle of fear. But there was no awe of the Holy Presence. Whatever this was, it wasn't of God.

The Apostle rose to his feet, staring into the blue fire. He wasn't sure what to do. Should he rebuke it as a demon? Or would a quick exit be the better part of valor?

Then he heard another sound in the midst of the wind, something familiar and impossible: a human voice.

"The wager is fulfilled."

That's when a bullet streaked out of the blue mist and ripped through the Apostle's head.

* * * *

TRANSCRIPT: NewsNet Live Tonight with Alicia Tellara

ATellara: Good evening, thanks for tuning in to NewsNet Live Tonight. I'm Alicia Tellara. Our top story today: the seemingly impossible disappearance of portions of one of history's most sacred texts. The Bible is the reference book of faith for more than two billion Christians worldwide. And now it appears that every copy, everywhere, is missing more than half of the New Testament, the latter portion of the Bible. We're not talking about a publisher's error. We're not talking about vandalism. This is a completely unexplainable event. And it's sparking panic, regardless of religious persuasion. Riots are reported in hundreds of cities, and the latest estimates put the death toll at over 10,000. Tonight we'll take a look at the historical, religious, sociological and scientific perspectives on this event. Starting us off here in the studio is Dr. Jonathan Trent, professor of theology and history at Perelann University. Good evening, Dr. Trent, and thank you for being here.

JTrent: My pleasure.

ATellara: First of all, tell us how you found out about the missing texts.

JTrent: Well, probably like a lot of people did. I have a personal meditation time that includes Bible reading. Two nights ago, when I picked up my Bible, I noticed it seemed thinner and lighter. At first I thought my wife had bought me a new one, until I started paging through it.

ATellara: And what did you find?

JTrent: It was the same old Bible, the one that I've had since I was a teenager. But it wasn't complete anymore. It stopped halfway through the 39th verse of chapter 15 in the Acts of the Apostles, which is the fourth book in the New Testament. The last two and a half verses of that chapter, the other 13 chapters in Acts, plus the remaining 22 books after it, had disappeared.

ATellara: Let me interrupt here for a moment. We're putting that last verse on the screen for our viewers. The verse reads: "And the contention was so sharp between them that they departed asunder one from the other."

JTrent: That would be the King James Version. There are other translations as well.

ATellara: Tell us what's happening in this passage.

JTrent: It involves two apostles, Barnabas and Paul, preparing to go on a missionary trip, about the year 50 CE. It was their second journey, revisiting the cities of the central and eastern Roman Empire where they'd preached a couple of years earlier. The two men had an argument about whether to bring along a third man, John Mark, who had abandoned them on their first trip. They settled their dispute by splitting up, going on separate journeys with different companions.

ATellara: Would you say it's a strange place for a book like the Bible to end?

JTrent:I'd call it the greatest cliffhanger of all time.

ATellara: And yet this change is true for every Bible, no matter where, no matter what language or translation or when it was published. Is that correct?

JTrent: That's right. More than that, the change is reflected in every reference book that's been looked at so far. I understand even the Codex Sinaiticus, which is a handwritten version of Scripture dating back 1,600 years and considered the oldest copy in existence, is missing the same texts. It's simply incredible!

ATellara: Some skeptics are claiming that this is a conspiracy by Christians, a cheap gag to get attention for their religion. What's your response?

JTrent: Two billion people somehow colluding to tear out sections of their Bibles, all at the same time, just to get on the news? That's too silly to comment on.

ATellara: Dr. Trent, is there any possible explanation for this event?

JTrent: I can't imagine what.

ATellara: Talk to us for a moment as a historian, then. What's this mean?

JTrent: If you're asking how these specific changes impact our understanding of that era … well, it's an interesting question. Let's assume for a moment that the Bible has always ended at that spot in Acts. And suppose that instead of going on separate journeys, Barnabas and Paul simply abandoned the idea. That makes it less likely that there was a third or, as many historians believe, a fourth missionary journey. Now, those journeys established the foundation of the Christian church across the region, and ultimately the world. Without them, the growth of the movement would have been quite limited. Likewise, the apostolic letters in the Bible—Romans, Galatians, and so on—would never be written. And the other letters, the ones by Peter, James, Jude and John, likely wouldn't see the light of day, either."

ATellara: Are you suggesting, Dr. Trent, that history has been changed?

JTrent: Uh … no, I'm not saying that at all. Keep in mind that we still remember what happened after verse 39. We haven't forgotten the portions of the Bible that are missing. So history isn't changed. I'm simply indulging in a thought exercise.

ATellara: But we're still left with the mystery of the vanished texts. Thank you, Dr. Trent, for taking the time to be with us today. We've heard the theological and historical perspective. Now let's hear what science has to say. Joining us remotely by video is Dr. Rachel Baylor, a physicist at the American Theoretical Research Institute. ATRI is an independent lab funded by research universities and foundations to support cutting-edge scientific studies. Dr. Baylor, good evening, thanks for joining us.

RBaylor: Happy to be here.

ATellara: Dr. Baylor, I understand your area of expertise is temporal physics. Can you describe what that is for our viewers?

166

RBaylor: Sure. Simply put, I study the fundamental characteristics of time. Only recently have we started to explore the idea that time can be understood in the same way that we know and study chemistry or biology or the other basic sciences.

ATellara: That's interesting, because we just heard Dr. Trent talk about how history would have unfolded if the events in the missing portions of the New Testament hadn't happened. He says history hasn't been changed. What's your view?

RBaylor: Speaking from the standpoint of science as we understand it today, I'd have to agree with him.

ATellara: No time-traveling DeLoreans, then.

RBaylor: I'm afraid not. Great movie, but little scientific support.

ATellara: So you're saying it's absolutely impossible to change the past?

RBaylor: No, I'm saying we don't know any way to do so based on our current knowledge. If we look at my area of study, which is temporal resonance, or measuring the flow of time itself, we—

ATellara: Hold on, Dr. Baylor. Measuring time? Isn't that what my wristwatch does?

RBaylor: Not really. Your watch is an arbitrary means of tracking our perception of time. I'm talking about measuring time itself—what makes time do its thing.

ATellara: And what have you found?

RBaylor: That there's a lot more research to do before I can start talking in absolutes.

ATellara: Including if it would ever be possible to somehow interfere with time, to change history, or make portions of an ancient book disappear?

RBaylor: Well … yes. But let me repeat what I said. All the science we know today says you can't change the past.

ATellara: One last question, Dr. Baylor. Let's say someone did interfere with history and caused the changes to the Bible and other reference works. Wouldn't our memories change, too, as Dr. Trent suggested? In fact, wouldn't our entire society change, given the historical influence of Christianity?

RBaylor: Okay. Hypothetically, based on my understanding of temporal resonance, yes, all of those things would change. History would unfold differently, and our memories would be rewritten. But it might not happen all at once. The disruptions in resonance would create waves that would flow through history, making changes as they go. It's like writing your name in the sand at the seashore. Each wave takes away a little bit of your name until nothing is left.

ATellara: Are you saying it's possible we may see more changes like the vanished Bible texts?

RBaylor: No. I'm simply answering your hypothetical question.

ATellara: You said we don't have the ability today to change the past. Can you rule out future science being applied to altering the course of history?

RBaylor: I'd say you are in a purely speculative realm that no one can speak to.

ATellara: Very well. Thank you for your time, Dr. Baylor. That was Rachel Baylor of the American Theoretical Research Institute. We're going to take a short break, and then we'll be back with more on this incredible story.

* * * *

The cameraman removed his earpiece and nodded at Rachel.

"We're clear," he said. "Thanks for doing this on such short notice, Dr. Baylor. We really appreciate it."

Rachel nodded and turned back to her computer, ignoring him as he disassembled his camera and left her lab, security guard in tow. Alone again, she swept her eyes across the colorful squiggles splashed across the large monitor, following their peaks and valleys, rolling the implications around in her head—and trying not to be frightened.

Baylor hadn't been entirely truthful with the journalist, a fact she resented more than regretted. Rachel, quite rightly, didn't trust Alicia Tellara, who had a well-earned reputation of sandbagging her interviewees. Greater scientists than Rachel Baylor had been tricked into discussing topics like the sentience of lobsters and whether plants have feelings. But Rachel's boss had insisted she do the interview. "It's great publicity for the institute, and you can calm the masses at the same time." So she reluctantly agreed, preparing to dance around the inevitable speculation that someone was screwing around with time.

Trouble was, Baylor's computer said someone was doing just that.

Temporal resonance was, by her own admission, a crazy idea. It was based on the notion of tachyons, faster-than-light particles that had long been considered theoretical. Baylor's studies in Lorentz invariant field theories had led her to a new hypothesis: that tachyons traveled so fast, they occupied all points of time simultaneously. Baylor sometimes called them "eternal guitar strings," stretching across the whole of space-time, from its future demise to its big-banging birth. Or vice versa. Major events somehow plucked those guitar strings, playing a tune that Baylor's computer could interpret. Such events ranged from the incredibly huge, like an exploding sun or colliding galaxies, to the comparatively small, like pivotal moments in human history.

The music of time was temporal resonance.

One particular note had been struck in the year 50 CE. It resonated to the present, drawing colorful squiggles on the computer screen. That note wasn't there yesterday.

Rachel cast a nervous glance toward the collection of optic lines, metal boxes and other technology piled on the bench beyond her computer desk. From out of that pile rose a metal ring, about two feet across, set atop a black pedestal of blinking lights.

For the hundredth time that day, she wondered if she should do it. Admittedly, she wasn't thinking like a scientist. She hadn't done all the studies, hadn't teased out every possible outcome.

There were dangers—that much was certain. Yet, with a few simple commands, Baylor might solve a mystery now terrifying the world. Or she might make things worse.

"Everything okay here, Dr. Baylor?"

Rachel lurched, startled by the return of the security guard. She turned toward the doorway, which the well-built man easily filled.

"Other than the heart attack you just gave me, we're good."

The guard chuckled as he stepped into the lab. The door swung closed behind him.

"Sorry about that. You just seemed a bit distracted after the TV guy left, so I wanted to make sure you were okay," he said. His voice carried a rich southern England accent.

Baylor smiled as she studied him. His hawk-nosed face wasn't familiar, though that meant little; Rachel paid scant attention to the comings and goings of ATRI staff. His affable nature suggested he'd been around for a while. But Rachel couldn't recall ever seeing him before.

"I appreciate the concern," she said politely. "Just be sure to knock next time."

"Of course."

The man continued to loiter, which made Rachel nervous. It was late on a Friday night, meaning the ATRI compound was largely abandoned. This stranger was taking far too much interest in her.

"Mind if I ask about that contraption on your bench?"

"It's a tachyonic field sensor," she replied. "Part of my research."

"Into temporal resonance?"

"How did—?" Of course. He'd been there during the NewsNet Live interview, gleaning a little knowledge in temporal physics. Harmless enough. Still, this guy wasn't scoring well on Baylor's internal trust meter.

"Yes. It tracks change waves in resonance."

The guard nodded. "And since the particles that form resonance are ever-present, my guess is you can correlate specific historical events with change waves, right?"

Rachel's spidey sense was screaming at her now. "Excuse me," she said, "and please don't take this the wrong way, but you seem to know a lot about temporal resonance for a part-time security guard."

He grinned. "I just have an honest curiosity."

An instant later, he had a 9mm pistol aimed at Baylor's head.

"And a theory I'd like you to test for me."

Rachel froze, staring into a gun barrel that seemed as big as a cannon. Her hands gripped the armrests of her chair to keep the rest of her body from trembling.

"What do you want?" Her voice was surprisingly steady.

Keeping the pistol pointed at her, the guard locked the lab door and moved closer to the scientist. "Nothing you weren't already considering, Dr. Baylor. Oh, we know a lot more about your research than you think. Tolman's paradox. Or tachyonic antitelephony, which I believe is the term you prefer."

"And 'we' are?"

"The Parabolani. I doubt you've heard the term." Rachel folded her arms and fixed him with a frosty glare.

"The Parabolani were a fanatical part of the clergy formed in the third century CE. I believe the term literally means 'risk takers' because the original Parabolani risked their lives to care for people with contagious diseases. But they also served as thugs from time to time, the most infamous example being the murder of the philosopher Hypatia in the early fifth century." She smirked at his look of surprise. "I double-majored."

The guard nodded. "Impressive. As you can see, I'm not here on behalf of the church. But the Parabolani are indeed risk-takers. We accept seemingly impossible tasks for significant wagers. I'm part of a doozy right now. And you're going to help me."

Baylor snorted. "One, that isn't going to happen. Two, even if I wanted to, what could I possibly do to help you?"

The guard's smile broadened. "I'll say it again, Doctor: tachyonic antitelephony. Sending a message back in time."

"You heard me on the news. It can't be done."

"Oh, but it can, Dr. Baylor. And you know it. Not just a message, either. An *object*. One that will forever change history."

The guard fished in his left lapel pocket and pulled out a small disk, which he tossed at Baylor. She caught it by instinct. Curious despite her fear and anger, she looked it over carefully.

"A genetic profile," she said. "Human?"

The guard nodded. "Did you hear about that break-in at a basilica in Rome a few months ago? It was all over the news for a day or two. It seems a certain influential apostle's coffin was, shall we say, 'aired out' a bit. No discernible violation of the remains, of course. We're not that insensitive."

"Just enough to get a viable DNA sample," Rachel concluded.

"Which you can use to correlate against a change wave, using your own resonance metrics. Enough, I believe, to zero in on the person and the moment that caused the wave."

Baylor shook her head, amazed and angry. The man knew far too much about her research. Even her superiors didn't know that she could, with the right data, identify precise moments, people and actions in history linked to disruptions in the timeline. Assuming her twisted captor let her live, she planned to have a pointed discussion with ATRI's board of directors about security.

"So what?" she said, no longer trying to manage her annoyance. "Even if I find this apostle of yours at a specific moment in time, what are you going to do about it?"

The guard held up his pistol.

"I'm going to kill him," he said simply. "In fact, the evidence suggests that I already have."

* * * *

Uploading the genetic profile and launching the timeline search took Rachel the better part of the night. While the computer scanned tens of billions of change waves in a tiny portion of history alone, she initialized the tachyonic field sensor. A hum of power, barely within the human hearing range, vibrated the air of the laboratory.

"You're wasting your time, you know," she said as she fine-tuned the instrument. "Assuming it works at all, tachyonic antitelephony can only be used to send messages, like radio signals. It's not a time machine."

The guard was standing at a nearby lab bench, calmly assembling the pieces of a sniper rifle he'd retrieved from a hiding place in Baylor's laboratory. It was a bolt-action FN Special Police Rifle, common in law enforcement and easy for an armed security force to obtain. As he tested the lever movement of the bolt, he sighed impatiently.

"Don't insult my intelligence, Doctor. We both know you're lying. You've figured out how to use tachyons as a transport mechanism."

Damn. "Alright, I'll stop underestimating you," Rachel said. "But if you're planning to leap through a magic doorway into the past, you're going to be disappointed."

He nodded. "On that point, we agree. The portal you create will handle, at most, a mass of 15 grams. Anything larger would be shredded by the forces involved. Rest assured, I have no intention of becoming the world's first dead time traveler."

"But as luck would have it," the guard added, "a .308 Winchester bullet checks in at just 150 grains. That's just over 10 grams. We have room to spare."

Rachel looked up from her labors. She was starting to understand just how insane this guy was.

"You're going to shoot a man from 2,000 years in his future?" she asked, incredulous. "That's crazy!"

The guard glowered at her. "I'm respectful of your work, Dr. Baylor. Please be respectful of mine."

"But it's futile! The man you're trying to kill is already dead!"

The guard lifted his fully assembled rifle and hitched a leg over the corner of the lab bench. "You're right. And given the evidence, the Apostle died the way I want him to die: before his time. But you of all people should understand, in the physics of time, cause doesn't always precede effect. We've seen the effect. From where you and I sit, the cause hasn't yet occurred. And it must, before he firmly establishes a religion that has cursed humanity for two millennia."

Suddenly, Rachel Baylor understood what he was trying to do.

"The missing portions of the Bible," she said. "That explains everything. You're going to kill the Apostle before he begins his second missionary journey. That means the Bible ends in Acts, the Christian church fails to gain a foothold, and all of history changes."

The guard gave her a small salute. "Excellent summary. But please don't miss the true beauty of the plan. Simply eliminating Christianity would massively upset the timeline. That's why I'm not trying to assassinate Jesus. Regrettably, we still need Christians to guide history. My goal is simply to take away much of their power—and wipe out the bloodbaths done in the name of their lunatic movement."

"Aren't you forgetting the good things done by the church?" asked Rachel. "Yes, they've caused a lot of horrible events, but they've also cared for the sick, fed the hungry, sheltered the homeless. Have you worked out all the possible scenarios, how history might unfold with a smaller Christian influence?"

"We're not entirely without scientific expertise, Dr. Baylor," the guard replied. "The Parabolani are more numerous and learned than you think."

Rachel's computer suddenly chimed. The guard leaped from the bench.

"You've found him!"

Baylor studied the data on the screen. She wasn't surprised to see that the search had landed smack on the spike she'd noticed earlier. She could even pin down the location: along the Orontes River, just outside Antioch in Syria.

"Initialize the tachyonic field, Doctor."

Rachel stared at him. He and his shadowy group of gamblers had amazing insight but no common sense.

"You can't do this," she said. "You have no idea how it will work out. No one could. No scenario can be that precise."

"You forget, we've already seen how it will work out. Look around you."

Rachel shook her head. "That's narrow thinking. I've been studying temporal resonance for a long time. History has a way of repairing any damage."

The guard chuckled. "Are you suggesting history is sentient, Doctor?"

"No. But I do believe it has an author. And God won't be edited."

Her captor raised an eyebrow, surprised by the turn of conversation.

"My research was incomplete. I hadn't expected a theological debate with you," he remarked. "But you're wrong. The edit has already happened, even though I haven't wielded my pen quite yet. That disproves your hypothesis. Now it's time to prove mine." He nodded at the metal ring on the lab bench. "Turn on the field. *Now.*"

"If I refuse?"

In a lightning-fast motion, the guard tossed the rifle to his left hand and drew his pistol with his right, taking deliberate aim at a spot between Rachel's eyebrows.

"Don't force me to kill you this way, Dr. Baylor. I respect you immensely, really I do. Enough to have followed your research closely. Enough that I can probably initiate the tachyonic field myself. But that's wasteful on so many levels."

Rachel snorted. "You expect me to believe you're not going to kill me when this is all over?"

"On that point," the guard sighed, "you'll just have to trust me."

Baylor continued to stare defiantly, arms folded.

The guard pulled the trigger.

One thing for sure, he was an excellent marksman. The bullet whizzed by Rachel's head, so close that she felt it brush the edge of her tightly pulled auburn hair. An instant later, it buried itself in an old file cabinet on the far side of the lab.

"The next one," he said coldly, "won't miss."

Whatever goodwill they'd once shared was gone. Rachel couldn't help shaking as she turned to her computer and, with a few precise keyboard taps, initiated the field.

As the low hum grew in volume and pitch, the large metal ring on the table began to glow with Cerenkov radiation, a gorgeous blue light that signaled the presence of particles moving faster than the light.

The shine intensified, spilling into the confines of the ring as if it were a mist, swirling and sparkling in random patterns.

Then something moved within the mist. It was like staring at a poor analog TV signal; Baylor could make out a ghostly, indistinct shadow drifting beyond the field. As the energies within the ring grew stronger, the image began to clear.

She saw a man. A man from the past.

Clearly of Mediterranean descent, he was bearded, and his head was covered with a linen headdress. His body was wrapped in a long cloak, probably made of wool. She couldn't make out any color other than Cerenkov blue—which, to her sudden astonishment, was probably what the man of yesteryear saw as the tachyonic field linked their two points in time. Around the man was darkness; it was nighttime in Antioch on the Orontes.

"Congratulations, Dr. Baylor," whispered the guard.

"It's him, isn't it?"

"If your research is everything you believe it to be," replied the gunman, an ever-so-subtle question in his tone.

Rachel wanted to stoke his doubt, however small, but she failed. Her confidence was apparent—which meant the man peering at them was one of the most famous religious figures in history.

The guard holstered his pistol and placed the sniper rifle on a chest-high supply cabinet a few feet from Baylor's computer. It was the perfect spot for sending a deadly bullet through the field. He shifted the bolt on the rifle and set his right eye near the sniper scope. The man was firmly in the crosshairs.

"The wager is fulfilled," the guard announced.

He pulled the trigger—just as Rachel threw herself at him.

Their bodies collided, and the guard was knocked off balance as his rifle erupted. Rachel watched in despair as the bullet streaked through the metal ring. Its passage shattered the careful balance of energies, and the tachyonic field collapsed.

But not before she saw the Apostle clutch his head and fall backward.

Failure. But she couldn't think about that now. She was about to face off with a trained assassin.

The guard was trying to scramble to his feet as Rachel leaped on him, flattening him on the floor again. He lay on his back, grasping her wrists as she tried desperately to hit him, claw him, do anything to stop him. But he was remarkably strong, too much so for the deskbound scientist.

"What a shame," the guard remarked. "Now I'll have to kill you after all."

He pulled up his legs until they were between him and Rachel, and then shoved her up and over his head with incredible force. Baylor somersaulted helplessly through the air, landing on her back with a bone-crunching thump. She cried out in agony and rolled over, her face to the floor.

The guard rose to his feet and reached for the pistol in his holster.

It wasn't there.

Rachel Baylor lifted her head. "Looking for this?" she asked coldly.

The gun in her hand fired three times.

He was dead before he hit the floor.

* * * *

TRANSCRIPT: NewsNet Live Tonight with Alicia Tellara

ATellara: Good evening, and thanks for tuning in to NewsNet Live Tonight. I'm Alicia Tellara. Another day, another impossible event. Just 48 hours after major portions of the New Testament vanished from every copy of the Bible around the world, the texts have mysteriously reappeared—with one major change. Back with us in the studio tonight is Dr. Jonathan Trent, professor of theology and history at Perelann University. Dr. Trent, what's happened now?

JTrent: As you said, Alicia, the most amazing thing. The New Testament has been restored, every word as it was before, to every Bible everywhere. Even the Codex Sinaiticus is whole again. And every reference work has been put right. But we're left with one significant change: the author.

ATellara: What do you mean?

JTrent: Well, throughout history we've venerated the Cypriot Jew named Joseph, more commonly known as Barnabas, as the greatest apostle in the New Testament. Once an enemy of the new Christian movement, he eventually became a follower himself, a man of great faith. He led at least three missionary journeys and wrote the epistles, letters that were published in the New Testament and laid the foundations of the early Christian church. He was executed by the Romans around 67 CE, and most historians are convinced his actual remains are interred in a basilica bearing his name in Rome. Scientific studies of the remains back in 2009 support that belief. But in the restored Biblical texts, Barnabas is no longer the author. Paul of Tarsus is.

ATellara: For our viewers who aren't up on their Bible knowledge, who is Paul of Tarsus?

JTrent: He was Barnabas's partner on the first missionary journey. There was a pivotal moment in their relationship, oddly about the time where the texts disappeared earlier, after they argued about John Mark. Before yesterday, history recorded that Paul took another assistant, a man named Silas, and went to Cyprus. Barnabas took John Mark on what became the second great missionary journey. That's what history used to tell us. Now their roles have been reversed.

ATellara: Reversed where?

JTrent: In the Bible, and in every history book and reference book in the world. Barnabas basically vanishes after chapter 13 of Acts. There are a few historical texts, all changed since yesterday, that now say he and John Mark went to Cyprus. One obscure source, which we can't confirm, suggests Barnabas suffered some sort of head injury that limited his ability to travel and minister.

ATellara: So you're telling us that Paul is now the greatest apostle, the author of all those Bible books, the one who dies in Rome and is buried in the basilica?

JTrent: Yes. As incredible as it seems, history has been changed. But as far as we can tell, only on this particular point.

ATellara: What does that mean for history, Dr. Trent. And for us?

JTrent: It's hard to say. The Bible's words are the same. The theology is unchanged. The history of the church remains as we remember it. We simply have two people swapping roles. I suppose a deeper study might reveal more, but I doubt we'll have the chance.

ATellara: Why?

JTrent: Think about what Dr. Baylor said on your show last night. If someone has manipulated time, our perception of history will soon change. We'll forget all of this. We'll always remember the Apostle Paul as the major driver of the early church and the author of the epistles.

ATellara: I have to say, Dr. Trent, I find this very unsettling.

JTrent: Don't worry. In a few days, you won't. No one will.

* * * *

In the solitude of her living room, Rachel Baylor tapped her TV remote and turned off the television. She let the silence reign for a long time.

History had been altered, yet preserved. She knew only what had catalyzed the change, and that she'd played a part in it. The saving of history, the rearranging of the players to protect its outcome—well, the credit for that belonged to someone else.

She reached for the black-leathered book resting on the table next to her couch. She felt its familiar heft, smiled at the worn pages. History had changed; the waves were washing across the beach, shifting the sands of time. But she'd already grown comfortable with the new narrative:

"Paul, a servant of Christ Jesus, called to be an apostle and set apart for the gospel of God ...."

THREE HOURS

The kid no longer was. Gone were the pudgy cheeks, cowlicked mop and that fresh, insatiable curiosity. Twenty years had scrubbed them way, leaving a hawkish face, shaved head and a surly attitude.

Still, you'd think our reunion would have summoned a wistful joy in me. Seems the pistol aimed squarely at my skull took the charm out it. That, and the blood spattered on his shirt.

"Just tell me, old man!" His voice rasped like a rake on a rock garden. "When did you crack it? You always said you would. I saw it happen." He cocked his head toward the small window to my workshop.

"So, you've become a thug and a Peeping Tom," I sighed. "Quite a resumé you've built for yourself."

The kid wagged his pistol at me like a shaming finger. "That's the best you can do? I can't believe I used to think you were somebody special."

Ouch. Had the years taken away even that? The hero worship I once cherished?

We had met on a dare. As his friends had hidden in the bushes, the young lad had knocked on my door to confront the crazed inventor. I had thrown open the door; he hadn't run, and I hadn't frothed at the mouth. Instead, we had shared some lemonade and the first of many marvelous conversations. His inquisitive mind had brightened my own love of science. For a time, we had pursued the quest together. But while the years had preserved my passion, they had robbed him of his. That hurt worst of all.

I took a long, slow look at my workshop. Rows of computers stood seven tall on sturdy steel shelves, with cables and wires spilling across the concrete floor. The multihued spaghetti made its chaotic way to a circular metal platform, six feet across, on the far side of the room. The stuffy air shivered with an electric hum.

It was impressive to behold—and a sign of obsession known only to madmen and therapists. Yet it steadfastly refused to offer me a suitable lie.

"When did you find out?" I asked quietly.

"Last night. The rabbit. It appeared over there"—he pointed across the lab—"before you zapped it on the platform."

At least he hadn't lost his keen eye. "Pretty impressive, kid. That happened in one five-thousandth of a second."

"Not so impressive. The window is single-paned, and you talk to yourself."

"So I do," I chuckled darkly. "Well, then. It seems you and I are the only two people on Earth who know that time travel is possible. What are you going to do about it?"

The kid said nothing. He just stood there, smirking.

"Planning to sell the story to some sleazy tabloid? Or maybe you're here just to rob me. Either way, you're out of luck." I flung a sweeping arm at my electronic menagerie. "No one will believe you. And you're looking at all my wealth. Every dime of savings, every maxed-out credit card, is here in this lab. Face it, kid, you've come up empty."

At my words, his smirk suddenly erupted in an unsettling laugh.

"This isn't about ripping you off. I just need a favor."

That was the last thing I expected. Gone twenty years, he bursts into my workshop with a gun in search of a *favor*?

"What do you want?" I asked.

"Simple: Make it never happened."

"What?"

"Make. It. Never. Happened."

I shook my head, confused. "That doesn't make any sense."

"Send me back in time. Three hours, to be exact."

There it was—the timing, the bloodied shirt. It all became clear.

"You hurt somebody. Maybe … *killed* somebody?"

His unstable humor flashed away.

"It was self-defense! All I wanted was the money. Damn clerk pulled a two-shooter from the cash drawer. A *two-shooter*! Didn't know whether to laugh or blow him away."

Obviously, he'd chosen the latter. I'd heard the sirens earlier, stopping up the street. Probably the all-night liquor store. And I knew the night clerk, a pleasant young man with a family. So the blood on the shirt must be——

I felt sick to my stomach.

"You're insane."

The kid took a step toward me, pushing his gun at my head. "And you have a death wish!"

"Pull the trigger, then!" In a mindless fury, I grabbed the barrel of his pistol and shoved it between my eyebrows. "You think you're a big man? You think you've got it all figured out? You're a stupid son of a bitch!"

"You'd better shut up, old man!"

I shook my head. "Maybe you know how to kill someone, but you don't know shit about temporal physics. I used a quirk in quantum theory to time-jump that rabbit a five-thousandth of a second into the past. You're talking three hours—*54 million times* further back! That's unthinkable!"

"If you want to live, you'll find a way."

Sotto voce, purely evil, yet delivered with all the innocence of the child he once was. It chilled and confused me. Until that moment, I assumed he wanted to go back and stop the crime from happening. But what would motivate a killer to undo a murder he didn't regret?

"Who said I was undoing anything?" he answered my question. "I have no intention of saving his life. He pulled a gun on me! That piece of filth deserved to die!"

So if not to undo the deed, then——

Came the dawn.

"You're going back to create an alibi."

The kid smiled broadly. "Beautiful plan, don't you think? While the earlier me is busy offing the clerk, I'll be at the police station, reporting the 'theft' of my wallet. The evidence at the scene won't matter. I can't be in two places at the same time—or so everyone will think."

"I could tell them the truth."

The kid wagged his head. "You said so yourself, who'd believe it? But just in case you want to try, don't forget that I'll still be around." A giggle bubbled out of him. "In fact, for three hours there'll be *two* of me."

Still pointing the pistol, the kid tiptoed across the sea of wiring until he reached the platform.

"Send me back, old man."

"I'm telling you, it's not that simple," I insisted. "The test you saw was one of six time-jumps I tried on rabbits. It was the only one that worked."

That wasn't true, but I wasn't concerned about a little white lie. For the first time, I saw a shadow of uncertainty flash across his homely face.

"What does that mean?" he asked.

"It means this isn't worth the risk. Come on, kid, it's been a lot of years, but you can't be that different! You can't have lost everything that you were. The wonder, the compassion. Tell me that child is still inside you!"

He looked at the platform beneath his feet, at the humming computers, at the gun in his hand. Trying to decide, trying to sort out a potential future and a potential past.

I seemed to have the advantage for a moment. Tragically, I chose to press it.

"Even if you go back, it won't change anything. The clerk will still die, and you'll still be a murderer."

The moment passed.

"You're wrong!" he screamed. "I won't kill him—the other me will do it! I'll be innocent!"

"No!" I shouted back, furious at his change and my own stupid mistake. "You still killed him here, in this time. No high-tech alibi will wash his blood from your hands. 'Make it never happened,' you said. Take your sin away." I shook my head. "Sorry, kid. That's God's work, not mine."

"I'm *warning* you, old man!"

There was no mistaking his intent. Or my choice.

It took just three keystrokes. The last I saw of him, he was grinning wildly, awash in a cascade of blue Cerenkov radiation—the telltale glow of a time warp.

As abruptly as it began, the danger was gone. But the tears in my eyes weren't due to relief.

The morning news wailed at length about the murder. Beneath the bellowing headlines was an image from the store's security camera. The killer's face was clearly visible. The caption identified him.

Funny, I never knew the kid's name before then.

There was no mention of his alibi. In fact, the cops had no idea where he was. Warrants were issued, manhunts ensued. All proved useless. They never found their fugitive.

But I knew exactly where he was.

My time machine had one peculiarity: It twisted time without twisting space. Immeasurably brief time-jumps with my rabbits kept them inside my workshop. But the bigger the jump, the farther away the rabbits appeared.

The universe is always moving, always expanding. My time machine couldn't cope with it.

I'm pretty much past the guilt now. But sometimes the nightmares still come. I see him, I witness that brief, agonizing, final moment of life, when the kid beheld the blue-white Earth moving silently along its ancient orbit.

Two hundred thousand miles and three hours away.

GABBATHA

Inside jokes are the best thing about time travel.

Slipping himself into an ancient work of art, or a bit of classical literature, never failed to amuse Rhys Timofey. But he stopped after two screwups—letting a woman play with his cell phone in a 1928 film, and forgetting to remove his Oakleys for a newspaper photo in 1940. Both incidents caused brief internet uproars decades later.

There was another reason to cease his cameos. It never occurred to him that one's biology is anchored to one's place in time. Weigh that anchor, and eventually you do irreparable harm.

Deep in the introspective haze from a Dvin brandy, which he shared with Churchill at Yalta, Timofey figured he could survive one more journey. Should he return to his own time? Or make a permanent home in the past?

The decision proved surprisingly easy.

A few hours later, Timofey stood in a broad, paved courtyard bathed in torch light beneath a cold night sky. He hugged himself, trying to keep warm. Across the courtyard, wearing long tunics and loose-fitting coats, a handful of men huddled, murmuring among themselves. Timofey knew what they were up to.

Turning, he beheld a stately portico and the immense fortress from which it protruded. Made of stone and ringed with an ornate colonnade, the structure spoke of wealth and power. Inside, Rhys knew, were walls adorned with painted characters from mythology, intricate mosaic floors, luxurious curtains, and sparse but expensive furniture.

Right now, those fancy walls and tiled floors bore witness to a pivotal moment in history—a moment Timofey was there to change.

He was, of course, aware of the dangers of tampering with history. Writers from Bradbury to Zemeckis had given ample warning. Indeed, in his early travels, Timofey would check his shoes for stomped butterflies and avoid contact with female ancestors. But eventually he realized time had a way of repairing itself, absorbing discontinuities as a pond absorbs ripples from a tossed stone.

To actually *change* history, you needed to do something significant at a pivotal moment.

Rhys glanced toward the eastern sky, noting the first hints of encroaching dawn. In a few minutes, a verdict would be delivered from the portico. That verdict would be driven by politics, loud voices and veiled threats, standing for all time as the greatest travesty of justice in human history.

Timofey would not allow it to happen again.

The crowd grew larger. Rhys could see the men knew each other. This confirmed a lifelong suspicion. For a moment, he regretted that he could no longer travel through time and admonish the millions yet unborn who would wrongly blame this injustice on an entire culture rather than on a few conspirators.

Blame.

The word lodged in his mind, nestling against a centuries-old question: How was it possible? A few dozen men—cajoled, bullied, or merely self-seeking—had committed an epic wrong, forever changing the course of history. It was hard to believe. Perhaps what was about to happen here was more than met the eye, more than a few voices demanding a verdict of guilty and a penalty of death.

But what? Rhys knew the account of this moment. He'd studied every relevant text. The criminals were assembling; in minutes, they would assume their immoral roles, begin the cruel choreography, and condemn an innocent man.

Innocent.

Another word that wouldn't exit his thoughts. A fascinating contrast, these two opposing words. He wasn't sure what it meant. He knew only what was happening to that innocent man right now, somewhere beyond the portico. Agony. Humiliation. Deep sorrow.

The morning sun slowly edged over the horizon, casting pale-yellow rays upon the portico. As if on cue, a balding man, pink-cheeked and slightly pudgy beneath his official-looking robe, emerged onto the platform. He carried himself regally—too much so, exaggerating his swagger to a skeptical audience. He strode to the edge of the portico and stared at the crowd with unabashed contempt.

Then he turned aside, allowing someone else to join him.

The newcomer was a shuffling ruin of a man. After hours of torture, he barely managed to stand upright. His legs quivered with unbearable pain and fatigue. His breath came in short, agonizing gasps. His face was a grotesque mask, peppered with bleeding cuts and nasty bruises. The plum-colored cloth wrapped around his thin body was darkened with large splotches of blood. Crimson rivulets flowed from a ring of braided thorns shoved cruelly upon his head.

But the most pitiful, gut-wrenching thing was the unfathomable grief that glistened in his swollen eyes.

The portly official gestured to the new arrival, making sure every person in the astonished crowd got a good look at what was left of him.

"*Idoú o ánthropos!*" he shouted. "Behold the man!"

Timofey did just that. He looked again at the prisoner, really looked. And gasped in horror.

What he saw now was no victim of torture, no blameless captive awaiting a rescuer from across time. Instead, he beheld something unbearably hideous. It was as if all that was evil, from everywhere and everywhen, was poured upon the man. Every ghastly thing done, every repulsive thought entertained, it all ebbed and flowed and dribbled before Timofey's eyes. That such repulsiveness could exist, that God Himself would tolerate it for an instant, was beyond comprehension. It was unrighteous, irredeemable. It screamed to be destroyed.

And the deepest, soul-shaking horror of the monster was that it looked just like Rhys Timofey—not just in appearance, but in his full nature. It was the sum of his every deceit, his every unspeakable word or deed, his every fear and desperate act, a gruesome reflection of his foolish and failed existence laid bare.

Rhys searched for a hint of decency in the thing, desperate for a glimmer of hope, a modicum of good enough. He begged for it. He wept for it. But it wasn't there. He knew instinctively that something else needed to happen first. And here, at this crossroads of time, this crucial juncture of humanity's story, Rhys was witness to it.

To destroy the Evil, Innocence had willingly embraced the Blame.

At last, the crowd roused itself. The men began to shout, feeding a frenzy that burst through Timofey's shock and revulsion. He couldn't turn away from what he saw. He couldn't demand justice as he'd planned, couldn't stand firm for what was right, couldn't defy the crowd that he so hated.

Because the image he had seen, he hated it more.

And so he joined their cry. He knew he must—for his own sake, and for the sake of humanity, now and forever.

"*Stavróno! Stavróno! Stavróno!*"

"Crucify!"

"Crucify!"

"*CRUCIFY!*"

FLASH OF LIFE

Where irresistible fiction meets immovable truth. That's the oncology ward at South Addison General.

Fiction was the conjured cheer of nurse aides who wiped brows and bums with all the passion of an automated car wash. Truth was the Florida-orange binders that hung on the beds, each filled with the cold facts of a patient's downward spiral.

For the aides, however, Hap Lister held a less cynical view. Some of them really had heart. You could see it in their eyes, the way they looked at you, not through you. Teej was one of them, an Irish concoction of redheaded fire and soothing compassion. She cheered every improvement in a patient and wept at every passing. That's why some, like Hap, hung on for so long. They didn't want to hurt her.

"You're eating better," Teej observed, looking up from Hap's binder. "A month ago, you insisted you were on the Final I.V."

Hap had made up that morbid euphemism. He knew how much Teej hated it.

"They always order pizza on the night shift. Had to hang around for that," he rasped. Pure oxygen streaming through his nasal cannula worked like steel wool on his vocal cords.

Teej smiled at him. "Get off the I.V. and keep down a few cans of Ensure. Then we'll talk about a slice of pepperoni."

She hung the binder back on the bed and headed for the door, pausing to—

… didn't see Dr. Baines walk in …

"Look out!" Hap wheezed.

—say goodbye. She didn't see Dr. Baines walk in. They collided. Teej stumbled backwards, arms flailing as she toppled over the visitor's chair and landed on the floor with a yelp.

Baines rushed to her side. "Are you all right?" he asked, clearly shaken.

A teary-eyed Teej nodded. Afraid she was injured, Baines peppered her with questions, but Teej waved him off. "I'm okay," she said, climbing gingerly to her feet. "Just my pride is bruised."

Baines kept apologizing even as Teej, forgiving the doctor seventy times seven, left the room. Still he had the last word, shouting one more pitiful "I'm sorry!" down the hall.

"Well," Baines said, turning to Hap, "that's certainly the stupidest thing I've done all morning. I hope she's really okay."

Fearing another mantra of regret, Hap interrupted him. "Let it go, Doc. I'm sure she'll live. And speaking of living," he smiled wryly, "tell me you brought that miracle cure with you today."

More gallows humor. Unfortunately, Hap Lister was way past medical miracles. Forty years, two packs a day. That's half a million cigarettes. Cancer had eaten away one lung and was three courses into the other. The outcome was certain, and Hap Lister was nothing if not a realist.

Nonetheless, Dr. Baines made a thoughtful show of perusing the orange binder. Hap sighed and stared at the ceiling.

"You're eating better."

"So I've heard."

Baines closed the binder, came around the bed and did a cursory checkup—heart, pulse, breathing. Hap endured the icy stethoscope without complaint. Finally, the doctor stepped back and folded his arms. Hap knew what was coming.

"You're going to tell me to go home."

Baines raised an eyebrow. "As a matter of fact, I was. When did you start reading minds?"

Hap grunted. "I don't have to be a psychic to know what's written in that binder." He swallowed with difficulty, and his gravelly tone softened a little. "I'm just … not ready to be alone."

Or to die alone.

Hap squeezed his eyes shut to stop a sudden flow of tears.

For a curmudgeon, it was the worst display of emotion possible. But it couldn't be helped. He would have to bear the tears along with his dread of solitude. Hap looked up again, marshalling enough pride to set his jaw and glare at the doctor. Baines nodded reluctantly.

"Alright. I won't send you home. But this isn't a big-city cancer ward, Hap. If someone else needs that bed, I have to let you go."

"Understood. And thanks, Doc. Really."

Baines smiled, reaching out to—

… hospital intercom sent out a loud, mournful tone. "Dr. Baines, report to ICU stat!" …

—squeeze his shoulder.

"Uh, Doc?"

The hospital intercom sent out a loud, mournful tone. "Dr. Baines, report to ICU, stat! Dr. Baines, report to ICU, stat!"

Baines whirled and ran from Hap's room, pausing just long enough to avoid any unsuspecting nurse aides in the hallway. Then he was gone.

Hap Lister sat alone, shivering in cold fear. He knew what Baines would find in Intensive Care.

And he had no idea how he knew it.

* * * *

Reg Foster's skin was the color of tapioca gone bad. Though dying of liver cancer, he managed to flop into his wheelchair every day and make a slow, painful round of the oncology unit. What motivated him was no mystery to his fellow patients: He, too, didn't want to be alone.

Right now, however, Reg felt neither anxious nor lonely. Instead, his red-rimmed eyes burned with skepticism.

"I'm a teacher, not a shrink," he told Hap.

"I didn't ask for a couch session. I know it sounds strange, Reg, but it's true, and I can't explain it. I saw Doc Baines knock Teej over *before* it actually happened!"

Reg shook his head. "Come on, Hap. You put hooch in your I.V. or something?"

"It's not funny, and I'm not making this up!" Hap snapped. "Look, I know the clinical name—*déjà vu*, the feeling that you've lived through something before. Everybody has it at one time or other. It's happened to me lots of times over the years. But now it seems worse all of a sudden."

"How so?"

"Well, like today. Baines was about to tell me I was too sick, that I should go home. Before he said it, I knew the exact words he was going to use. And then he got the stat call to ICU. I heard it before it came. I even tried to warn him! It's eerie, like watching a movie you forgot you'd seen before. You get this nagging sense that you know what's going to happen."

Foster folded his arms and slouched in his wheelchair, taking breath after slurpy breath. The scowl on his face finally registered with Hap.

"Fine. Forget I brought it up."

"Now don't get your shorts in a knot!" Foster growled. "You have to admit this is pretty bizarre. A lot of strange things occur to terminally ill patients. Emotional and physical things."

"Go away, Reg!"

"You know, *déjà vu* is a symptom of an epileptic seizure. Maybe you should talk to Baines again."

Hap gave a loud, obnoxious snort. "Great. As if dying of cancer wasn't bad enough."

It certainly wasn't the third act Hap would have penned for his life's script. The end should have been brighter, like the rest of his story. Harold J. "Hap" Lister—decorated fighter pilot, brilliant inventor, rich entrepreneur. He'd turned his tinkerings into a successful career designing aircraft control systems. Nearly every jetliner sketching a contrail across the sky carried Lister components.

He was a hero in his home state of Maine, a local boy made extraordinarily good. He'd worked hard, obsessively hard, forsaking every distraction. Family, friends, none of those things got in his way. And financially, at least, he had been amply rewarded.

Death by lung cancer wasn't fair.

Hap could have gone anywhere for treatment. He chose South Addison, a small town hugging the coast of downeast Maine. The hospital was a regional operation, treating old lobstermen who spent lifetimes inhaling tobacco, diesel fumes and fish guts as they ran their traps day after ocean-heaving day. But for Hap Lister, South Addison was home. If nothing else, it offered a chance to revel in a few final accolades before he died. A few more awards, a little more ink, a bit more well-deserved glory.

Until his mind and body conspired against him.

"Okay," he sighed, looking at Foster again. "I'll bite. What else causes *déjà vu*?"

Even mortally ill, Reg Foster could slip easily into the role of lecturing professor. "Some experts say our memories get mixed up when we experience something that's similar to a past event. Others think it happens when the way your brain processes an experience gets out of sync, so you remember and live through an experience in the same instant. And there are other ideas, like reincarnation, time travel and the paranormal. I'll skip those."

"So you're telling me that—"

… Mrs. Welch. Postoperative aneurysm …

Hap gulped. "Mrs. Welch is dead."

Reg sat up in his wheelchair, surprise and sorrow etching his long, jaundiced face. "Yeah. You heard?"

"Not exactly." Hap took a deep breath, desperately trying to calm himself. "Postoperative aneurysm, right? That's why Baines was so upset by the ICU call. He was her surgeon."

Foster slowly backed his wheelchair away from the bed. "How did you know that? I was at the nurse's station just a few minutes ago when the postmortem came in!"

"It's just like before, Reg. In my mind, I saw you telling me."

"That's crazy!"

"Come on, man!" Hap burst out. "You used to be a big-deal college wag. They paid you to think. So *think*! I want to know, is it possible that I'm seeing the future?"

Reg kept staring at him, clearly wracking his brain for a rational explanation. None was—

... "No! Don't tell me! I don't want to know!" His last, ragged breath ...

—forthcoming. Hap gasped at this latest vision. That and the expression on his face said it all to Reg Foster.

"No!" Reg screamed. "Don't tell me! I don't want to know!"

With surprising strength, he spun his wheelchair around and fled from the room, shouting and crying all the way across the ward. Nurses flocked to comfort him, but he was inconsolable. Within minutes, Teej stormed into Hap's room, her freckled face aflame.

"What did you say to him?" she demanded.

Hap shook his head, too afraid to answer.

An hour later, Reg Foster took his last, ragged breath.

Hap had already grieved.

* * * *

The nurses held a little memorial for Reg in the hospital chapel. Hap skipped it; he'd abandoned the church scene long ago and had no desire to turn penitent now. Besides, he was too terrified to leave his room. The visions were becoming more frequent:

... Baines stumbled, spilling coffee on the bed ...

... "I'm engaged!" Teej squealed, waving her ring finger in the air ...

... Nurse Chapman cursed like a stevedore, damning every uncooperative vein in Hap's arm ...

Slices of Hap's life at South Addison General, experienced moments before they actually happened. He saw visitors before they visited. Read cards before he opened them. Guessed lottery numbers before the bleach-blonde TV hostess read them off the little Ping-Pong balls—though he resisted the urge to play. It was too frightening to be reduced to a game.

How long, Hap wondered, before his death was the featured preview?

There was one, admittedly minor, solace in that thought. It's said that, at death, your life flashes before your eyes. And Hap Lister's had been a truly stunning life, full of treasures that dazzled his mind's eye. Faced with his passing, such a playback would be something to savor—

... *"I was hungry, and you gave me nothing to eat."* ...

Hap lurched, startled by the sound. Sound? He hadn't actually heard a voice. The words, laden with sadness, simply formed in his mind. It was an unsettling experience. Hap fumbled for the control unit beside his pillow—

... *My God, it hurt!* ...

—and pressed the call button.

... *Nurse Chapman bolted from his bedside. "Ellen, we've got a code blue!"* ...

He waited. No one answered. No one came. Hap pressed the call button again with all his might.

... *"I was thirsty, and you gave me nothing to drink."* ...

"Who's there?" Hap demanded, his voice cracking. Only the hiss of oxygen and the clicking of his IV pump replied.

... Teej stood at the foot of his bed, hand covering her mouth, tears falling on her smock as they wheeled in the crash cart ...

It's not supposed to be like this, Hap insisted. Where was that flash of life? That would show the value he'd brought to the world. It would justify everything.

He stabbed the call button again.

... "I was a stranger, and you did not invite me in." ...

What did that have to do with anything? Hap wondered, fighting panic.

... "I can't get a pulse, Doctor!" ...

The dam of self-control gave way. Adrenaline surged through his thin, ravaged body, and he smashed the control unit against the bedrail.

... "I needed clothes, and you did not clothe me." ...

But what about everything he'd accomplished—his inventions, his business? Why wasn't he seeing those things?

... The electrodes discharged against his bared chest, twisting his body like taffy ...

Hap gripped the dented bedrail, struggling for every breath. Time! There wasn't enough time! But there were always good intentions—

... "I was sick and in prison, and you did not look after me." ...

"When?" Hap gasped, his brittle voice shattering against the sterile walls. "When did I see anyone hungry or thirsty or sick or in prison? It's not my fault, and this isn't fair! Show me all the things I did right!"

That's when Hap Lister realized what was happening.

This wasn't *déjà vu*. It wasn't even life—for that was the very thing already flashing before his eyes. Teej. Doc Baines. Reg Foster. They were merely the final images in the replay he'd desperately sought. Now, at the moment of death, Hap revisited every second of his sorry existence in a frantic search for any redeeming moment, any instant when he might have looked beyond himself to the least of those around him, when he might have reached out to them, when he might have shown a little compassion.

But no such moment could be found. Not anywhere. He'd never embraced the truth of it. And now he could embrace nothing at all.

My God, it *hurt*!

And … the flash of life ended.

And … Nurse Chapman bolted from his bedside. "Ellen, we've got a code blue!"

And … Teej stood at the foot of his bed, hand covering her mouth, tears falling on her smock as they wheeled in the crash cart.

And …

HEARSAY

Tipley was past tired, past patient, and way past deadline. The city council meeting had gone late; he had no time for Benny Warren's foolishness.

"Look," snapped the young reporter as he jumped into his battered Chevy, "even if Mayor Dalkins' wife *was* a strip-o-gram dancer in college, it's not a news story!"

Gray-haired, jowly, his once rigid stature now faintly stooped, Benny still managed to intimidate. He snarled at Tipley through the driver's window.

"Don't lecture me, you little twit! I spent 52 years at that newspaper of yours! I know what makes a good story!"

"Benny. The woman died of cancer a year ago."

"And that matters?"

Shaking his head, Tipley started the Chevy and, to his later regret, fired a parting shot.

"I never knew retirement turned old reporters into bitter old gossip mongers!"

The shot found its mark. Benny's heart shattered as Tipley roared off.

He stood in the moonlit parking lot—alone, as always. No family or friends. No causes to champion. Just the night, his memories, and that inner cry to feel valued again.

Despondent, Benny turned and climbed into his ancient pickup truck. There he had two big revelations:

One, someone else was inside the cab.

Two, it was a good thing heart disease didn't run in his family.

"Relax. I'm a friend," the man said.

"Hell of a way to show it, scaring me like that!" wheezed Benny. "What do you want?"

"The same thing you want: to do something that matters." He grinned, his face mummy-like, a disturbing image in the darkened cab. "You've felt useless since you retired. Irrelevant. Am I right?"

Benny looked away.

"We can help each other." The stranger held out his hand. Resting in his palm was an enormous gray capsule, as big as Benny's thumb.

"What is that? A drug of some sort?"

"Of some sort. Technically, it's called a neuromorphic catalyst. It realigns the electrical impulses in the brain to exchange and process wireless data." His hideous grin grew wider. "Think of it as the entire internet in a pill."

"That's the silliest thing I've ever heard!" Bennie snorted.

The stranger brought the capsule closer. "Imagine if you could find out everything about anyone—*just by looking at them*. Every name and detail from every database in the world. It's a journalist's dream. No secrets. No spin. And you, Benny Warren, in control of it all."

Benny snorted again. But he couldn't peel his eyes from that pill. "You don't believe me? Prove me wrong."

"Okay, fine." Benny snatched the capsule and, amazingly, swallowed it whole.

"I should point out," the stranger said, "that you may experience some stomach upset."

That's when the capsule exploded in Benny's gut.

* * * *

An incessant *tap-tap-tap* drew Benny to consciousness. He opened his eyes, astonished to see daylight. Equally astonishing was the pain in his head and stomach. And then there was the policeman, calmly rapping at the pickup's window.

"Hey Benny, you okay?"

Benny turned his aching eyeballs toward the officer—and gulped.

Incredibly, a stream of bright yellow text swept across his vision, like a news crawl on a TV screen. Benny rubbed his eyes and looked again. The text magically reappeared:

```
    Jonathan Randolph Wells … age 27 … Deputy, Ryan
County Sheriff's Department … wife: Anne Michelle …
children: Robert Randolph, age 7, Jessica Jane, age 5 …
```

The words scrolled on, describing the life of the young officer: son of an abusive father, ROTC grad, a brief career in professional wrestling—

"Benny?"

The old man was speechless. His aches faded as he marveled at the data on Deputy Wells flashing before his eyes. While it disturbed him to see so much personal information so easily gleaned, Benny needed little effort to thrust that worry aside. Think of the possibilities!

Mumbling a lame excuse to Wells, Benny started the truck and drove straight downtown.

A stroll along the crowded sidewalks proved this neuro-*whatsit* pill was everything the stranger promised. A glance at anyone summoned a cascade of information. Benny soaked up every tidbit about the passersby, including a few community leaders.

The head of the tourism bureau suffered from depression.

The business club president never repaid his college loans.

The mayor's wife really *had* done strip-o-grams.

Benny gleefully scribbled these discoveries in a notepad, savoring renewed dreams of journalistic fame. Where should he begin? Breaking small-town news? Or exposing the underbelly of political corruption in Washington?

Still mulling his future, his spied a scruffy, muscular man sipping a beer outside a popular sports bar. Once again, the old reporter felt a thrill sizzle through him as yellow text leaped into view:

```
    Armand Matisse … age 37 … convicted murderer …
reported escaped from federal prison …
```

The thrill turned to ice in Benny's chest.

In seconds, Armand Matisse's criminal record was laid bare, and it wasn't pretty. Murder, rape, assault—a career marked by vicious brutality.

That's when Matisse caught Benny staring at him.

Benny averted his eyes, but it was too late. Scowling, Matisse quaffed the last of his beer and headed in Benny's direction.

Trying not to panic, Benny turned and melted into the shuffling mass of shoppers. He soon lost sight of Matisse. Relieved, he walked on until the crowd thinned near the edge of the business district. Between the last trinket shop and the credit union building was a narrow alley. A security guard stood nearby, sipping coffee. He was armed.

Benny ran up to him. "I need your help! There's this guy—"

The words congealed in his throat as an enormous shadow fell over both men. Benny turned and found his nose in the chest of Armand Matisse.

"Let's talk," Matisse growled.

Benny doubted he would enjoy that conversation.

He shoved the murderer backward, spun around and knocked the guard's steaming coffee down his uniformed chest. As the guard screamed in pain, Benny clawed for his gun. By then Matisse had recovered his balance and was lunging for Benny, forcing the old reporter to abandon the gun, duck the man's grasp and flee down the alley.

"Wait! Come back!"

Benny did neither. He ran for his life, dodging piles of building supplies scattered across the alley. But the flight was short-lived, ending abruptly at a chain-link fence topped with razor wire.

Benny was trapped.

He turned, heart pounding. Matisse was coming toward him at a slow trot. The security guard hadn't followed. Maybe he was calling the police. Too bad they wouldn't arrive in time.

Matisse was just a few feet away now. Yellow text scrolled across Benny's vision, repeating the horrible crimes for which the huge convict had been locked away.

No doubt another would soon join the list.

Benny's right foot slipped beneath him. Glancing down, he saw a piece of metal pipe, roughly the size of a baseball bat. He grabbed it and held it aloft.

"Stay away from me!" he snarled. Matisse stopped. Drowning in his terror, Benny didn't notice that his pursuer was suddenly worried.

"Mr. Warren, you need to put that down!"

Benny was horrified. *He knows my name!*

The journalist was trapped with a cold-blooded killer who, inexplicably, knew him.

What choice did Benny have?

He leaped forward and brought the pipe down on Matisse's head, feeling the wet crunch as the man's skull caved in. But that wasn't enough, not nearly enough to feel safe again. In fear and rage, Benny struck Matisse over and over, driving him to the ground in a bloodied, gasping heap.

Then, at last, the gasping stopped. Matisse lay still. Forever still.

"My God—*CUT!*"

The shout came from above. Startled, Benny looked up and saw a platform attached to a fire escape five stories overhead. There, to his surprise, stood the stranger who had given him the pill.

Next to him was a man with a video camera.

The stranger, clearly trembling, gripped the railing as he stared at the gruesome scene. "You killed him!" he stammered. "I can't believe it!"

Confused, Benny glanced back and forth between the dead murderer and the two men above. "What … what's going on?" he demanded.

The distraught pill pusher looked at him.

"You never questioned any of it. Never asked if it was truth or hearsay. And now … dear God!"

"What the hell are you talking about?" Benny shouted.

"He wasn't a real murderer. Matisse was an actor."

Something sucked the air out of Benny's lungs.

"A what?" he wheezed.

"An actor. He was part of our setup." The stranger waved a quivering hand at his companion. "We're shooting a cable reality show. We fed you the data you saw. Garbage, most of it. Gossip we heard, or stuff we made up. We wanted to film your reaction … for the show!"

Benny's reaction, what was left of it, lay dead at his feet.

The blood-slicked pipe fell from his hand with a loud clang.

The only other sound in the alley was his own whimpering.

And a distant siren.

206

SACRIFICIUM

The beast's scream ripped the raw night air.

Josh whirled, completely surprised by the attack. The predator's flame-white eyes bore down on him. Josh grasped a splinter of time to fling his body out of the way.

Then, with sudden indifference, the beast withdrew, heaving a long, indignant howl.

Josh rolled out of the snowbank where he'd thrown himself. Adrenaline still tingled the nerves in his skin. While it took the edge off the deep-reaching chill, Josh knew the warmth would soon fade, just as the falling snow gradually obscured the shrinking taillights of the "beast" that had only been a passing car.

Josh climbed to his feet slowly, painfully. Wedges of bitter cold lodged in his joints, and his coat hung heavy with snow. He trudged on, shuffling through the piles of white lining the roadway. With snowplows idled by the blizzard, the streets lay nearly impassable, with few courageous enough to venture into the storm. Josh's surroundings were cold, dark and empty.

He had never felt so alone.

In truth, his loneliness had little to do with the nasty weather and lifeless streets. The ache had troubled his soul for a week, ever since Mara threw him out of the house.

Even now, Josh hadn't figured out why. He'd merely accepted his exile as temporary. Later, when he returned home, no one was there. The door stood locked, the house empty. It was clear his adopted mother had left for good.

That was a problem for Josh, still an apprentice in the delicate art of self-sufficiency. Mara always took care of him, doting on Josh from his earliest memories. Now his life had changed forever, a lesson driven home by the bitter wind.

That wind intensified, stirring snowflakes in tiny white zephyrs. Josh hardly felt its bite anymore. He was too hungry to notice, too numb to feel and too despondent to care.

Josh continued his slow, staggering trek. The only sound was the gale that sometimes moaned as it bent itself around the stacked buildings nearby. That, and the soft tinkling of tiny lights that hung on thin wires overhead. Josh paused a moment to stare at them, bright and lively sparks in a dark, forbidding place.

The arctic air finally drove Josh into an alley between two buildings. Largely sheltered from the storm, Josh caught a whiff of old motor oil and garbage. The latter intrigued him most. Josh hurried down the alley, his eyes alert. At last he discovered a large trash bin, its heavy lid open to the night.

Salvation! Josh rushed to the container and vaulted over its lip, plunging into an ocean of half-frozen, half-eaten food. Notions of dignity fled from his mind, destroyed by his ravenous hunger.

"What the—?"

Josh's feast ended abruptly. An enormous man, dressed in a white shirt and an apron straining to cover his considerable girth, appeared at the bin's edge. Furious, he reached in and grabbed Josh by the throat.

"Get out of here, you tramp!"

The man displayed amazing strength. He lifted Josh clear of the bin and tossed him onto the cold asphalt. Before Josh could scramble to his feet, the man began kicking him viciously.

"Worthless vagrant! Go dig in someone else's garbage! We're a *respectable* restaurant!"

Josh didn't defend himself. He simply leaped up between kicks and bolted. The man pursued him, but even with Josh half-starved and mostly frozen, the obese cook was no match in an all-out sprint. A moment later, Josh was back in the street, his blond hair dancing in the frosty gale. The wheezing, cursing, vomiting cook never made it out of the alley.

Josh fled across the abandoned street, past darkened buildings and beneath the rows of twinkling lights. He wanted to cry, but his panicked flight wouldn't allow him that luxury.

There was only running. And the cold—the cold of his past and of his present, both rejecting him.

All that remained was the unknowable future.

Josh didn't slow down until he reached a snow-blanketed plain. There he stopped, drawn by its empty serenity. Far across the unbroken snowscape squatted a steel structure. Its sharply pitched roof had sloughed most of the snow to form tall white bunkers. Neatly bisecting one bunker was a short ramp that led to a small alcove.

Josh saw the opportunity for shelter and forced his weary body toward it. The alcove beckoned a hundred yards away; it felt like a hundred miles. Josh could no longer feel his legs. His body no longer shivered. Ice caked his eyelids and threatened to freeze them shut. But shelter was so close now—a final chance at sanctuary.

Unfortunately, his sanctuary was already occupied.

The man looked incredibly old. His face was the color of a scaled fish, his eyes red-rimmed and swollen. Even here, protected from the wind, his shabby clothing—a tattered sport coat and pants, a pair of cotton work gloves and a Detroit Tigers baseball cap—fell pathetically short of keeping him warm. He huddled in one corner of the doorway, his knees pressed against his chest, as if to make himself a smaller target for the cold.

The man's first reaction to Josh's presence was to defend his territory.

"This place is mine!" he snapped in a steel-wool voice, feebly waving his baseball cap in Josh's direction.

As before, Josh remained silent. An argument wasn't worth the energy. But neither was another painful excursion into the night, assaulted by the merciless wind. Regardless of the man's protests, Josh's odyssey must end here.

The man seemed to recognize this. His expression softened. He lowered the cap and stared at Josh. A tiny smile played on his stiffened lips.

"Looks like we're both in the same boat, eh?" the man said as he carefully pulled the hat over his thin, gray hair. "Even tonight, of all nights, neither of us has a place to go. No one to take care of us. Eh?"

Josh made no reply. With patience, the man might yield and let him stay. The alcove was too small for both of them, but they would manage. They had to.

And there was another reason for Josh to wait, though he didn't quite understand it. A feeling, both old and new, emerged from within his chilled body. Something from deep in his past, from when Mara first held him in her arms, threatened to burst forth, to transcend his own loneliness and fear and cold.

"You gotta forgive the ol' Roamer," said the man, spitting a bit as he spoke. Josh realized he had no teeth. "I don't have much of my own. And even this place is mine just till the cops run me off." The man chuckled, a painful sound.

"But hey, seein' what night it is and all, don't seem right to kick you out. Guess you can stay."

Relieved, if still a bit wary, Josh edged closer to the man called Roamer. He wasn't yet comfortable with this stranger, and the incident in the alley was fresh in his mind.

Roamer saw Josh's timidity and honored it.

"Don't blame you. Can't trust no one these days. But me, I never did nothin' to nobody. A little employment trouble, that's all. Nothin' bad."

He coughed, deep and startling.

"And yeah, there's the horses. A little bad luck, that's all. Then there's the whiskey. Do like the whiskey. It helps the hurt, let's you take another look at life, eh?" He fixed Josh with a pleading stare. "I never done nothin' to no one. Never did."

His head slowly fell back against the steel wall of the alcove. They shared a moment of silence, disturbed only by the wind and the sprinkle of ice crystals against the building.

Roamer sat up again and locked his bloodshot eyes on Josh.

"I got nobody, you know?" He sobbed from sorrow, from cold, from despair. "No one cares, I guess. But never done nothin'...."

The eyes closed; the voice trailed off.

Josh studied Roamer for a long time. Each breath the old man took was a little shallower, a bit more ragged, than the one before. But Roamer's troubles clearly went beyond the physical. Josh could hear it, feel it, even if he couldn't comprehend the depth of the man's pain.

Then again, maybe he could.

Like Roamer, Josh had been cast aside, rejected by everyone in his life. The two were not so different. Their lives followed parallel courses, their hearts burdened with the emptiness of being unwanted and unloved.

And now it seemed that, on this night Roamer called special, they would share a similar death.

Josh found the thought abhorrent, unacceptable. Yet it fed that strange feeling inside him, causing it to burn in his heart and whisper to his cold-fogged mind. The voice compelled, giving direction where none existed before, shining a beacon for two lives cast adrift, bringing an overwhelming sense that, somehow, death was not the only option for them.

Josh heeded that still, small voice. He crept closer to the old man.

* * * *

A citrus sun broke through flat, blue clouds clinging to the eastern horizon. Chased from the sky, stars of newfallen snow glittered in the morning light, untouched by any significant heat.

Officer Peter West was not so lucky.

"*Dah*—!" he cried as his police cruiser thumped through a snowbank, jostling the foam cup of steaming coffee in his right hand. Near-boiling liquid instantly raised two painful blisters at the base of West's thumb. Cursing, West steered the cruiser into an empty parking lot at the edge of downtown. He stopped the car, set aside his coffee and began nursing his wound.

A cop's sixth sense prompted a glance, and then a double take, toward a nearby building.

There was a body sprawled at the front door.

West grabbed his microphone and called for an ambulance. As he stuffed his head into his hat and clambered out of the cruiser, the radio spit a four-tone alert for the paramedics.

He doubted that the call would do any good. The previous night's blizzard had plunged windchills near zero, driving the chances of survival just as low. West approached the body quickly but reluctantly.

What he found startled him.

The doorway contained not one but two individuals, one on top of the other. The man underneath was severely frostbitten, but his shallow breathing and thready pulse bore proof he'd survived the night. West pulled back the man's baseball cap to get a better look at his face.

"Roamer!" he gasped. The vagrant was a frequent guest at the local shelter.

The figure atop Roamer had no pulse that West could find, and his limbs were cold and stiff. He'd died hours before—probably not long after he'd placed his body across Roamer's, sheltering him from the storm.

Saving the old man's life at the expense of his own.

A distant siren tickled the frosty air, but Officer West didn't notice it. His mind fully embraced the mystery of Roamer's savior. Why would he do it? Why would he sacrifice his life to save a worthless old man?

It reminded West of an ancient maxim he'd heard in his youth, something eminently appropriate on this morning of miracles.

"'Greater love has no one than this,'" Peter quietly recited, "'that one lay down his life for his friends.'" He paused, then added, "I guess that's true for more than people."

West carefully removed the body of the golden retriever from atop Roamer and cradled it as the paramedics waded through the snow.

Cradled it and tried not to cry.

Then he looked into the old man's face once again.

"Merry Christmas, Roamer," he whispered.

THREE MILES

Author's note: This isn't a fiction piece; it really happened to me. I share this experience in the hope that it might offer you a bit of reassurance, a glimmer of hope in a time of loss.

"True wisdom comes from pain." That's a song lyric, or a line from a quote-of-the-day calendar. We read it, perhaps nod in uncomfortable accord, and then let the sentiment slip away, for we would rather gain wisdom by other means.

Yet life often reveals the harsh reality of that statement. Pain comes as a raging storm, thundering with fear and despair. If we hold on, if we persevere, then wisdom gently follows as sunlight peeking from the clearing clouds, casting a stunning rainbow at the retreating tempest.

When I stepped into the predawn silence of March 9, 2004, neither torrent nor sunshine was evident. There was only the frigid air and a faint haze blurring the winter stars overhead. Still, a spring-like energy coursed through my body as I trotted down the driveway and onto the street for a warm-up jog. Within a short distance, that energy lifted me to a solid, comfortable run.

Perhaps my training is on the upswing at last, I thought. Having been a runner for nearly a quarter-century, with many miles and races pounded into my feet, the last four years had proven frustrating. It began with my second-ever marathon—18 years after my first—in which I improved my time yet fell 12 minutes shy of qualifying for the legendary Boston Marathon. I'd struggled with a kind of malaise ever since—lethargic morning runs, and a constant weariness spiked by the stresses of a high-pressure job.

213

But by 2004, I was feeling better, stronger, and more confident as a runner. Maybe I still had a shot at that dream trip to Boston. I was already mapping out my strategy, gradually ramping up my training for a qualifying race in the fall, then joining the marathon masses at the starting line in the quaint New England town of Hopkinton, Massachusetts, the following spring. I could picture the crisp Patriots' Day morning, the growing excitement of the noodle-thin runners, the welcome release of the start, the screaming girls at Wellesley College, the brutal hills at Newton, that last turn to the finish on Boylston Street.

But first there was this run—a quick, three-mile jaunt.

I glided along the abandoned streets, my steps light and rapid, my breathing steady, my heart pounding partly from the effort and partly from a deep, satisfying joy. Already I could tell this would be one of those magical runs.

Near the one-mile mark, the course took a turn into an unlit linear park that twisted DNA-like alongside a gurgling creek. Light snow on the asphalt pathway swirled around my feet with each floating step. It was a glorious morning, and I picked up the pace.

What would soon happen didn't come without warning. About half a mile into the park, my right foot slipped on a patch of black ice hidden beneath the snow dust. I tottered but stayed upright, stepping quickly off the trail to gain better traction. Relieved, I jogged slowly for a moment, studying the pathway ahead. It appeared ice-free, though still thinly layered in pristine snow. I returned to the trail, tested its safety with a few strides, and felt reassured. The black ice had been an anomaly.

My pace quickened again. As I passed beneath a long archway of trees, my mind raced ahead gleefully to the warm months and all the running that lay before me.

And then my left foot slipped.

There was no way I could stay on my feet this time. I twisted in the air, hoping to minimize any damage the coming impact would cause. Despite that effort, my left leg ended up tucked beneath me as I landed. Hard.

Something inside my leg exploded. Raw screams ripped the darkness, shattering the silence over and over again. It took a few moments before I realized those screams of agony were my own.

My head cleared as the pain in my leg dulled to a fierce, persistent throbbing. I found myself on my back, clutching my left knee to my chest. Gingerly, and a bit fearfully, I stretched out my leg, letting my heel rest on the asphalt. I might as well have dropped it on a bed of nails. I gasped in pain and hugged my knee again.

I didn't want to look at my leg. Besides, it was probably just a twisted ankle. A couple of days off, maybe some icing, and everything would be fine. I'd be back to running, back on the training schedule, back on the road to Boston—as long as I didn't look.

Don't look. You really, really, don't want to look.

I looked.

I saw my left foot pointed inward at an unnatural angle. Dumbfounded, I tried to straighten it. It remained unmoved. For a bizarre moment, I marveled as my brain barked orders but my foot paid no attention.

I couldn't deny the truth any longer. This was no twisted ankle. I had broken my leg.

This meant deep trouble. I was on one of the lesser-used stretches of the park at an early hour in the dead of winter. It could be some time, perhaps hours, before someone came along. With a raspy voice, I called out for help, but there was no one to hear.

I was on my own.

Walking was clearly out of the question, and the nearest exit was a gated service drive nearly a quarter of a mile away. How was I going to get out of the park?

I paused long enough for a simple, desperate prayer, counting on God to fill in the blanks as He invariably does. Then I looked around for anything that would improve my plight. After thrashing about in some frost-stiffened undergrowth, I found a stick to serve as a crutch. It wasn't very sturdy, but it would have to do.

Standing was a slow, painful and terrifying exercise. I carefully avoided putting pressure on my injured leg, but just being upright heightened the pain. I could feel the foot and ankle swell, straining against my shoe. Balanced between my good foot and the wobbly stick, I took the tiniest step forward.

To my relief, everything held.

I tried it again. Still good. Once more. Okay. It was terribly slow going, but each teetering step brought me a few inches closer to salvation.

So intent was I on my escape plan that I forgot one crucial variable: the black ice lurking beneath the snow.

My makeshift crutch, bearing almost all of my weight, suddenly found a third patch of ice. The stick leaped completely from my grasp, and I fell to the pavement once again.

Right on top of my broken leg.

The screams this prompted were animal-like, full of sheer agony, fear and fury. Later I would learn that the two falls collectively snapped my tibia in two places and shattered my fibula, the long outer bone of my left leg. As far as my skeletal structure was concerned, my foot was flying solo.

And I was still stuck in the middle of the park.

Exhausted, fighting the pain, I turned to the one option left. Rolling over onto my hands and knees, elevating my lower leg to keep the injured foot from dragging, I began to crawl. My hands grew wet and numb as I pulled myself through the light snow. I crossed a small bridge and continued along the winding path, passing the time by calling out "Help!" and "Fire!" and all the exclamations that are supposed to summon rescue. But again, there was no one to hear.

At last I reached the service drive and its gated entrance. A narrow dirt passage near the creek snaked around the gate. I carefully crawled through the dirt, near the bubbling water, and continued the slow, hand-over-kneecap journey up the service drive to the empty street.

Now I was fairly close to home, but my cold, stiff hands and battered knees would take me no further. Instead, I lay at the side of the road and waited for a car to come by. Because of the early hour, the wait was eternal. At last, three motorists came along and stopped to assist. One had a cell phone, which I used to call my wife and ask if she wouldn't mind too much giving me a lift to the hospital.

The next few hours were a jumble of pain and resignation. This injury was beyond the healing of cast, crutches and rest. Surgery was necessary, and even that would have to wait a week until the swelling subsided. Then two titanium plates and a dozen screws were added to my body, holding my broken bones together as they mended and then encompassed the metal for eternity.

But that was just the beginning. There were multiple casts, months of sleeping in a bed in my living room, being helped each morning with baths and dressing. I returned to work three weeks after the accident, coming home each night worn out, my ankle swollen and throbbing. Crutches were my constant companion for more than 12 weeks, and a stylish cane carried me a few weeks more. Physical therapy moved with frustrating slowness from pool to workout room, an intense and tiring four months.

Through it all I struggled with a profound sense of grief. I'd lost something incredibly precious. How many of life's fears, unknowns and disappointments had I reasoned through in miles upon countless miles of running? How could I face that life without the smooth cadence, the steady breathing, the miles passing beneath my running feet?

As it turned out, the prognosis wasn't quite that bad. My doctor promised I would run again. But my long-distance days were over. No lengthy trail runs on hot summer days. No training logs filled with hundreds upon hundreds of miles and memories. No Boston Marathon.

And yet there was a lesson to be learned. The blessing hadn't been taken away; it had merely been transformed. The storm had passed, and even now wisdom was beginning to peek from behind the clouds.

Four months after the accident, I ran for the first time—three pool lengths in chest-deep water, harnessed to my physical therapist. As a smile slowly crept across my face, I saw a glimmer of that sunlight, a hint of a colorful glow.

But I wouldn't know the wisdom in all its glory until much later.

That time came on another cold winter morning. In ominously silent darkness, I walked alone from my home to that same service drive at the edge of the linear park. I slipped around the gate, grateful for the good-natured greeting of the creek below. With some trepidation, I slowly retraced the path that I'd crawled exactly one year earlier. Within minutes, I was at the scene of the accident.

For a third time, I fell—this time on purpose, and to my knees. I thanked God for the years I had spent as a distance runner, and for allowing me to continue to run. I thanked Him for healing my body. And I thanked Him for the wisdom I'd gained. My running had been about reaching a mythical goal. Now it was a way to celebrate life and health, of simply being.

I stood and glanced upward at the same fuzzy stars that had watched me suffer a year before. Then I began to run.

I passed over the small bridge, following the winding path with increasing confidence and rising speed. Sweeping past the service drive, I continued on—through the cathedral of trees, onto the street at the trailhead, then arcing back toward home, finishing that long-delayed three-mile run, my heart and my life awash in a dazzling rainbow.

AFTERWORD

I write with the hope that people read, enjoy and reflect on my stories regardless of background or belief. Still, it's important to note that my writing is strongly influenced by my Christian faith. Sometimes the influence is overt, sometimes subtle, even tenuous. But it's always there.

That said, you won't find "turn or burn" preaching in this book. What drew me to Christianity is Jesus' simple message of *faith* in God, *hope* in Christ, and *love* in action. It's a call to act justly, to love mercy, and to walk humbly with God. That's why I'm frustrated by the many people in modern churches who taint that message with siren songs of power, politics, prosperity and prejudice. No wonder Jesus aimed his harshest words at religious leaders.

Jesus often used parables, or stories with a point, to get people to reflect on their motivations, to challenge their assumptions and biases, to point them back to God's simple message. Such self-reflection is neither easy nor comfortable, but it's necessary—and it's what I try to prompt with my stories, even as I use them to challenge myself.

Nearly every tale I write connects to a passage from the Bible. If you're interested in those links to the stories in this book, here they are:

Coveting Fields, II Samuel 12:1-12; *The Chasm*, Luke 16:19-31; *A Speck of Sawdust*, Matthew 7:3-5; *All the Stage a World*, James 5:1-6; *What Might Have Been*, Deuteronomy 5:32-33; *Have Not*, Haggai 1:5-6; *Locum Tenens*, Hebrews 10:5-14; *Thicker Than*, Ecclesiastes 5:13-14; *Moksha*, Esther 4:14; *Enmity*, Genesis 3:1-19; *The Good Person*, Romans 3:21-31; *Pièce de Résistance*, Proverbs 16:18-19; *Random Precision*, Luke 9:24-25; *Telephone Tag*, Luke 12:16-21; *Superhero*, Luke 18:1-5; *The Margin*, Luke 10:25-37; *A Sheep Oneself*, John 1:1-18; *Throw of the Dice*, James 3:13-18; *Ghostwriter*, Numbers 23:19-20; *Three Hours*, Romans 7:21-25; *Gabbatha*, Luke 22:54-62; *Flash of Life*, Matthew 25:31-46; *Hearsay*, Proverbs 26:20-23; *Sacrificium*, John 15:12-15; *Three Miles*, Isaiah 40:31.

Must you look up those passages to enjoy these stories or get something out of them? Not at all. This isn't intended as a Bible study manual. People across the spectrum, from theologians to atheists, have told me that my stories have spoken to them. I find that profoundly humbling. I want my stories to entertain, I want them to challenge mindsets, but I also want them to bring hope to those who feel hopeless.

Still, should you choose to look up these passages, you may discover a deeper perspective on a story, or the passage, or your life, or all three. It's a perspective that I invite you to explore.

ACKNOWLEDGEMENTS

Were I to list all the people who have influenced me as a writer, I'd need to publish another book. Nonetheless, there are a few I need to mention here, people to whom I'm indebted for their support, encouragement and involvement:

Norma and Bill Sootsman, Richard and Cindy Chambers, and Beverly Forsyth and Leonard Calvert, parents and in-laws who encourage me (and especially Mom, the voracious reader, awaiting her signed copy in Heaven); siblings Keith, Terri, Dan, Kelly and Linda (RIP); Cari Rutkoskie of Words Matter, LLC, for her stellar copyediting; Laura Hosler and Lori McNeill of GreenStreet Marketing & Design for the amazing cover; Jim Lester and Paul Fazio, spiritual mentors who have nurtured my creative writing for many years; Dean Hauck of Michigan News, a champion of homegrown authors; Meg Vollick and her wonderful students, who have hosted me in the classroom and celebrated my writing; Evelyn Goodwin, my friend and most encouraging fan; James Cawley and my many, many friends (too many to list, but you know who you are) I came to know through *Star Trek New Voyages*. Finally, thanks and love to my family—Tyler, Tobi, Ryan, Kailynn, Rowan, and especially my wife, Terri, who makes this life's ride worth every moment.

ABOUT THE AUTHOR

Rick Chambers is an award-winning communications consultant, author, screenwriter and former journalist. In addition to many short stories and professional articles, his written works include a science fiction novel, *Radiance*; three literacy/ESL novelettes; and he was the screenwriter for two episodes of the award-winning, web-based fan series, *Star Trek New Voyages*, and two episodes of an anthology series titled *Chronicles*. He resides in Michigan with his wife, Terri.

Other Books by Rick Chambers:
> *Radiance*
> *Anything But Free*
> *Something To Hide*
> *Casey's Grudge*

Made in the USA
Monee, IL
02 June 2020